Emerald to Pounamu

A Midwife's Odyssey

Marie-ann Quin

Jeff.

It is so lovely to share my new Book with Faye's dad.

I have heard such lovely things about you from your daughter and Ian.

Arohanui

Marie-ann

A catalogue record for this book is available from the National Library of New Zealand.

Soft cover ISBN 9780473675493
Ebook/mobi ISBN 9780473675509

Cover Artwork by Kat Quin 2004

This book has been printed using sustainably managed stock.

Design & layout by Stuart Bradfield, Dublin, Ireland
Printed in New Zealand by www.yourbooks.co.nz

Acknowledgements

First and foremost, without the bravery and steadfastness of my ancestors I would not be here today to write this book. The stories I have gleaned over the years of their journey to New Zealand, and settling into life in this country, inspired me to write this, my first novel. It was only by chance, through discussions with family genealogists, research and meeting with the wider family members, that my belief of being the first nurse/midwife in the family since Florence Nightingale, was dispelled. I am so grateful to have the genes and examples of such strong, determined women and men who have guided my journey to pen this story.

The Alexander Turnbull Library has been a tremendous resource for the research I undertook in the beginning, with ships logs, births and deaths on board ship and immigrant details. I am grateful to the families who arrived on the *"Skiold"* from northern Germany with my ancestors, who have given me permission to incorporate some of their own ancestors' stories into this book, most especially the Bruning family. Mine are not precise accounts of actual events as the passage of time changes history, and poetic license is used, but still, they were invaluable to me.

I have worked alongside many amazing midwives in my fifty year career as a nurse, Plunket Nurse and midwife. I have interviewed some of these women. Because the book I set out to write, about the changes in Midwifery since the settlers came to New Zealand up until now, through sheer volume of content, has morphed into 3 or 4 books, their stories will continue to be used as the saga progresses. Chris Storey and Judy Lockie are just two of the midwives whose stories and mentorship have inspired me.

The incredible mothers and babies I have cared for in my career and their diverse birth events have given me the foundation and inspiration for each of the birth stories in the chapters. Despite modern medicine, technology and education, the strength of women giving birth, along with the fact that giving birth and being born is still fraught with dangers, never ceases to amaze me. Even after all these years, the valued gift of attending the arrival of a new family member is an honour.

My own family have been incredibly supportive. My daughters Esther, Katherine and Laura, each in their own way, have contributed immensely to my completing of this novel. Their wisdom, knowledge, artistic gifts, work ethic and ruthless guidance have enabled me to perfect this book to be my best literary achievement. My husband, Pat, has done all those chores that would normally distract me away from writing and has been my side-line 'go-to' for a variety of facts and elusive words. Kia ora te whanau, I love you beyond words.

Many thanks go to my Midwifery colleagues, most especially Kimai and Jackie along with a cartel of interested friends, family, colleagues and followers who have willingly critiqued and buoyed me along to completion of the book. Thank you, Aaron, for coming up with the perfect title.

Thanks go to my friends from Northern Germany, Birge, Conrad and Alina who have helped me with Plattdeutsch and some special times exploring near the area my ancestors emigrated from.

Last, but not least, grateful thanks go to the professional guidance I have received from the team at The Write Practice, Lesley Marshall at Editline, Patricia Bell at Bellbird Words Proofreading, Editing and Writing Services, Kat Quin-Gemmell at Illustrated Publishing for the cover design, Esther Harcourt for her knowledge with words, writing, German and keen competitive streak to work alongside me in the 100 day Book Challenge. Stuart Bradfield generously offered to format the book and, with his partner Clare Mason, has helped me with everything Irish. Patricia Bell surprisingly added her Irish knowledge and guidance during her proofreading.

Although I punched the keys on my laptop to produce the book, this creative product has opened my eyes to the fact that there is always a huge team and a community and a lifetime of experiences behind its completion. Kia ora, Veelen Dank and thank you to my awesome community.

Part 1

"A Life Changing Journey."

Chapter 1

What a grand day, Bedelia thought. Bedding was laid out on the deck to air and dry. For the first time since the ship had set sail from London four weeks ago, the boxes and trunks of the Irish colleen and the other steerage passengers could be brought up on deck. They stored all the worldly goods of their owners, who took the opportunity to restock, replenish and in some cases sell off unwanted items. Some had brought extra provisions for the unknown requirements of the many months they would be on board the ship and for the life in the country they were bound for, so far away.

Many of the passengers had spent the first few weeks confined to their bunks with seasickness, made worse by the rough weather and high seas they had sailed through. Bedelia felt lucky to have found her sea legs straight away. She had immediately taken on the role of caring for the women who were laid up. The narrow bunks made being confined even more debilitating and disheartening. As she walked over the deck Bedelia saw, by the mattresses out to air, that the men were assigned a rather longer berth than the women. She and her sister had been given a list of recommended supplies and the mattress, with its specific measurements, was one of them. The bedding to go with it was also on the list of required items.

The day was fair, with only a light breeze to fill the sails. Tremendous calico sheets of canvas billowed and flapped. The masts and booms creaked as the ship was carried along by the following wind. The weather today was in stark contrast to that which the immigrant ship, the *Catherine Mary*, had endured since heading south into the Atlantic from Gravesend.

Bedelia's auburn hair shone in the sunlight. A scattering of freckles crossed her satin skin from above her fine cheekbones. The little brown specks joined at the bridge of her nose, telling the tale of a childhood spent outdoors. Her green eyes sparkled.

Taking care to be out of earshot of the officials conversing on the upper deck, Bedelia whispered to the young man sitting a couple of feet from her, "What would be your name? Do you have family travelling with you?"

"Michael it is," he said in a low, gravelly voice. "My travelling companion, his name is Keenan. I have aboard my brother Patrick and his wife Moira with their children, Seamus and Bridie. They stay in the family section of steerage. Myself and Keenan, well, we are staying in the men's quarters in the stern. We don't see a lot of my brother and his family, but you will have met them, for sure."

Nodding, Bedelia said, "I think I may have seen them, although the families have their own area. So where would you be coming from, Michael?"

At his reply Bedelia jumped up suddenly, then popped down just as quickly as she noticed his hand waving for her to sit. "Templemore! Why, I am coming from Scarriff, County Clare. Just two days' journey by road, it is," she said, being sure to turn her back to the upper deck as she fossicked through her cabin trunk.

A harsh voice boomed down from the poop deck just yards away. "Mind yourself, young lassie, I have my eyes on you two. You know the rules," the matron said.

Bedelia knew the risk she was taking sharing a few words with this stranger. The single women were not allowed to fraternise at all with the single men aboard. In fact, the two sexes were kept quite separate during the night and the day. Women had their area in the aft of the ship, and Bedelia had discovered that only the matron, the captain and the ship's doctor held the keys. The families were in the middle and could be reached from the women's compartment, but the women had little contact with them. The men had more freedom, being permitted on deck longer than the two hours allotted to the women. Very rarely were they there at the same time.

Segregation of the single men and women had seemed strange to Bedelia, who took an interest in everyone she encountered. She had often been warned that her familiarity with strangers was likely to get her into trouble, but that didn't stop her. When she had first learnt of this separation on embarking, she had wondered, "Why, for the love of Jesus, do we need to be kept apart?"

Turning his back on the matron, Michael whispered as quietly as he could, "I see you have some preserves. Would you care to exchange them for some linen I have myself? My family ran a drapery store, but we had to sell up with me Mam and Da passing on. These were a few things I guessed might come in handy in the colonies."

Bedelia glanced into his trunk. She liked the finely stitched items she could see on top, for they reminded her of the special doilies her nan had made for the chest of drawers that had stood in her childhood home.

Michael continued, "I don't have the tailoring gift like me Da. My hands are made to do harder toil."

Bedelia nodded in agreement as she took in the size of his mits. She could lose both her hands inside one of his, she thought. Michael was tall and lean with a mop of black hair. He would tower above Bedelia when he stood. His smile was almost obscured by his full ginger beard. His eyes spoke to Bedelia of a warm and caring man, one whom she felt could be trusted.

Bedelia pulled out her own goods to trade. "You may have the plum or the peach, but mind, I want the jars back when you have emptied them," Bedelia said. "I have heard tell that these will come in handy when settling into our lives in the new country, so I have."

Michael stroked his fiery beard. "Who are you travelling with?"

"My elder sister Veronica. Our passage was got on a note. We have heard that young women are sought after in the colonies, for work and such. Why is it you ask, then?"

"I wouldn't have considered for a moment that a young colleen like you would be embarking on such a momentous journey alone." Michael smiled.

"So where would you be setting eyes for, then?" Bedelia said.

"We're looking to lay our peg down in Australia. My brother and his family have been promised work on a farm out of Sydney town. Myself and Keenan may look for labouring work to put money together to purchase some land."

Bedelia's face was beaming as she carefully placed the fine linen in the box Uncle Paddy had made for his nieces. She leaned back, rearranging a rich red lock that had come free into the bundle of hair tied loosely behind her head. She caught sight of the matron and the captain heading their way and signalled to Michael, then quickly concentrated on sliding the items she had retrieved, into a cloth baggie. Bedelia knew it wasn't worth getting on the bad side of anyone in authority on the ship. She had already seen the results of that.

Soon after they had set sail, Bedelia had witnessed the punishment of a sailor. He had been tied to the mast and given "five of the best", as the captain called it. Bedelia considered the sailor's misdemeanour to be a very minor error. He was guilty of dropping one of the first-class passenger's trunks as he single-handedly hauled it up the gangplank. Although Bedelia had been told

Captain Seeley was firm but fair and that he needed to keep a tight rein, her stomach turned at the cruelty and injustice of this act.

Patrolling the deck, the ship's matron held herself erect, her diminutive stature offset by her ample bosom. Fierce hazel eyes peered from behind her spectacles. The wispy grey hair tied firmly back in a bun accentuated her stern demeanour. Mrs Pentwick was employed to see that the single women weren't exploited and that they behaved in a seemly manner. She had made this quite clear when she introduced herself on that first day aboard and told the women that she was there for their welfare.

Bedelia had heard the captain tell one of the first-class passengers that so far, Mrs Pentwick was one of the better matrons he had endured. Although she was not employed by him, the passengers were aware that the matron was under his jurisdiction for the duration of the voyage. She received free passage for her efforts, certain privileges and a small gratuity on arrival at their destination -if it was deserved.

Bedelia had also observed what a bulwark the matron was when protecting her charges from "the attacks of lecherous brutes", as she described the single men and crew aboard the ship. "The single women's quarters are like a honey pot to a swarm of starving bees," she said to the women. "I have worked in a girls' boarding school too long to be blind to the shenanigans that can go on." As she spoke, Bedelia thought she resembled a hornet ready to attack.

In one of the rare quiet moments between storms, when most of the women were unable to rise for a meal, Mrs Pentwick had confided in Bedelia that she wanted to settle in the colonies, as England had nothing left for her. Hers was a childless marriage, so she had taught for years in a West Yorkshire school where her husband worked as the caretaker. She was following Mr Pentwick to Australia, as arranged. He had set sail just six months previously. There had been no word from him and would likely be none, as any letters would likely pass like two ships in the night.

Once the matron and captain were safely past and out of earshot, Michael and Bedelia continued their conversation. Michael said that when the ship had first left England he felt queasy with the constant rolling of the ship, but to escape the close and putrid hold he made the choice to weather the storms on deck. His companion, Keenan, did not fare so well. "He remained below, as sick as a dog," Michael said. As long as he stayed out of the way of the crew working the sails, Michael's presence was ignored. He would don his weatherproof jacket and brogues and hole up towards the rear of the ship, where he could watch the wake as the ship ploughed through the foaming seas. It was there he got the benefit of fresh air; something lacking in steerage.

Bedelia nodded firmly in agreement.

Making the Irishman's acquaintance and hearing the familiar lilt of his voice caused Bedelia to think of home with a twinge of sadness. Despite their simple upbringing on the tenant farm, Bedelia knew they had been loved beyond words. Veronica and Bedelia had been happily oblivious to their circumstances until losing their four younger brothers and sister to starvation and disease, followed closely by their da. Their mam had died in childbirth one year before the rest of the family.

Uncle Paddy, their mother's brother, was their guardian, but he was unable to take the sisters in. He had never been married and worked as a shepherd on a farm, where he spent many weeks in the back country living in a basic hut made from sods of earth and tending herds of animals in the surrounding hills and valleys. Although educated and once a man of the cloth, when hard times struck he was forced into a solitary life of guarding sheep rather than God's flock.

If it hadn't been for the Poor Law Guardians rescuing them to the Scarriff Workhouse, Veronica and Bedelia might have met the same fate as the rest of their family. After they had spent some time sewing in the workhouse, close to the south end of the River Shannon, Uncle Paddy told the sisters about the company that was recruiting women to emigrate to the colonies. At first Bedelia couldn't imagine that kind of life for them. But as she pondered the reality of the days spent putting one stitch in front of the other, the thought of a new start excited her. She was finally able to convince her elder sister that it may be the best option for their future.

The local Board of Guardians had strict standards when considering applicants for emigration. Once accepted, Bedelia and Veronica's fares, provisions, food, clothing and transport to Gravesend were seen to, as well as medical examinations and vaccinations before boarding the ship.

Uncle Paddy also helped the sisters with some of the extras required for the voyage and their future. He had carefully stored some of their parents' treasures after their deaths. These were packed in the bottom of their box. "The family Bible and your mam's handiwork are no good to me," he said. "Take care of them, for the threads and pages carry the memories of your homeland."

As they boarded the ferry and said goodbye to their uncle, their only close relative left living, Bedelia knew they would likely never see him again, nor the beautiful hills covered in a carpet of rich green. But she held back the tears. She had to be the strong one.

Bedelia's thoughts returned to the present. She had to go check on her sister. She parted from her new friend with a grin and a nod, for the matron and the captain were returning their way.

Back in the single women's quarters, Veronica's wan face peered out from her sleeping place just below Bedelia's bunk. She looked very fragile from the barrage of the sea's fury, Bedelia thought. Their mattresses were adorned with covers they had delicately stitched themselves. The material had been gleaned from any scraps they had been able to rescue during their time in the workhouse. Despite the simple fabric, the love and time taken over each stitch would not be lost on those who cared to take a closer look. Bedelia was most proud of their efforts and also grateful for the gift of stitchery, which came from their mam. On wintery nights in their childhood, she would take the girls to the one lantern they possessed and patiently show them the art of turning a plain piece of rag into an item of beauty and usefulness.

"Won't you come for a stroll around the deck, Vonnie? It'll do you a treat. The sun's shining, so it is, with a lovely fresh breeze blowing," Bedelia said.

"Not just now. I feel so weak that I fear my legs won't hold me up," Veronica said.

"Oh, and by the by, I met a nice fella who swapped some of our jam for a swatch of linen. I believe I was the winner there. We'll even get the jars back." Bedelia related her morning's pleasure with enthusiasm. It felt so long since she had been excited about anything.

As she finished her story, she looked at Veronica with fresh concern. "Do you want me to get anything from the box? We may not be able to get at it again for another month."

"Yes please. If I might have the shift with the forget-me-nots I sewed on the bodice, and another pair of stockings? I feel a freshen-up might just set me right to feeling better."

"What about one of the sweet treats from our box as well?" Bedelia said, hoping to coax her sister into eating something other than the broth she had been sipping since setting sail.

"Oh no, but thanks for thinking of me. You've been an angel over these last awful weeks. For that I'm truly thankful. Sure I'll be fine and dandy now the seas have settled."

Bedelia was grateful to see the shine return to her sister's brown eyes. Her curly chestnut hair was still bedraggled and matted together from sweat, sick and the tossing around in her cot.

"How about I bring a basin of warm water to freshen you up? I can wash your hair if you'd like," Bedelia said.

Veronica's eyes lit up. "Why that would be dandy, Dee, if you don't mind."

Once the task was completed and she had gently combed the tangled hair into ringlets, Bedelia felt satisfied with her morning's work. Veronica's locks shone in the beads of sunlight streaming through the hatch.

The gong rang for the midday meal, and Bedelia's friend Isla Quin shouted, "Dinner time!" Isla was the first herdsman, and it was her duty to collect the meals and hot drinks and bring them from the central galley to the single women's compartment. Bedelia was sometimes called upon to help Isla carry the large pot, so she knew that Isla had been up since dawn with her tasks. Isla was under Matron's supervision and was responsible for taking care of the single women's stores, all these having been carefully weighed and doled out on Monday. Porridge was always the breakfast meal. Long benches surrounded the large table at the centre of the quarters for those well enough to sit and share the meal.

Like the day before, dinner was salted pork and pea soup.

"Well, this is a change from the preserved meat and potatoes last week, and I have grown a bit wearisome of the salted beef and rice from the week before, so it's lovely to have a change." Bedelia winked, making Isla laugh.

Isla reached for her calico bag hanging alongside many others on a hook screwed into the beam above the table. She pulled out her bowl, spoon and a mug. The other women followed her example and soon Isla was dishing out the contents of the pot to those waiting at the table.

As she ladled, she started giggling. "Did yer remember the new dish the stormy Bay of Biscay concocted?" Isla said. "It was surely a change from the same old slops we dish up daily here."

"Oh aye, I've never before had tea and raisins mixed with bread and broth. Softest bread we've had all month. Ha ha!" Siobhan said. As she recounted the mishap, all present at the table and within earshot let out whoops of laughter. Even the matron, who usually kept a restrained presence, joined in.

"I do recall the wee smile you lot set on my face with your laughter even though I was too weak to know why," Veronica said from the confines of her bunk.

On the calmer days at sea, meal times at the long table conjured up happy memories of Bedelia's childhood; of the family sitting around their kitchen table, laughing, teasing and sharing the day's escapades over a meal. At other times the few women who were able sat around sharing stories of their life back home. Cook had told Bedelia the communal table was made of sturdy kauri, a durable wood brought from the colony, along with beams for the masts. It was scrubbed clean every day by one of the women who had been given that task.

Just as Mrs Pentwick was sitting down to her meal, Maggie slipped in behind her. Bedelia spotted the young girl and realised she had taken full advantage of the freedom on deck while everyone was occupied sorting through their stowed belongings. Bedelia had noticed that Maggie had the bare minimum of possessions in her small box, so it must have only taken her a short time to get what she wanted.

"Mrs Pentwick, do you have plans for our afternoon?" Bedelia quickly said.

As Mrs Pentwick began to explain her intentions, Maggie slid into her seat at the end of the form and winked at Bedelia. "Well, that was a fine dinner, can I have a tad more?" Maggie said as she proffered her clean plate to Isla.

"No," Mrs Pentwick snapped, "you cannot even have your first serving, young madam. If you scallywags think you can pull the wool over my eyes then you may as well think again."

Under the table Bedelia found Maggie's hand, passing her a slice of bread folded over with a good dollop of jam inside. Out of earshot of the matron, Maggie recounted that she had met a young lad named Danny. They had found a quiet place to talk behind the neatly twirled piles of ropes from the rigging. "He told me that the ropes resembled the ringlets in my hair both in colour and in shape. He was so sweet to say such a thing, wasn't he just?"

She told Bedelia they had shared a few memories of their carefree younger days playing and exploring in the lush green countryside nearby. "It surely takes my heart home."

Maggie had confided in Bedelia during one of the long, stormy nights that she was travelling with another family from the market town north of Dublin. They had taken her under their wing out of kindness.

"Danny is travelling with his older brother and his wife and baby," Maggie said. "They're the only family he has left in the whole wide world." She told Bedelia that Danny had to stay in with the single men because of his age. His brother and family were in the family section, along with the family she was travelling with. "I feel sure they must know each other by now."

Veronica suddenly let out a shrill scream from her cot. The women around the table turned in alarm to see a large grey ship rat scuttle away to a gap in the partition.

"No matter how hard I try and how many times I see them, I just can't abide one running over me. It fair gives me the willies, so it does," Veronica said.

Bedelia was at the opposite end of the table to Mrs Pentwick, facing the open hatch. While the others were distracted by Veronica's distress, she noticed one of the women sidling furtively into their quarters looking rather dishevelled. Bedelia recognised Therese, her skirt in disarray, one of her breasts having partially escaped from the confines of her bodice. Her fair hair was hanging loose and her eyes were scanning here and there. Therese placed her finger on her lips as she looked at Bedelia and shook her head in Mrs Pentwick's direction. She slipped into a dark space at the end of her bunk.

The meal passed without further incident. Several of the women, who had brought down preserves newly retrieved from their boxes, had been generous with sharing their stock.

"The bread today was altogether made more delicious by the treats," Siobhan said as she licked the remnants of the jam from her lithe fingers. "It's been quite the day. It surely was a treat to breathe the clean air, feel the sun-beams warming my face and not be tossed around the deck." She and the other women on cleaning duty stood to clear the table and make room to wash the dishes. Despite the usual complaints about the food, it had all been devoured.

Cleanliness, orderliness, industry and self-improvement were the matron's principles, which she reeled off every day to the women in her care. She made it clear that in her job as chaperone, ensuring their moral improvement was secondary only to protecting their virtue. Mrs Pentwick also took on the job of patiently teaching reading, writing and arithmetic to her charges. Many of them had limited ability, as school had not been a priority for poorer families. The matron also supervised sewing projects and other handcrafts.

Although a few women had brought their own materials, which they had retrieved from their trunks in the morning, much of what Mrs Pentwick pull out from the box she produced was donated sewing and reading materials supplied from missionary and other benevolent societies. Out came skeins of wool, both plain and dyed in a variety of colours. Knitting needles carved from light wood to turn the yarn into chosen articles of clothing sat alongside the tightly rolled balls. Along with swatches of cloth to stitch into quilts, and larger rolls of various patterns to do with what they wanted, came basic sewing accessories like buttons, needles and cotton threads of many colours.

"My, what a treasure trove," Bedelia said as she picked up the soft-spun hank of wool and some needles, choosing a pattern for a pretty but practical shawl. She turned to Mrs Pentwick. "Please can you help me get started with this? I'm not the best at reading a pattern, but once I've got the way of it I'll be all right."

"That's a dandy choice, missy, but I believe it will be quite above your ability," Mrs Pentwick said with another rare smile.

"I'm sure we can work it out together," Bedelia said, thinking the matron's morning in the sunshine might have melted her icy resolve a tad. She appeared to be less vigilant and a little less severe.

The afternoon was whiled away on stitching, knitting, reading and writing - both letters home and diary entries, if the girls had the words to do so. Mrs Pentwick hovered to offer assistance. Some women were industrious and some chose to sit and chat with their companions despite persistent prodding from the matron.

While Bedelia worked out the pattern for her shawl, Veronica, still seated in her cot, used the quill somewhat awkwardly to pen a simple note home to Uncle Paddy, with the matron's guidance. She and Bedelia had only managed a few years at school. Veronica was eighteen years old which gave her two more years of schooling, an advantage over her younger sister.

Some of the women were chatting about what they may do on their first stopover of the voyage. Earlier in the day, when all the cabin trunks had been fetched up from below, the captain had told the passengers they were bound for Tenerife, where the ship would be taking on supplies and fresh water for the next leg of the journey. Veronica's letter could be sent from there.

Further down the table Molly sang an Irish dirge. Her sweet voice rang out the words with such emotion that it brought back scenes of the rolling green meadows and home fires burning bricks of peat on the grates. "Skibbereen" was familiar to most of the Irish on board. Bedelia felt a catch in her throat as she joined in the familiar words of the song she had learnt in the workhouse. *Why did that have to happen to our families?* Bedelia thought. *I know many of the other women have been through what we have ... but why did we make it through the troubles and not the others?* Despite avoiding talking about it, Bedelia knew in her heart that the hard times had killed many or changed the survivors' lives forever.

"Oh Molly, that was so beautiful, but could you please sing something livelier," Veronica said. "I'm getting pretty homesick right now and hearing something more cheerful might lift my spirits a tad."

Siobhan jumped up from her stitching and skipped over to her bunk. Tucked away in a leather case was her fiddle, a treasured possession given to her by her grannie, she had told the sisters. She could play the instrument by ear, and as soon as she put bow to string all those present brightened up as the first few notes rang out. "Whiskey in the Jar" sang its own lively tune. Those from Ireland sang along as they knew the chorus, at least. Molly and Siobhan could peel off the verses. Some of the others, who had the energy, got up and danced in time to the music.

Bedelia thought that the most heart-rending item of these few hours was a folk song sung by Siobhan in Gaelic, accompanied by Molly on the tin whistle. The eerie tune crept out of the hatch and through the gaps in the partition. It attracted an audience of all those within earshot on deck and below. Necks craned and eyes peered but no one dared step foot on the ladder or through the gap in the partition. Mrs Pentwick's glare prevailed.

The afternoon passed quickly. They had barely put away their cleaned plates from their dinner when a message arrived from the ship's doctor. One of the crew called down the hatch that assistance was needed and that Bedelia was his preferred helper. This personal request was quite bewildering to Bedelia.

"I am at a loss to know why the good doctor would be wanting to call for a snippet of a girl like you," Mrs Pentwick said, looking down her nose through her spectacles.

Bedelia followed the cabin boy to the deck above. He beckoned her towards the cabin occupied by a missionary family travelling to New Zealand. As she was ushered into the small but well-furnished cabin, the woman lying on the bed let out a loud moan. She breathed heavily through a gripping pain as she held herself below her abdomen.

Bedelia looked around at the occupants of the cabin. One was the ship's doctor and another was the woman's husband, the preacher, Mr Ashcroft. He conducted the Sunday services in the cuddy when the weather permitted. The two men were engrossed in conversation and, to Bedelia's surprise, seemed relaxed about the condition of the woman in the bed. Peeking over the wooden bed-end were two pairs of wide and frightened eyes.

Bedelia knew immediately what was happening. She gave her hand to the woman, who squeezed it tightly as another pain surged through her from the tightening of her womb. Bedelia could feel the hard mass as she placed her hand on the woman's distended belly. The children's terrified eyes grew wider and the little girl started to cry.

Bedelia caught the doctor's eye. Without hesitation she said, "Now I'd be suggesting that these little ones have an adventure. The other ladies, where I'm staying, have been having fun with some music. You may have caught the tunes earlier."

When the doctor gave a nod, Bedelia turned to Mr Ashcroft. "I'm sure they will be well cared for by my companions, and Mrs Pentwick is there also."

When he gave a sign of agreement, Bedelia turned to the children and said, "My, you'll have a grand time, sure you will."

The cabin boy, who had waited for direction outside, was given the responsibility of guiding the children to the women's quarters. Bedelia said, "Now be sure to tell Mrs Pentwick that these little ones are wanting to hear the music we were enjoying earlier."

Bedelia was familiar with labouring and birthing as she had been present at the births of her younger brothers and sisters in their tiny, two-roomed cottage - not by choice, but by necessity.

Oh, it's been such a long time since I helped Mrs Murphy with Mam, Bedelia thought. Despite this, she set to readying the room for the impending birth. She turned to the ship's doctor for some guidance, and was bewildered again that he appeared to show little interest in what she was doing as he and Mr Ashcroft continued their discussion. Without further ado she shrugged her shoulders and went about the tasks she knew were necessary preparation.

As another wave of pain washed over the woman. Bedelia knelt beside the bed, quietly and gently talking. "Mrs Ashcroft, you are doing just fine, keep breathing through the pain and hold my hand if you need. Is there anything else you require?"

"I am so hot … can you find a cooling cloth?"

Bedelia reached for one of the cloths she had found on the bureau, dipped it in the porcelain bowl with the water she had taken from the matching jug and placed the wet cloth on the woman's forehead. She poured a cup of water from the jug and encouraged Mrs Ashcroft to take some sips.

Meanwhile the doctor carried on talking to the preacher, who in turn seemed relaxed and comfortable with what was happening to his wife. As the conversation progressed it was clear to Bedelia the topics they were discussing were to do with all things medical. *The preacher must be a medical man also,* Bedelia thought.

While there was a lull between pains, Bedelia popped her head out of the cabin door and saw the boy was back again awaiting further instructions. "What's yer name boy?" she said.

"Jim," he said as he fidgeted nervously, pushing back his blond hair that had strayed into his eyes.

"Have the little ones settled with my companions?"

"Why yes, miss. They are busy with some drawing and the girls are playing some music. It be so lovely. I couldna help meself but I had to watch for a while until I got the look from the matron."

"Now Jim, I need you to go fetch me some things. Get some boiled water from the cook. Mind that you carry it back carefully. Oh, and some old, clean rags. Now off you go and mind you don't tarry."

Bedelia stepped back into the cabin and Mrs Ashcroft reached out for her hand as another wave of pain flooded through her.

"Breathe slowly now," Bedelia coached, "in and out, in and out." She placed her hand on the woman's swollen abdomen and felt a small movement from within. It pleased Bedelia, for she had learnt that feeling the baby moving inside was a good sign. *I'm surprising myself with the lessons from Mrs Murphy that are coming back,* Bedelia thought.

Bedelia also noted that the crisp, white nightgown Mrs Ashcroft was wearing had neither dampness nor blood stains on it. This was another sign that her mam's midwife had taught Bedelia to watch for in the progress towards a birth.

The fact that the doctor was busily chatting to the preacher also set Bedelia's mind at rest that the confinement was progressing well.

No sooner had that thought passed than Mrs Ashcroft experienced another violent pain. She let out a scream, and Bedelia knew that this, and the other sounds coming from Mrs Ashcroft's throat, were signs of an imminent birth. At that moment the bed was flooded with a gush of clear liquid with an odour Bedelia recognised.

Mrs Ashcroft screamed again. "The baby is coming, I can feel it!" With that, the doctor and preacher abruptly ceased their conversation and came to the bedside to make ready to assist this baby into the world.

There was a tentative knock at the cabin door. Bedelia opened it a crack to reveal Jim carrying a large jug, steam emanating from the top and a swathe of rags slung over his shoulder. Bedelia placed the rags under one arm and took the jug with two hands, closed the door with her foot and crossed the cabin to place all the items on the bureau. After she had poured some of the water into the washing bowl, she put a few rags in to soak and asked the doctor what else he needed.

"Just something warm to wrap the baby in."

Bedelia went straight to the bundle of neatly folded, clean linen she had discovered on a chair in her earlier reconnaissance of the cabin. She took a couple of items that resembled wraps from the pile and discreetly placed them inside her tunic. *The baby is going to be here very soon,* Bedelia thought as she relived the excitement she had experienced as a girl helping her mam's midwife.

"Your body heat is the best warmth for a baby," the midwife had explained.

The doctor was ready with his hands near the small opening at the bottom of Mrs Ashcroft's nightgown. He had placed a sheet over her legs; an attempt at discretion and modesty for these godly people. Bedelia thought *Mam would have laughed at that* as she remembered her saying, "When you have children, Dee, you leave your dignity at the bedroom door."

The next moment Mrs Ashcroft made a bovine noise, grunted, pushed and the baby's head could be seen between her legs. With another push the rest of the baby's body was born and the wee girl let out a loud cry as she breathed for the first time. Mr Ashcroft announced proudly, "It is seventeen minutes to the hour of eight."

"Congratulations. You have a healthy wee daughter, Mr and Mrs Ashcroft," the doctor said.

Bedelia could not hold back the tears for the safe and speedy arrival of the missionaries' third child. They were tears of relief, tears of joy and tears of grief at the memory of the tragic loss of her own mother and baby sister. That birth had been the last one she had witnessed before this happy event.

Bedelia could see that this overwhelming surge of emotion, with the safe arrival of a new baby, was relished by all those involved. It is truly a miracle in this hazardous world, she thought.

Bedelia wrapped the baby in the warm cotton sheet she had removed from inside her bodice. She placed the baby as high on Mrs Ashcroft's chest as she could manage with the ropey cord still attached. There was a brisk bleed following the baby's birth, and the doctor skilfully delivered the afterbirth as he watched for more bleeding.

Remembering the explanations from the midwife, Bedelia knew that this was always a birth practitioner's tense moment; another time of tremendous concern. She had been told that excessive bleeding was one of the most common reasons for the loss of a mother in childbirth.

Bedelia knew this only too well. Memories flooded back of her little sister's birth. She had witnessed the midwife's struggle to stem her mother's bleeding and watched frightened and helpless as her mother's blood loss rapidly drained her life away. The event came back to Bedelia like it had only happened yesterday.

The doctor felt the middle of Mrs Ashcroft's abdomen in the area where the pregnant bulge had once been and took Bedelia's small hand. He guided her as she cupped her hand inside his. She felt a large ball-shaped object at Mrs Ashcroft's navel. The doctor led Bedelia to firmly massage this with her hand. She could feel the change and hardening of this shape as she rubbed until it became about the size of a large closed fist.

"Well done, Bedelia," the doctor said, "I felt sure I could rely on you as the best helper for me on this ship. I have noticed how able and willing you have been to administer to those in your cabin who have been stricken during the rough weather."

Bedelia glowed with the doctor's praise but knew there was more work to do. Her next task was to assist Mrs Ashcroft to get into a comfortable position so she could offer the baby her breast to feed. The little stranger nuzzled in, licked the golden drops off the end of the pink nipple, then with a wide mouth latched to the breast and began sucking. Bedelia knew how important this most natural form of feeding was to the baby's future health and nourishment.

The doctor explained to Bedelia that in the twenty-four hours following the birth it was crucial to watch and perform the womb massage if there was any concern about a woman's blood loss, and he turned to Mr Ashcroft with an enquiring look.

"I am familiar with the procedure and the benefits and will call you for help if necessary," Mr Ashcroft said. "And thank you, young lady, for your attention to my wife. We are very grateful for your care."

Bedelia took a little more time to set the cabin right. She offered to wash the wet and bloody items soiled during the birth.

"There is no need, thank you, we have good help to tend to our daily needs and house-keeping," said Mrs Ashcroft.

With that, Bedelia begged leave to return to her quarters, with the promise that she would see the children safely returned to their parents.

As the sisters settled for sleep that night, Bedelia confided, "Oh Vonnie, I still feel the excitement of what I witnessed. The birth of a baby is the miracle of life, and I feel so drawn to helping women with this, as I was when Mammy had the little babies. The doctor was saying really nice things about my help. He said it would be worth my while to look for a position with a monthly nurse or midwife when we settle in the new country."

Veronica smiled. "That's wonderful, Dee. It's certainly not for me. I'm leaning towards looking for a position in a home with a young family. I so enjoy being around children, but ones with a bit of age on them. I can also cook and clean, so that's the way I want to go. I know I would like it. The preacher's children, who came down here this evening, were so lovely; we had a lot of fun. We were able to do some drawings in my notebook then Molly played her tin whistle and Siobhan taught Jacob and Sarah a jig. They loved it."

The sisters turned over in their bunks, bidding each other goodnight. Bedelia's mind was busy reliving the birth. She couldn't switch off the doubting voice in her head telling her she was too young, too ignorant, didn't have enough experience. *Why did the doctor and preacher just stand by and leave me to work out what was needed while Mrs Ashcroft laboured?* she thought.

Bedelia considered how she and Veronica would be able to find positions, enabling them to stay close while pursuing their individual work. She snuggled down under her quilt and followed her sister as she slumped into an exhausted sleep of dreams for their future.

Chapter 2

Excitement was rising. The first mate had called "Land ahoy!" Tenerife was the first land sighted since they had departed England.

It was six in the morning. The sun was about to rise and the rays crept over the water as though a lantern were being carried up towards the horizon. The bustle on board fuelled Bedelia's anticipation. Already numbers of Portuguese peddlers had arrived beside the anchored ship in their small boats with baskets full of oranges, lemons, bananas and lovely bunches of flowers, varieties never before seen by the sisters. The vendors were calling out their wares in broken English.

Bedelia and Veronica, who had now perked up, were among the first passengers ready to disembark. The Portuguese ferry boat had tied up alongside the *Catherine Mary*, ready to transport those passengers wishing to visit the port town for the day. Although they had but a few pennies to spend, the sisters had agreed that this experience could not be missed.

"When will we get this chance again?" Veronica spoke Bedelia's exact thoughts aloud.

The girls were wearing their lightest dresses and bonnets, for they had been warned it would be very hot ashore. The atmosphere reminded them of their excitement when visiting the country fair as children, and yet the whole scene was so strange and new.

As they were helped onto the wharf, men and women squatted along their path ready to sell their goods. The passengers who had the money found it difficult to barter. Luckily Mr Ashcroft had come ashore with this group, and he was able to converse and help the buyers with his knowledge of the French and Spanish languages. The sisters had been told by the first mate that these vendors were used to the many English speakers who visited their port. They found it convenient to pretend ignorance when securing a sale.

Some of the passengers bought fresh eggs, others bought fruit. Bananas, they were told, could not be taken on board the ship as they were a bad omen; a ship carrying them would be lost at sea. Bedelia and Veronica had never seen nor tasted one, so they bought a small bag of oranges instead. "I can almost taste these before I even peel them," Veronica said, licking her lips.

A passenger was so intrigued by a man with a parrot jabbering away on his shoulder that he was close to buying it until the preacher warned him that the captain would not let it aboard. The sisters stopped to look.

"That bird looks to have been splashed with all different colours of paint. That may be why it's squawking in protest. I'm sure I would be," Bedelia said, giggling behind her hand.

Veronica was able to purchase stamps for her letter home to her uncle. They could leave it there to be sent with the next ship heading for England. "Isn't it a wonder," Veronica said. "Here we are across the seas, and I can imagine the surprise Uncle Paddy will get for sure, when he visits Scarriff and the store keeper hands him this letter. It's worth our precious pennies to give him this treat for his kindnesses."

Bedelia was intrigued by Tenerife, a quaint little town with its wide streets and flat-roofed houses with a backdrop of beautiful mountains.

Townspeople were heading towards a church in the centre of the square, so the sisters followed the group. Bedelia noticed some of these women wore simple dresses with a kerchief tied over their heads. Others, whom she presumed were of a higher class, wore black dresses of finely made, intricate lace with a matching square of the same material draped gracefully over their heads. They were carrying pretty parasols and fans.

No one questioned their presence, so the girls took a pew at the back of the church with a genuflect and a sign of the cross made respectfully as they bowed towards the altar.

They scanned the building, their eyes wide and mouths agape. Bedelia put her mouth close to Veronica's ear saying, "I've never seen such beauty. Will you look at those grand ornaments!" A brightly polished golden chalice sat atop an altar covered with a white satin cloth, which was appliqued and embroidered with gold thread. The splendour of the adornments here surpassed those in the simple church they had attended back home.

The congregation rose in unison and in glorious song as the priest, in his lavishly stitched vestments of white and gold satin, paraded in carrying a golden staff with a cross on top. He walked at the rear of his entourage, who slowly and reverently made their way up the aisle, each heading to their designated place at the front of the church.

The prayers of the mass, said in Latin, came naturally to Bedelia and Veronica and the girls stayed for the entire service. They watched the familiar way the congregation used their rosary beads and noticed how devoutly they prayed. It made Bedelia homesick, remembering mass her family had attended in their village church at least once a week.

As Bedelia and Veronica left the steps of the church, they stopped to let a man pass. He was leading a cart carrying produce and drawn by oxen. Six donkeys ambled along behind, tied to the rear of the cart. The man wore a dirty white shirt that hung loosely from his frame and trousers with a blanket fixed around his middle. He stopped in front of the sisters and gestured until they understood that he was offering them a ride.

Veronica declined, but Bedelia nodded enthusiastically. The man indicated he wanted a penny for the ride. The girls looked at each other and Bedelia glanced down at the handkerchief holding their meagre pennies.

"I am thanking you for your trouble, but no it is," Bedelia said as she shook her head.

The man leading the cart let out a jovial laugh and beckoned Bedelia towards a donkey. The shake of his wrist indicated he was happy to give her a free ride. Veronica hooted with laughter as the donkey, with Bedelia holding on tightly to the bridle, her legs splayed like a wishbone over its sides, trotted down the road towards the market.

Bedelia arrived just beside where the crew from the *Catherine Mary* were loading full barrels of water and supplies of fresh produce for the ongoing journey. Michael appeared just in time to offer Bedelia his hand to dismount. He had come to shore on one of the later ferries. Somewhat out of breath, Veronica caught up to her sister.

"That was such fun," Bedelia said as she slid down from the donkey with a big grin on her face.

Michael said, "This is my companion, Keenan. We're going up to see the gardens. We've been told they're full of beautiful flowers of all sorts not found in Ireland, and there are fountains and the like."

After shaking Keenan's hand, Bedelia turned to her sister. "And this is the young fella I told you about. He's the one I met the other day we had our trunks out. His name is Michael, and this is my sister Veronica."

"Pleased to make your acquaintances," Veronica replied with a prim little giggle and a curtsy.

"Oh, no need for any formality, Vonnie, these men are one of us. They just come from over the valley in Templemore."

Bedelia turned to Michael. "Have your brother and his family come to explore too?"

"No," he said, looking down at his hands, "their young Bridie has a fever and is quite poorly, so they were unable to leave her."

"I saw there was a sickly little one in the family section. I offered to help, but they were managing with the doctor's care. I hadn't figured they were your family, Michael."

"That was kind of you, Bedelia," he said.

"Just call me Delia," she said. "I prefer that. Bedelia sounds such a mouthful, so it does."

"Thank you, I'll be glad to do so. Would you both like to take a turn of the gardens with us?"

"That would be just grand, Michael," Bedelia said as she did a little skip around to face her sister.

"I hope you don't mind, but I won't come, as I haven't much energy left. I've done more already than I have been able to do for weeks," Veronica said. "Now be off and enjoy the gardens. I'm just going to sit here under the tree and watch the men toiling with the ship's supplies. Mind you stay close to the others from the ship, Dee."

There was a bench seat just beside them with a clear view out to the *Catherine Mary* and beyond. Veronica sat down and started peeling the orange she had picked out of her bag. Bedelia caught a glimpse of her sister smelling it. She hoped it was as delicious as she remembered. They were such a delicacy and rarity as children, they often had to share one between the lot of them. She vividly recalled the juice that squirted out with every mouthful of each carefully dislodged segment, freshening her tongue with that distinct sweet flavour. The succulent liquid that escaped down her wrist, before she took the next bite was so clear in her imagination that she very nearly took an orange to eat on her way. She grinned. She caught her sister's satiated smile as they walked away, Veronica capturing some of the juice with a slurp of her lips.

The seat Veronica had found was close to the bustling activity of the dock. "I'm pleased, so I am, to see Vonnie enjoy some sustenance at last. She will be safe sitting right there, I think," Bedelia said to her two escorts.

An hour later Bedelia, Michael and Keenan returned to join Veronica, in time to take one of the last boats ferrying the passengers back to the waiting ship.

"Vonnie, words aren't enough to tell you of the beauty we've just seen in the gardens," Bedelia said as she handed her sister the small bunch of brightly coloured tropical flowers she had picked. "I've never seen the like before. Keenan helped me with the names, but really, there are too many to remember. What did we see?" Bedelia said, turning to Keenan.

"Oh, I remember now," she said before either of the men could answer. "There were orchids, plants with prickles on them you wouldn't want to touch, but with the prettiest, most unusual flowers. And some of the trees had branches like fat ladies' arms holding bunches of thick blades of grass. I don't know why they're called Dragon Trees, I don't, not that I've ever seen a dragon."

Bedelia was thinking how nice it had been to spend time on land after weeks of that endless rolling of the ship. She wished they could stay a bit longer in this exotic place, so different from home. She would have liked to explore more.

After dinner that night, lying together in the confines of one of their bunks, Bedelia prattled on about Michael. She was so excited and wanted to share everything they had experienced on their outing.

Veronica whispered close to Bedelia's ear, "For goodness' sake Dee, slow down. I'm getting a little weary of hearing about that man. Michael did this, Michael said that. You'll have to be careful that Matron doesn't see you fraternising with the men folk on board this ship. And besides, we really don't know him from Adam, so don't get yourself smitten. You might be disappointed."

"Go on with you, Vonnie. Don't be showing your green eyes just because I've found a friend who just so happens to be a man. There's nothing more to it than that. And besides, he makes me laugh. And in this god-forsaken life we've been given so far, a good dose of laughter goes ..."

Bedelia stopped mid-sentence. She and her sister hadn't bickered like that for a long time. They stared at each other for a moment, then burst into tears as the floods of emotion for all they had endured together spilt out. They lay there, clinging to one another, sailing towards the unknown. The feeling of separation from their homeland widened even more for Bedelia.

It was only several days later, as the sisters were taking a turn of the main deck, that they noticed the activity at the rear of the ship. Bedelia wondered what several of the crew were engaged in. She whispered to Veronica, and they approached the bosun to ask what was happening.

"Ma'am, we are measurin' our speed. Would you care to come aft and I'll explain?"

"We'd be mighty pleased, thank you for your trouble, sir," Veronica said.

The bosun led Bedelia and Veronica onto the poop deck. Bedelia knew this area was restricted to the passengers travelling in first and second class. The cabin passengers usually kept their distance on this part of the ship, out of bounds to the "riff raff", as Bedelia had heard them being called by a man with a very upper-class English accent.

The bosun pointed to the sailor handling a length of rope. "Here, watch what's happenin'. You see the log is tied with rope. The rope is havin' knots at equal distances along its length and is wound up in a bobbin, makin' sure it runs freely. Now that sailor over there, he's in charge of the sand glass, which takes the sand through in ten minutes of the clock."

Bedelia could see the first sailor was making ready to throw the log of wood, shaped like a slice of pie, over the stern of the ship.

The bosun continued, "The number of knots along the rope that roll into the sea in the time the sand glass is emptied is noted, and the workin' out is made for how many knots we travel in one hour. That then becomes the speed we're travelin'; perhaps twelve knots. Simple as that."

"Why thank you, sir, for your explanation," said Veronica. "The nuns at the school I went to before the … well, they said I could do my sums. What you have told us has made some sense to me."

"So where would you be coming from? Can you tell us about your home, sir?" Bedelia said.

The bosun puffed his chest out and with a big grin said, "I know the ship and the ports we dock in like the back of my hand. I have been at sea many more years than I lived in the home where I grew up, so ask me about Robin Hood's Bay in the north-east of Yorkshire, and I'd be at a loss to tell you much, but ask me about a ship and I'll tell you all the workings from the tip of the mast to the bottom of the hull."

"I'm thanking you for your trouble, sir. Now we'd better be off. I can see our being on this deck is getting some of the passengers upset," Veronica said.

The sisters stepped down from the poop deck under the disdainful gaze of several first-class travellers. The girls held their heads high. Veronica said, "Well, that surely put some noses out of joint, so it did."

Bedelia poked her tongue out and wiggled her hips as she strode confidently down to the main deck, nose in the air. They knew there couldn't be any complaints, because they had been formally invited. "So there," Bedelia said, giggling.

After the midday meal, Bedelia's offer to help nurse Michael's ailing niece was finally accepted. The doctor explained that the child's condition had worsened and there were grave fears for her recovery. She had endured a fever for days and not let much more than a few spoonfuls of broth and water pass her lips. Her rosy-red cheeks and lips stood out in stark contrast to her pale little face. Her glazed eyes, quite sunken, were encircled by dark rings.

Bedelia gently coaxed the little girl into taking some more liquid and even gave up one of her Tenerife oranges to be squeezed into the water as an enticing treat. She cradled the child's small head in her lap and gently wiped her brow with a cool, damp cloth.

Looking up into Bedelia's eyes wistfully, Bridie seemed to have the knowing eyes of an old soul.

The energy of the child's parents, Moira and Patrick, was spent from many sleepless nights tending to their daughter. They were only just managing to eat themselves and see to their young son Seamus's everyday needs, and were grateful for the respite given by Bedelia nursing Bridie.

Bedelia ate the stew her sister brought through to the family section and offered Bridie a small spoonful of the gravy. The child pursed her lips tightly and closed her eyes, turning her head away.

After the family had settled for the night and sunk into a deep and exhausted sleep in the larger berth they all shared, Bedelia found a small area at the base of the bed to sit for her night vigil.

By two in the morning Bedelia knew the little girl's life was slipping away. Her breathing had become shallow, her pale body limp, and her parched lips had turned from a deep rose colour to a grey-blue hue. Bedelia gently roused the parents, sure that they would want to spend time with their daughter in her last hours on this earth.

"If you want me to stay, I would be willing. I know your distress will be great as I'm sure we're losing the fight and your little Bridie's time with us is drawing to a close."

"Please do, if you will," Patrick said. "You have been such a rock for us even in this short time, and we see so much love and caring in your eyes for our Bridie. Can you see if our Michael can join us?"

Bedelia knew it was forbidden for single men to enter this area, but she felt the matron and the captain may be compassionate enough to allow it in these circumstances.

"Mikey has such a soft spot for our young ones and they for him," Patrick said.

"Would you be wanting the preacher to come? He is a man of God and as good as any priest to see your little colleen into heaven," Bedelia said with a quaver in her voice.

Patrick was hardly able to speak as he nodded his assent.

Bedelia woke Mrs Pentwick and asked her to send for Michael and the preacher. She returned immediately as she was loath to spend any more time away from the family than was necessary.

Only a short time passed before Michael's sleepy and concerned face appeared around the curtain dividing the women's quarters from that of the families. The Wesleyan missionary was just behind him.

As soon as Michael saw his little niece, tears welled in his eyes and he looked questioningly at Bedelia. She shook her head slowly, tears pricking at her eyes.

Michael moved forward and kissed his niece on her forehead as she lay limp in her father's lap. He took one of each of Patrick's and Moira's hands as they watched the life slowly drain from Bridie's body. The messenger of death had entered their midst.

The preacher prayed and said his ministrations for the repose of the innocent child's soul. Bedelia knew a Catholic priest would have administered last rites, anointing the child with oil while those around prayed with rosary beads, but Mr Ashcroft was the only holy man on the ship and the family seemed comforted that he was there.

The little girl's last breath left her body and there was silence all around. Suddenly Moira let out a shrill keen. All those in steerage were roused, but no one moved, as they all knew what this meant. Many of the others in earshot joined the family as they prayed for the safe passage of the sinless creature into heaven. Bedelia started and the others followed, saying, "Eternal rest grant unto her, O Lord, and let perpetual light shine upon her. May she rest in peace."

A resounding "Amen" came from all corners of the families' and women's quarters.

Bedelia held Michael's hand as he, too, wailed with grief for the loss of yet another family member. Bedelia wondered why, after witnessing so many deaths of family members in the preceding years, a person would not become numb and immune to death. But she knew that another death brought back the memories of all those other loved ones lost. She thought at least her countrymen know how to mourn and show their raw emotion and grief. The keening seemed to allow that sorrow to pass more quickly.

After Michael and Mr Ashcroft had left, Bedelia washed Bridie's wasted body tenderly and dressed the child in her best outfit, with a little help from the sobbing mother. By dawn the small body was wrapped and sewn into a sail cloth with a bag of sand tucked inside to weigh it down. After a short and solemn service by the missionary, Bridie was commended to the deep.

Chapter 3

The atmosphere was oppressive. The feeling among the passengers was tense. "Mrs Pentwick is becoming a real fiery dragon now. Nothing we can do is right," Bedelia said to Isla, as they carried the steaming broth up from the galley. That really was the last kind of meal she felt like in this sweltering heat. Nothing in Bedelia's life could compare to the humidity they were all suffering.

Several calm days had passed, during which they had seemed to make little or no progress. The women in steerage were allowed up on the deck throughout the day. Normally this had only been permitted in the late afternoon, but the heat in their living space was so suffocating that some were falling sick just from the lack of fresh air. The doctor advised a little leniency in the rules, but the matron's watchfulness had not let up.

"Four eyes are surely better than two," Mrs Pentwick said to the doctor as they walked the deck. Bedelia smiled as she wandered past the two chaperones, noting their serious faces and alert eyes darting here and there.

A large sail cloth had been erected above the main deck to shade that area. The women had reduced their clothing to light shifts, with just enough cover to keep decency in the searing heat. A spare barrel of water was sacrificed for the passengers to dip a rag in to cool their foreheads and another with a jug to keep their drinking vessels full. These barrels were being emptied at great speed.

Bedelia stood at the railings looking out to sea as she listened intently to the conversation going on above her on the forecastle. "The doldrums," the first mate explained to a group of first-class passengers, "is a belt of calm and bafflingly light winds. It is common north of the Equator, between the north and south trade winds. We could be stuck here for days, and some ships have the misfortune to be stuck for weeks."

Even at night, heat seemed to emanate down from the deck into the hold. The men and the crew were permitted to set up their hammocks on deck on whatever structures or posts they could find, in order to sleep. The women had to sweat it out sleeping below deck with the hatches open and the ladder removed. "To prevent any straying for a night rendezvous," Mrs Pentwick told them.

Bedelia noticed the lack of ease as the crew went about their work. She mentioned this to the doctor when they met on deck one day.

"The crew, and more so the captain," he said, "have deep superstitions about the cause of being caught in these extremely unpleasant weather patterns. They would rather be racked by heavy seas, squalling rain, sleet and strong winds."

"I'm sure I wouldn't," Bedelia said.

"I agree," said the doctor. "I could barely function in the last storm we went through. The crew say at least they feel they are getting somewhere with the stormy weather, but the relentless heat and lack of movement appear to play havoc with minds." He went on to say there were many superstitions on board a ship, and some unfortunate incidents were blamed on simply saying "Goodbye" or "Good luck". One day Bedelia and several passengers had seen the captain confiscate a hat belonging to one of the men, saying it was a bad luck omen if it was lost overboard.

As the pitch bubbled in the seams of the deck, the stifling days seemed interminable. The ship inched sluggishly along and Bedelia wondered if they were doomed to be stuck here for eternity. It was as close as she imagined Hell's heat to be if she dared sin against God. She recalled the priest's sermons at mass, preaching Hell's fire and damnation to sinners who strayed from the Holy Father.

With so much time to think, even this unpleasant recollection of the threats coming from the pulpit brought tears to her eyes as she thought of home and the familiar, happy places of her childhood, the comfort of the warm fire in the grate and the light downy feeling of their shared quilt. Recollections of her mam's soft, welcoming cuddles and Da's sturdy lap were fading memories. Bedelia smiled as she recalled the treat if you were the one lucky enough to sit on his knee, the others sitting at his ankles, while their father sang favourite songs, tapping out the beat on the bodhran positioned on his free knee.

Bedelia was brought back from her daydream as the ship stirred and the sails creaked and those looking towards the horizon took in the cry, "Wind to the starboard!" A small breeze had whipped up the mirror glass water to a ripple and then stronger gusts of wind produced tufts of white foam catching rides on waves of deep blue sea.

After a pleasant night's sleep, one of the first in many days, the ship's passengers were called together on the deck. Excitement and expectation spread as the doctor shared with Bedelia a peek through his eyeglass. He was explaining where she needed to look in order to see the Equator, a mark of the line they were about to cross. Bedelia persisted in pursuing the line in the distance. As she moved her eyes slightly back, freeing her lashes obstructing her view, an incredible sight of the line and a large wave heading towards her caused her to jump back. It had felt so close and so ready to swamp her on the deck.

The doctor let out a hoot of laughter. Bedelia realised she had been duped and joined his laughter, the doctor revealing the small thread he had placed across the sight glass of his scope.

"You just wait, you'll be sorry, you will," she said, a huge smile on her face.

A sharp trumpet sounded from the forecastle along with a guttural roar. They were welcoming Neptune on board. Bedelia had heard the male passengers being warned by the crew to have a few coins in their pockets.

Bedelia and Veronica noticed the preacher's children on the poop deck and waved to them. The children tapped their mother on her arm and Bedelia could see they were pleading and pointing to the women on the main deck.

As she cradled her wee baby in its woollen shawl, their mother conferred with her husband, then nodded to her children. The wind had whipped up, and while it held a warmth from the newly risen sun, it was still brisk enough to require the baby, Catherine Mary, shelter from it. Bedelia had found out that babies born in passage were often named for the ship on which they had been brought safely into the world.

Sarah and Jacob skipped happily down from the poop deck and headed straight for Veronica, Siobhan and Molly. "You know we're going to see Neptune. He looks after the middle of the world," Sarah said.

The women laughed and bent to listen closely to the children as the din from the pending show rose. Michael had joined Bedelia, with his nephew Seamus beside him. Bedelia introduced the two young boys, who hesitated for only a few moments in their shyness and very quickly connected.

"Young ones are all the same no matter where they hail from. They're happy to find someone of the same age to spend time to play with, so they are," Michael said.

A makeshift carriage covered in a Union Jack, drawn by five men dressed as animals supposed to represent marine monsters, arrived from behind the captain's cabin. It was carrying one of the sailors decked out as Neptune, complete with a swab for a beard, a couple of mops for hair, and a crudely made crown placed on top of his head. The other occupant was another sailor depicting Mrs Neptune. Seamus called out, "Look, she has hair on her face!" as the couple were carried down from the forecastle.

The carriage was accompanied by other crew members fantastically dressed as a policeman, a doctor, a barber and his clerk and a bear with his keeper. The bear was the cook togged out in the skin of a sheep. With its black face and white woolly coat, it no more looked like a bear than Neptune's wife looked like a woman. The barber carried a large pot and all the men were laughing loudly.

The entourage approached the poop deck and shook hands with the captain, wished him a good voyage and had a glass of rum all round. After parading around the deck, they returned to the base of the forecastle, where Neptune and his wife danced, Mrs Neptune showing more leg than was seemly in polite society. The passengers cheered. The dance concluded and the five sea monsters disappeared.

Neptune held a large book. He opened it, calling out the name of the first victim. "Mr Hall!"

The men echoed the call. "Mr. Hall!"

The crew reverberated "Mr Hall!" and the rest of the assembled crowd took up the chant until it felt like even the sails were echoing the call.

Mr Hall was seized, blindfolded and brought to the bath some of the crew had set up earlier. It was filled with water with a wooden board placed across it.

Neptune asked, "Have you ever crossed the line afore?"

Mr Hall dubiously tilted his head, attempting to capture a sliver of light, his fearful face betraying his uncertainty as to the fate that would befall him. "I haven't, sir."

"What will you give to lighten your punishment?" Neptune persisted.

"I don't know," said Hall, "I'm not sure. Oh," he said as he realised the game, "what about a bottle of porter?"

"A bottle of porter!" Neptune complained bitterly. "Can't you do better than that?"

With that, the barber mixed the pot he held containing a vile liquid made from tar and the filth collected from the bottom of the animal enclosure. The stench emanating from the pot made any person close by have no doubt as to its contents.

"Two bottles of porter," Hall pleaded.

"Done," said Neptune.

The barber stepped up, slapped Hall's cheeks with a paintbrush soaked with the mess from the pot, scraped it off with a crude replica of a razor and tipped the young man back off the board into the bath. He was then ducked a couple of times by the bear and his keeper.

Hall gingerly exited the bath drenched to the bone, his face dripping blood from his close shave.

Over the next hour more men were subjected to the same degrading punishment if they couldn't come up with the goods that pleased the King of the Sea. The crowd screamed with laughter, as much at the response from the victims as at the antics of the actors carrying out the punishment. Other men looked mightily relieved when they had not been singled out.

Once Neptune and his accomplices had disappeared, the entertainment moved on to include everyone with musical talent and those others keen to join in the festivities with dancing and singing. It was all a welcome relief from the usual tedium of life on board.

Several sailors had musical instruments; one had an accordion, one a mouth organ and another a bodhran. The Irish drum looked just like their da's, Bedelia thought. It was held in one hand from behind, which could control the pitch and timbre, and beaten in the front with the other hand holding a short double-ended drumstick made of wood.

Siobhan and Molly stepped up after getting their instruments from below. The musicians stood in a huddle to discuss which tunes they had in common, and the session began.

There was much foot stomping and clapping. Michael jumped up to join in with a jig and a reel. Bedelia looked on briefly, surprised and pleased she and her friend had another thing in common. He started a hard shoe dance and, at his invitation, she adeptly followed his lead, which in turn drew a surprised look from him. He went this way and she went that as they matched each other's movements. In no time at all they had the passengers whooping and calling out for more, easily stepping into a complementary rhythm as if they had been dancing together all their lives.

Once the scene had been set and shyness pushed aside, each of the men approached one of the women. They readied themselves for the set dancing that ensued, called by the second mate. This was very popular and none of the women were left seated, including the matron. Even Moira and Patrick shed their sadness for the moment and joined in. Mrs Ashcroft was able to join her husband when the doctor offered to hold the baby.

The children ran around the periphery of the dancers, watched carefully by the first mate and the captain, who were standing behind the helmsman in charge of the large spoke wheel. When resting after an exuberant reel, Bedelia noticed these three crewmen seemed dedicated in their vigil. She realised the dangers when the children got too exuberant and moved too close to the main deck railings or the taffrail on the poop, needing to be ushered to a safer place to play. The little ones were having the time of their lives together, squealing with delight. Bedelia smiled.

Around mid-afternoon the dancing died down, and the cook and his assistants brought up the feast they had been preparing for days in readiness for this celebration. All the crew, who had spent many years on the sea, were very familiar with the events that went on when crossing the Equator. Some crew had set up the tables to take the sumptuous food. The pig had been on the spit for many hours, tended and basted by the kitchen hand while the cook was taking his part in Neptune's visit.

Roast potatoes, pumpkin, cabbage and fruit brought on board in Tenerife were in serving dishes on the table. Bedelia thought there was a feel of celebration about the fare, although she was unfamiliar with the richness of some dishes, especially the steamed fruit puddings dripping with lashings of brandy sauce.

"What a treat," Bedelia said to Michael. They were still catching their breath after the last dance, both red-faced and sweaty from the exertion.

After the meal the children were ushered off to bed, but the captain gave the single passengers, and adults without children, permission to carry on celebrating with music and dancing. The matron, doctor and captain took their posts as chaperones on the deck.

Veronica had regained her strength and was having her sixth dance with the first mate. Bedelia had only danced with Michael and the doctor and continued with Michael for the rest of the night. They were gently touching and holding each other when the chaperones' attention was elsewhere. Neither had eyes for anyone else. Bedelia's heart was bouncing out of her throat more from emotion than the exertion of the dancing. Michael didn't look at any other woman on the deck.

It was midnight before the captain called a stop to the fun. He, along with the doctor and the matron, ran a check on all their charges to see that no one had escaped their eagle eyes. Four were missing, and with all hands on deck, one couple, Maggie and Danny, were soon found. They were in a quiet place in the rear of the poop deck among the coiled ropes. Sound asleep in each other's arms, they were fully attired, much to the relief of the matron and their families. The other two were finally found behind the livestock pen in the midship hold, *inflagrante delicto,* as the doctor could be heard telling the captain.

The couple, brought up on deck, bedraggled and wrapped roughly in their clothes, were taken before the captain. The man was one of the cabin passengers and the woman was from steerage. Bedelia recognised Therese.

"That little hussy," the matron said to the captain. "She and her female travelling companion have been my nemesis from the time they boarded the ship. Their cheekiness and defiance have been a constant trial." The passengers who had stayed up for the celebration were gathered around to watch the spectacle.

The captain raged that the gentleman had disgraced the etiquette of his class and the young woman was showing her gutter upbringing. They were banned from any future contact.

The captain had no real power over the gentleman as he was a first-class passenger who had paid his way, but the matron and the captain sentenced Therese to reduced rations and a month of floor scrubbing in steerage.

"From now on," Mrs Pentwick said in her sternest voice, "I will be watching over you and your friend like a hawk. I will not tolerate this behaviour. I will make sure there is not a repeat of this serious breach of ship rules. And that goes for the rest of you lot in my charge." Mrs Pentwick's eyes swept around the women gathered with such ferocity that no-one could be in any doubt as to her intent to carry out this threat.

It was certainly an event that set all the tongues wagging throughout the ship for the rest of the journey. "Tut tut" fell from the matron's lips with monotonous regularity. It irked Bedelia to see her fellow passengers turn their eyes aside when they came into contact with Therese. No conversation was permitted with her, as that would be seen to be bringing oneself down to her level; a great shame, Bedelia thought.

Chapter 4

The miles passed and the ship's journey proceeded. The winds became fresher and the passengers afflicted by seasickness took to their bunks once again, while Bedelia's assistance was called on more and more.

For the fifth day on end the ship creaked and broached, swayed, and climbed up and down the huge waves. If one dared or was even allowed to be out on the deck it would have made the hardiest person's stomach turn.

All the hatches were battened down, but despite that, the sea seeped in through the cracks between the deck timbers. Everything felt damp and dreary. The last of the evening light was creeping in through these gaps. It was too hazardous to use the lamps; they could easily be thrown to the ground. Despite the sodden conditions, if the wooden boards sealed with tar and combined with oil were ignited by the flames, it could lead to a devastating fire.

Meals were cold for the same reason. Those immune to the nausea caused by the harsh weather conditions dreamed of quieter seas and the plain but more palatable hot, cooked food.

Bedelia moved around the women's quarters checking on the women tucked in their bunks. She gathered the buckets brimming with the products of seasickness. As she bent to collect one of the last pails, she noticed Maureen doubled over in agony. She was in more distress than Bedelia would expect from seasickness.

As she looked at the young woman more closely, she saw a large blood-stained patch spreading out from under her nightgown. Bedelia called out for Mrs Pentwick to come quickly.

Maureen's companion Therese was peering out wide-eyed from the bunk above. Since her shenanigans some weeks ago, when they had stolen some moments out of sight of the others, Therese confided freely in Bedelia, who had been the only woman in steerage to ignore the punishment the others were imposing on her. It appalled Bedelia that anyone could send someone, in such close confines, to Coventry.

Despite Bedelia's tender years, she wasn't shocked to hear that Therese and Maureen had worked together in one of the oldest professions in the world.

Bedelia was aware of prostitution. She had encountered women who were coerced into the pleasuring and entertainment of men when she and Veronica themselves were forced, by their circumstances, into the workhouse. Bedelia mused that, when you were dirt-poor, there were few choices for women to avoid starvation.

Therese told Bedelia they had decided to leave the harshness of their conditions when they had seen the poster offering young women "of good character" free passage to the colonies. Their companions, who had worked in the brothel for much longer, knew the trapped life that lay ahead of them. They had encouraged these young girls to take this opportunity and run away.

Therese explained that all they needed was a letter written by a willing sponsor. One of the more benevolent of their patrons, from the finer society, agreed to help. Many such men frequented the "House of Pleasure". The letter came with a small financial assistance to obtain the required travel items for emigration.

Therese's fellow workers, she told Bedelia, felt that by assisting her and Maureen to escape their fateful future, they themselves had some sort of hope.

Maureen called out in pain. "Shite, Jaysus, Mary and Saint Joseph, what's happening? I've never felt the like of this pain."

Mrs Pentwick, who had responded to Bedelia's request for help, yelled back at Maureen, "Stop that blasphemy. I will not have such gutter language spoken in my presence. Get a hold of yaself."

Bedelia surprised herself as she took the matron aside and said sternly, "Mrs Pentwick, I will be needing your help and not your sneers, for I am thinking Maureen is in the condition and will soon be producing a little stranger."

Mrs Pentwick took a step back, her face betraying her absolute disgust. "These two women will be the death of me," she moaned.

"Mrs Pentwick, I'll be asking you to send for the doctor if you will." The matron unlocked the hatch and yelled for one of the nearby crew to go fetch the doctor. The sodden sailor, peering down from above, replied "Aye, aye ma'am."

It wasn't long before the same sailor returned and when the hatch was opened to his loud knocks, Bedelia turned to see a face that showed the news.

"The doctor be laid up in his cabin. The seasickness has got him bad," the boy said, shouting above the din of the storm.

Mrs Pentwick plonked herself down on the form at the communal table. "What are we to do, lass? I'm nay good to you, I've never so much as held a wee one."

Bedelia had already made an inventory of her requirements in her mind and she had set to preparing what meagre items she had at hand for the pending arrival. She sent Therese for some old rags, and would normally have asked for some boiling water. With no way of heating it, she would just have to do with a jug of water from the barrel. As instructed, Therese tucked some of the rags against her breast to use to keep the baby warm when it arrived.

Bedelia attempted to create an area in which to work. She put on her pinny to protect her shift, as she knew there would be no chance to do any washing for many more days. She sat beside the distressed girl, rubbing the small of her back firmly when she experienced another gripping pain. Bedelia knew this was extremely soothing because when her mam's time had come for birthing, she had called for Bedelia to do this for her. Even with her tiny hands Bedelia knew exactly where her mam needed her to rub, and how firmly.

It was clear from the size of the well-concealed bump now protruding from Maureen's shift that this baby was going to be small. It didn't surprise Bedelia that this girl's condition had gone undetected. Maureen was small, but her garments were loose and covered a multitude of sins. Bedelia smiled to herself at the double meaning of this thought, yet her heart was thumping in her chest knowing that she had to care for this woman and bring her baby into the world with no reliable help.

With most of the passengers in steerage being laid low by their sickness, the young girl's cries fell on many deaf ears, their own misery overshadowing what was going on in the bunk nearby. Bedelia could do little to alleviate Maureen's ordeal. She waited, patiently rubbing, as the hours passed, with an ear out for the familiar noises women made when birth was imminent.

Bedelia's mother had given birth not many hours after starting her pains. It was the memory of losing her mother when her last baby sister's birth had gone on and on that worried Bedelia. This was a time of considerable danger for both mother and baby. Bedelia had learnt that no matter how easily a baby might enter this world, future births could still be perilous. She presumed this was Maureen's first birth. She felt so responsible in her task, with no knowledgeable support - so very alone.

It had been a long night and now the dawn light began peeking through the portholes. Despite Maureen's exhaustion and exclamations that she was dying and couldn't go on, Bedelia welcomed the tell-tale grunting noises coming from the labouring woman; the baby was on its way into this world.

With one explosive push from Maureen, the bag of waters burst. The fluid, that had cradled the baby for months, gushed out. The walls of the baby's home were breached. Bedelia noted that the colour of this warm liquid was the green of the meadows of home. Even with her limited knowledge, Bedelia knew this was not good. A small peek of a baby's bottom followed and Bedelia's heart skipped a beat as she realised the baby was coming the wrong way around. She had no idea what to do next.

Because of the small size of the baby, the next powerful push expelled the legs, and half the baby boy's body revealed itself between Maureen's legs. His little legs started peddling; Bedelia knew the baby was alive. With the next push his face and head were born, his outstretched arms coming last as he fell into Bedelia's waiting hands.

Looking at her timepiece, the matron announced, "This little stranger is born at seven minutes past the hour of seven in the morning."

The baby let out a weak little mewl, like the kittens Bedelia had cuddled on the steps of her childhood home. She placed the little one straight onto Maureen's chest, up through the shift she was wearing, knowing the heat from his mam's body would be the best place to keep him warm. The cord, his lifeline, was attached to the yet undelivered afterbirth and was still beating.

Bedelia asked Therese for some of the warmed rags and placed them over the baby's head and exposed body. He gave a few more quiet gasps, then after some brisk rubbing from Bedelia his skin colour slowly changed from a blotchy blue to a warm pink as he let out a louder cry.

Bedelia was aware that the few passengers who had heard the night's events, and were well enough to understand the significance of the sounds emitting from the rear of the compartment, let out audible sighs of relief. This had been a long night of travail, from both the distressed sounds of the labouring woman and the incessant heaving of the boat.

Knowing her job was not done until she delivered the afterbirth, Bedelia realised it still appeared to be attached inside Maureen's womb. Her mam had always known to suckle her babies to encourage this to come. Bedelia remembered what the doctor had said after Mrs Ashcroft's birth. This small baby was struggling to breathe as he continued to make small gasping noises, his belly below his ribs labouring with the effort. Bedelia sensed that suckling would be too much for him to manage right now.

The mattress was already soddened with the products of birth, and still more blood was gushing out. Bedelia put as many spare rags as she could find under Maureen to sop up the residue.

Bedelia checked Maureen's tummy. It still seemed as big as before the baby was born, but was now soft and spongy. The cord was still attached to the little boy. Maureen, by this stage, had slumped back in the bed. Even in the dim light she looked as pale as the sheets she lay on. Her breathing had become quiet and shallow.

Bedelia knew she had to detach the baby from his mother. She called for the matron, who had been as useless as tits on a bull so far, Bedelia thought. "Mrs Pentwick, please fetch the sewing kit, for I am in need of some string and scissors."

Bedelia tied the string around the thin, flaccid cord in two places, just as she had seen Mrs Murphy do when her brothers and sisters had been born. She cut between the two knotted ties. The cord felt like the gristle on a chop and a small squirt of blood dripped from both ends. She picked up the baby from the new mother's chest, took the remaining warmed rags and swaddled the baby. She placed him gently in Therese's trembling arms and went back to the task at hand.

Bedelia felt so inadequate wishing the doctor was there to help. She was floundering in the dark unknown, frightened and yet determined to try her best for this young woman.

She had the feeling that the undelivered afterbirth was the cause of the bleeding, but she had no knowledge of how to proceed. She pulled on the protruding cord and Maureen moaned weakly. She massaged the top of the womb from the outside like the doctor had shown her after Mrs Ashcroft's birth, and this drew a louder moan as Maureen grabbed Bedelia's wrist away … and still there was more bleeding.

Bedelia looked with concern at the mounting pile of blood-soaked rags in the bucket Matron had fetched for her. As she changed the pile from under Maureen's bottom the bright red patch continued to grow. She asked the matron to check if the doctor was able to come and help now that the storm had eased a tad. A few long minutes later Matron returned.

Mrs Pentwick looked at the floor, avoiding the rookie midwife's eyes. Bedelia knew that she was still on her own.

She tried again to pull on the cord and massage the womb, to no avail. Maureen's skin had become cold and clammy. She took in a few quiet, uneven breaths. Bedelia, the matron and her good friend Therese, who was clutching the baby firmly to her bosom, watched as this new mother's lifeblood slowly drained away. Therese wailed in anguish and Bedelia's tears streamed down her cheeks. She was aware that even the matron, so righteous and judgemental, could not hold back the emotion of the moment and let out a hiccup of a sob.

There was no more to do for Maureen, this much Bedelia knew. She made the sign of the cross and reverently covered the dead woman's face with the tattered sheet. She turned to the little being who still had some life in him.

Bedelia tried to prise the baby out of Therese's arms with the assurance that she needed to tend to him now. Therese finally unlocked her grip and reluctantly handed the baby to her.

He was spluttering mucous and still making rasping sounds. Bedelia knew there was nothing for it but to use what God had given her to clear his airway. She had watched as her mam did this for one of her baby brothers as he struggled with catarrh. She turned away from the other women, placing her lips over the baby's tiny mouth and nose, and did what she had to do. Within seconds his nasal and oral passages were clear, and the baby let out a tiny but lusty cry.

"Three pounds of butter, I reckon this little one would weigh. We need to keep him warm and dry. Can I leave you responsible for that, Therese?" Bedelia said.

A nod and a sob were all Therese could manage as she took the little bundle, cradling him in her arms.

"I didn't ... I ... I didn't know about this, for sure I didn't," Therese repeated over and over.

Bedelia knew it could be days before the storm settled down enough to release Maureen's body to the sea. In the meantime, it was up to her to lay her out. It was the least she could do to honour this young woman, another product of the harsh life they had all left behind.

Tiredness from the long night, fighting to stay upright as the ship pitched and rolled and the overwhelming emotion of the responsibility she had shouldered were finally taking their toll. She had tried her very best, she knew that for certain, but surely she could have done more.

She washed the blood away as best she could, dressed Maureen and tenderly brushed the tangled and sweat-drenched hair, laying it upon her shoulders. All the while the tears rolled silently down her freckled face. *Oh, if only I knew more,* she thought.

Bedelia left Maureen on the irretrievable mattress. It would need to go overboard too. She wrapped her own rosary beads around Maureen's hands and covered her with the clean, threadbare sheet they had found in the dead woman's bag of supplies.

Bedelia had been taught that the presence of a priest was needed at the time of death, and to get him to perform the last rites before she passed away was vital in preparing the way to heaven. Failing this, at least her son could receive God's grace that his mother had missed out on.

Ignoring the matron's directive that the dead woman wasn't worthy, Bedelia sent for the preacher to bless Maureen's soul and to baptise the living product of her sin. Mr Ashcroft willingly performed the blessing of the dead and christened her son.

It was three more days before the storm abated and Maureen's body could be committed to the deep. Most of the women from steerage, some of the families, a few men including Michael and his companion Keenan, the doctor, the preacher and some of the crew attended.

Bedelia was pleased there were no hierarchical barriers when it came to death on board ship. The true nature of Maureen's past life was only known to Therese and Bedelia, although the gossipers felt they knew too. Many of the women knew that the saying *There but for the grace of God go I* applied when it came to life's trials and bringing new life into the world.

The heart-rending issue was that another wrapped soul, tied into his mother's arms, went with her forever to the deep that cold, cloud-filled day. The women had named him Desy. Despite all their attempts and the breast milk that Mrs Ashcroft had so generously shared, he had been born too early to save.

Therese and Bedelia, between them, had spoon-fed Desy with love and dedication day and night, but in the end it was his lungs that could not keep working, taking in that vital air he needed to survive. He had left the world only hours before the dawn service, almost as if he had known that his place was in the arms his mother who, Bedelia felt sure, would have loved him dearly given the chance.

At the end of the short service and committal, Michael approached Bedelia and gently touched her fingers with a look of tenderness and appreciation. Bedelia understood that news spread like wildfire, especially on a ship where the tedium of one day led into that of another. Gossip was rife and there were no details spared. She wasn't surprised that he knew it all. Her amazing dedication was on everyone's lips. "Bedelia," Michael said, "I'm so proud of what you have done and so very pleased to be your friend."

That afternoon, Bedelia, who was still exhausted, sat on her sister's bed and unloaded her experiences. Veronica was aware of the happenings three nights before, but had been laid so low with seasickness that she could be of no help.

"Oh, by the love of the Virgin Mary I have been initiated by fire into this profession of helping mothers birth their babies. I felt so powerless to do anything for that poor colleen, so I did. Thanks be to God I had such a lovely experience with Mrs Ashcroft's birth. I swear I would not be pursuing becoming a midwife otherwise."

"Oh Dee, I hear tell that you were just grand dealing with what was being thrown at you, and that Mrs Pentwick was worse than useless. I'm quite losing respect for her, so I am."

"I know that I am made for this work, Vonnie. I will carry it on when we get to the new country, but how do you get through these sad times when you get so emotional about it?"

"We wouldn't want you any other way, Dee. Compassion is so important at these times, and you'd have to be a rock or a Mrs Pentwick not to be affected by the good and bad things that happen, and that's for sure. All I know is that you have the gift and getting together with someone like Mrs Murphy, who can teach you the skills, is what you have to do."

Chapter 5

After the rough weather and the seasickness among the passengers had passed, the doctor sought Bedelia out. He sang her praises. Her handling of a very difficult situation at such a tender age and all by herself was most commendable. "Even I would not have been able to save the mother or the child," he said. "You have proven your ability beyond your years and your experience."

"Oh, doctor, I was trying to do what you showed me, and rub where you said to stop the bleeding but it just didn't work, and Maureen cried out in such pain."

"That was because the afterbirth had not come away from the inside of the womb. It would have been stuck fast and that method is not recommended until you have removed it," the doctor said. "You were not to know this, and you made the correct decision in not persisting. There are so many variables in birthing situations, and then many more different choices to make in midwifery. It is a profession you learn by doing. Reading about it in books may help somewhat, but experiencing it is what makes the knowledge stick."

He paused, then continued. "Would you consider joining me in New Zealand. There is a great shortage of skilled people and much need for your services in the colony. I am keen to work alongside you, guide and teach you the skills I know, although my experience of birthing is somewhat limited. Your aptitude in tending the sick will take you a long way, Bedelia."

"Where is it you're intending to set up practice when we reach the new country? My sister Veronica, she's all I have left in the world, and hopes to work with families, help in the house and with children. To be near each other is what we want, so it is."

"I am looking at a small town called Nelson. I have heard that it has a favourable climate and there is a growing settlement there," the doctor said.

"When we left the old sod my sister and I had no thought as to where we'd be wanting to lay down our roots. We knew it couldn't be any worse than the trials we've been through. The assistance of our Uncle Paddy was generous, and the Workhouse committee got us on the boat. We just have to trust in God's will to do the rest, by the Virgin Mary's love we do."

"Well, let us just wait and see," the doctor said. "I am sure there will be more than enough work to occupy all three of us when we disembark."

The weather was variable on the way down the western coast of Africa. Passengers were aware it was one of the main shipping routes on the journey to the colonies. "Ships tend to take the eastern route there, and when they're headed back to the old country they take the more hazardous route around the bottom of the Americas," the first mate told Bedelia and Veronica when they stopped to talk on one of their afternoon strolls around the ship. Bedelia had begun to notice this crew member always made a bee-line for them when she was strolling with her sister.

Other than the odd spell of rough weather or a sick child to tend to, there was little call for Bedelia's services. For this she was most grateful, and even more so that there were no more deaths.

They rounded the Cape of Good Hope with much gratitude for the fairer weather. The sisters took this as a good omen. They were told of the proximity to land when the captain pointed out the cape pigeons, which were flying around the ship taking advantage of the gusts coming off the sails. The birds would then dive down into the sea with their wings folded back, creating small plops of foam as they sought out their dinner. Later these creatures were joined by "Nellies", so-called by the sailors. "They live mostly in these waters around Antarctica," they told Bedelia and Veronica as they watched birds the colour of tea leaves adeptly twist and turn in the wind.

To top off the sisters' feelings of good fortune, one of the men up on the poop deck called out, pointing to a bird with a wingspan longer than that of the table in their compartment, "Lo, an albatross!" The massive white creature glided on the wind for many minutes without moving its wings, then, dipping one wing, circled the sails so closely you could see its pinions with their notched ruffles. Veronica and Bedelia were mesmerised.

The wind was brisk, but the sea gave them a more comfortable ride as the wind came from the starboard quarter at the rear of the ship. The water bubbled at the bow, with the ship leaving a long lacy froth trailing like a bride's veil as the wake went far into the distance. Bedelia and Veronica clutched their shawls, for despite being told it was nearing summer here in the southern part of the world, the temperature did not match their expectation. The wind felt just as cold as winter at home.

The call for lunch brought them back to where they were, having their turn of the deck. They watched the majestic bird wing its way north towards, Bedelia guessed, the land beyond the horizon. The captain had told the passengers that if the weather remained settled, they would be calling in to Port Elizabeth in the next few days for their final supplies before they reached Australia and then New Zealand.

"I cannot quite believe we are here near the bottom of the world, Vonnie. To think we are now nearly halfway to our new life. One side of myself is telling me to be thrilled and the other is scaring me out of my wits. I'm not quite sure which side to listen to."

Despite strong winds that the sailors called the Roaring Forties, so far the seas and weather had been kind to those on board. The passengers were told that it helped to have prevailing westerly winds as they sailed east, but they were warned that change could happen in only a few hours in this part of the world.

As they completed their rounding of the bottom of Africa the next day, the excitement rose and all aboard were called onto the deck to witness the spectacle. A family of whales appeared to starboard. Bedelia and Veronica were first to the railing on the main deck. They had a bird's eye view of the magnificent creatures as they breached from the water displaying their huge undersides of neatly pleated white flesh. All that was left on show was the gracefully curved tail ending in two opposing points as they re-entered the water with what looked like a cheeky flick and a splash. "This," the first mate told Bedelia and Veronica as he came up beside them, "is called fluking of the tail."

"Well, will you look at that. It seems as if the whale is waving to us," Veronica said "I have never seen the like before in all my days."

"I have seen this display on many of my voyages," the first mate told the sisters. He explained that the family of whales - for there appeared to be about twenty of them - consisted mainly of mothers and their calves. A few males acted as escorts, remaining on the periphery of the pod. "These are humpback whales," he said. "They come down to the colder waters to feed on the krill. They migrate up to the warmer climes of the tropics to mate and have their calves. They take a tad longer to grow their babies than we do, before they're ready to come into this world." He seemed proud of his knowledge and quite comfortable to share it.

Aware of her exploits as a midwife he turned to Bedelia adding, "They don't need your services lassie, they do the job just fine by themselves."

Veronica blushed, and noticing her unease, he quickly said, "So sorry, miss, I was just telling it how it is in life. No offence meant to your sensitivities." He continued, "Now listen to the different sounds coming from the males and the females. It's not so easy to tell which noise is from which whale."

The calls emanating from the pod were eerie, for some were singing and others produced a less than melodic and more haunting moan.

"It surely sounds like they're talking to each other," Veronica said, the high colour around her neck and face dissipating as her complexion returned to a normal soft pink.

The exciting spectacle lasted almost an hour, with the whales swimming alongside the ship as they played and performed. The massive creatures spurted water from their blowholes. They jumped out of the water, twisting in a feat surprising for creatures so large. As she noticed one whale's piercing eye, Bedelia was sure it was looking straight at her.

"It is quite like a circus," the preacher said as he joined the sisters with his children, who were squealing with delight at the whales' antics.

Michael had joined the enthralled audience beside Bedelia. "What a fine performance it is, for sure. Who would have thought that we'd ever see creatures quite as big as a train carriage acting like side-show entertainers at the village fair?"

"Will you look at that, for the calf is swimming beside his mammy. And he's not so little either," Bedelia said.

The ship finally pulled away from the whales' dinner table. The children waved to the whale family as if saying goodbye to some new-found playmates. The first mate was still explaining to the group the pod worked as a team to herd up their meal of krill and other small fish they encountered, with a salad of little plankton on the side.

The passengers continued to mill around. The encounter with the whales, matched with the fair weather at this latitude, was so rare that relaxation of the rules, of separation between men from women on-deck, was tolerated. The excitement lingered, with animated chatter about what they had witnessed. The captain decided to extend the experience, inviting the passengers to join him for the midday meal. "There may not be another opportunity to socialise all together before reaching your destinations," he said.

The crew and the men brought up the tables and forms from below and set them out on the deck. The meal bags were fetched by their owners. Isla went to collect the food that cook had prepared with Danny's and the cabin boy's help.

It was still the standard, bland fare, but the novelty of eating in the fresh air created a festive atmosphere. The men were permitted to join the ladies if they chose and even the cabin passengers were pleased to join in, bringing their tables as close to the others as the space on the deck permitted.

The first mate quickly found his place next to Veronica. Michael and Bedelia sat opposite them, with Michael's family on either side of the couple. The preacher's family politely asked if their table could be joined to theirs, with young Jacob and Sarah jostling for the seat closest to Veronica.

Musicians were encouraged to break out their instruments after the meal and dancing was a natural lead-on when the toes started tapping. Bedelia and Michael were discussing how much tedium the passengers had endured over the past few weeks, day in, day out. Confinement below decks, sickness and the intense discomfort of the rolling ship as it navigated the stormy seas were in stark contrast to the joy and laughter they were experiencing now. "It's beginning to really feel like spring now, and that summer is just around the corner," Bedelia said.

"The matron and doctor surely don't get to have the fun we are having," Michael said as the pair passed behind them. "Those being watched know to stay out of trouble, for they may be missing the chance to visit Port Elizabeth."

Bedelia was pleased to see Veronica and the first mate quietly chatting the afternoon away with the occasional interruption from Jacob and Sarah, as they excitedly relayed what they had just seen or done or were intending to do. Seamus had also joined them to play.

Maggie and Danny made sure they kept visible in order to not get into trouble again. They held hands under the table and continued to share their childhood experiences from back home, laughing together between joining in the dancing.

Bedelia and Michael had overheard some of their conversations, bringing back their own memories.

"Danny, do yer remember sitting First Holy communion when the priest took confession?

We didn't know what to confess so we made things up, so we did," Maggie added.

"My big one was lying," Danny admitted. "Oh, to be sure, I didn't even know what I had lied about, but it got the usual punishment of ten Hail Marys and ten Our Fathers."

Bedelia looked at Michael and laughed at the innocence.

"I remember the communion well," Danny said. "The body of Christ got stuck to the roof of my mouth, so it did. It was so dry and so stuck that I couldn't 'Amen' to Father O'Halloran. He got quite mad with me and kept saying 'Corpus Christi, Corpus Christi' 'til I started crying so loud that me mam had to come and fetch me from the altar railings. Me in my new suit and shiny shoes she had managed to scrounge from the neighbours."

"I was a sight for sore eyes, me nanny said, after she had sewn me a white lacy dress and veil. Cathleen O'Hara was as green as grass with envy, so she was," said Maggie.

Danny and Maggie got the giggles, and the others, who were within earshot, couldn't help but join the laughter.

"It's so lovely to see the young people happy and laughing; it fair lifts my spirits. I sometimes forget that's how it once was for us," Bedelia said.

The party had died down. Veronica said to her sister, "My, you two talked near until your tongues dropped off."

Bedelia smiled. "Well, you can't talk, and that's for sure. I noticed the first mate is pretty sweet on you, Vonnie dearest," she said, puckering and smacking her lips several times.

"Oh, get away with you Dee, it's nothing like that at all."

Bedelia winked at Michael with a huge grin on her face as they parted company, making a pact to join each other when they took the trip into Port Elizabeth.

Earlier Bedelia had been standing beside the matron and the doctor at the ship's railing hearing the matron say, "Well, this is a very pleasant and uneventful afternoon. Quite unexpected, but lovely all the same. I'm so much looking forward to meeting up with my husband when we arrive in Sydney town. I hope he received the letter I sent him on the *Mary Louise*, arriving afore us. After such a journey it seems it'll be no time at all 'til we arrive there. I wonder where Alfie has for us to settle."

"I'm sure it will turn out just fine for you, Mrs Pentwick," the doctor had said. "Sydney and the other towns in Australia are so much ahead of New Zealand in their settlements, there will be places to live and more than enough to do. Going on to Nelson, in New Zealand, necessary items to make life more comfortable are not so easy to come by, consequently I've come prepared for settling there. I intend to build my practice, therefore I have with me all the makings to furnish a small cottage and a room for my surgery."

The doctor continued. "My colleague, who travelled as a ship's doctor two years ago, has set up practice there. He wrote instructing me what was needed and I have heeded his advice. The Reverend Ashcroft told me that he was advised the same by some of the missionaries who preceded him. Apparently, besides his skills as a man of the cloth and a doctor, he has learnt some carpentry, which will hold him in good stead for what is required to settle with his family in New Zealand."

Bedelia noticed Mrs Pentwick had a satisfied smile on her face as she was heading towards the hatchway. She smiled as she heard the doctor and the matron heaving sighs of relief, counting the last of their charges off as present and correct. The chaperones parted company, and the matron followed Bedelia down into the women's compartment.

Chapter 6

During the night before their excursion to Port Elizabeth, one of the sailors fell from the rigging. A wind gust hit the ship and caught the man off guard. Although she was initially disappointed about missing out on the outing, Bedelia offered to stay back as she felt her help may be needed. The doctor told her that he feared the sailor had broken several ribs as well as his leg. He would have to manipulate the bone back into alignment before firmly splinting and strapping the limb.

"Thank you Bedelia, but I will need the help of some of the sturdier crew to hold him down. He will need to drink a substantial ration of rum before we begin."

He explained there would be slightly more yelling than she would experience when helping women in childbirth. He would rather passengers were not within earshot of the expected commotion and the language that may be used.

"I would like you to take my eye-glass, and I expect you to tell me about all the animals you spy with it," the doctor said as he handed her the long, shiny brass object.

Veronica and Bedelia managed to get on the same tender as Michael and his companion Keenan. As the crewmen rowed them in, they could make out some buildings close to the water while others stretched away up towards the hill at the back of the town.

The captain had advised all the passengers heading onto land to be wary of the animals they may encounter. "There are some you wouldn't want to meet with face to face. Stay close to the guides and heed what they say," he said.

The matron had decided to stay back to assist the doctor with the supplies he may need, and had already set to turning some worn linen into bandages. "I won't be holding his hand or rubbing his back," she assured Bedelia.

The party of sightseers pulled up beside the dock. A well-built blond-haired man with a tanned, weathered complexion called for them to come over. He held the reins on a team of two oxen to pull the wagon and wielded a large whip.

"What a funny way of speaking English he has, Michael," Bedelia said.

"I am thinking it's Afrikaans. The first mate told me they're called Boers, and have their origins across the waters from Scotland, in the low countries of Europe," Michael replied.

A man with darker skin than Bedelia had ever seen in her life sat beside him. His shiny face was the colour of the ebony cabinet in their local church. It was even more accentuated by the white teeth glistening from behind his lips. He wore a colourful smock top and loose drawstring trousers. On command from the other man, he jumped down from the wagon and scurried over to the boat. With one of his large bare feet planted on the wooden dock and his other steadying the small vessel, he helped each passenger ashore.

The group gathered their belongings, including some bread and dripping and a few slices of meat left over from last night's supper. A man of few words, Keenan said, "I insist on paying for the safari, for this is what we're about to go on. C'mon ladies, this is an adventure not to be missed."

As the ladies were being helped onto the wagon by Michael and Keenan, the black man let out a yelp. Bedelia let out a gasp, her mouth agape, feeling like she had been struck also. She was appalled to have witnessed the man in front whipping the other for no apparent reason. The party of sightseers sat silent for some time, absorbing this interaction. Michael took Bedelia's hand and stroked it tenderly, until it slowly stopped shaking.

When the shock had eased, they looked out at the sights from their places on the planks of wood on either side of the wagon. Bedelia was hardly able to stay seated. She looked this way and that as they reached the outskirts of the town. "What do yer think we'll see today?" she said. "I'm a tad afraid and yet I feel much excitement, so I do."

No one seated in the back of the wagon had any knowledge about the animals of Africa other than those they had seen in the drawings in books at school.

After an hour of rattling over a well-worn track, they stopped near a waterhole, close enough to see yet far enough away to be safe. The guide gave detailed explanations of all they may be about to encounter. Bedelia was transfixed. She could imagine from their wide, alert eyes that the others felt the same.

The guide warned the group they must remain on the wagon. Bedelia was reassured as she spied the large firearm he had positioned between him and the man Bedelia presumed was his servant.

As soon as they stopped, the group witnessed the many varieties of animals gathered at the oasis. They heard the noisy bustle as these creatures turned their attention to the task at hand, drinking the water with the massive fertile veld spread beyond.

The most unusual blue-grey birds were wading through the water, their long tail feathers trailing behind them. White birds with long bills and even longer legs and many green-grey parrots, squawking as they flew in and out of the mob of animals, added to the menagerie. The smaller birds were almost as varied in their colours and plumage as they were many in their numbers.

For Bedelia, the larger animals drinking at the waterhole were also a wonder to behold. The guide started naming each one as he pointed to them from the wagon: rhino, buffalo, giraffe, zebra.

Massive elephants with their thick wrinkly skin covered in the mud in which they had just been frolicking drank their fill of water, aided by their hose-like trunks. These majestic animals needed no introduction. They, like the whales the passengers had watched just days before, were traveling in family groups, and the baby elephants, despite being small compared to the adults, were large compared to the humans observing them.

The guide carried on pointing and naming the animals: cheetah, warthog, hyena and lion. Meanwhile he looked this way and that, alert, as he clutched his rifle.

Bedelia shared the doctor's eyeglass with the others so they could pick out the details of these wild animals from the safe distance, high on the wagon.

"Look at those huge cats, the ones with the spots. I guess that's a cheetah, and I know that one with all the fur around his head must be a lion. I've seen that in a book afore, so I have," Veronica said with excitement in her voice. "From here he looks like a cuddly pussycat with a purr to match."

"I wouldn't be stroking him at all," said Keenan.

"Here Michael, take your turn," Veronica said as she handed the eyeglass on. His eye moved to the deer-like animals with the horns protruding towards the sky in corkscrew spirals. There were several varieties of antelope, and as they moved on they displayed their agility by gambolling away across the plain.

The buffalo, with their foreboding horns, appeared to fascinate Michael. He kept the eyeglass pointed in their direction for the longest time, then said, "Why, they'd be so much heavier-looking than the bulls on our farms back home." He laughed. "I wouldn't have teased them and got away easily, like I did when I was a boy, that's for sure."

He handed the eyeglass to Keenan, who focused on and described the intriguing patterns that adorned the giraffe's body and that of her calf. The long wiry neck allowed the animal to browse the tall trees for the foliage out of reach of all other grazing animals.

Bedelia said, "Even you couldn't top that baby giraffe, Michael, as tall as you stand. I would like to see the both of you side by side."

"Well, I will not be hopping down from this wagon to see, young lady, and that's that," Michael said.

Keenan pointed to the unusual brown animal with two horns like large pointy warts on its snout. Folds of thick skin flapped down at the top of its forelegs, and hog-like ears pointed up from sad-looking eyes. "If that's not the strangest and ugliest creature I have ever seen in my life, I'll eat my hat," he said.

Just then Bedelia noticed the guide rapidly raise the firearm. He said something to the other man in his native tongue, then in the same alarmed voice said, "We will be leaving now." He flapped the leather leaders harnessing the oxen and they moved back down the track towards the town. The oxen, too, were showing signs of alarm.

The guide pointed to a very long, thick snake disguised in the dry foliage on the ground. The reptile, with its intricately patterned brown and cream skin, was slithering towards the wagon. It was only yards away. It had curled itself in such a way as to bely the actual length of its body.

Just as they were pulling away to put a safe distance between them and the snake, Bedelia and the occupants of the wagon saw the perilous possibilities of what they had just avoided. The snake opened its mouth so wide it looked as if its jaw was dislocating, and its fangs came down hard on the small, unfortunate creature it was stalking. It was so quick that the group had no idea what unlucky animal had met its fate. The guide said "The poisonous fangs will see its prey dead and then it will be swallowed in minutes."

"Spread out straight, that snake would be longer than me and as thick as my arm," Michael said.

Bedelia shuddered at the thought. She had never seen the like before and would hopefully not see it again in her lifetime. "I've heard tell that Australia has snakes, but in New Zealand there are mostly birds which they say are quite harmless," Bedelia told the others.

Michael looked at Keenan as he said, "Well, if that's what Australia will be dishing us up, I may be reconsidering my plans."

Returning to the port, the group descended from the wagon. They all agreed that they had enjoyed their excursion and felt fortunate for the guide's quick actions in escaping the snake. Keenan was about to give the guide a few more pennies than they had agreed upon, when they turned to see him whipping the black man again and again.

Bedelia jumped back, mouth agape. Rage ignited inside; her eyes grew fiery. Before Michael could stop her she marched up to the guide, who was still seated on the wagon. She stood up in her most Mrs Pentwick-like impersonation and said, "We thank you for your trouble in taking us for the grand safari and dealing with the snake, but we are not thanking you for the terrible way you have treated your man. You are a disgusting, despicable man, on whom we will be pleased never to lay eyes ever again." Bedelia stomped away, hands on hips, head high. Her companions applauded her grand performance.

On their way back to the ship Bedelia cuddled into Michael. Despite her confident display, she was shaking with the feelings of disgust, pity for the black man and shock at the appalling treatment of one human towards another.

Lightening the tense atmosphere, the crewman pointed to the penguins hobbling across some rocks beside the sea. "Their black and white feathers remind me of the habits worn by the sisters in the convent school we went to back home," Veronica said, giggling. Those were the days when school was still an option for their family. All the Catholic passengers in the tender shared the humour of these little "nun birds" Bedelia and Veronica had just renamed.

Chapter 7

From the south of Africa to Van Diemen's Land, the voyage had been the longest distance the ship had sailed in one leg. It had been an unscheduled port of call. The captain had told the passengers that he had been asked to deliver much needed supplies to the penal colony there. The large island was to the south of Australia.

Bedelia was frantic with worry, as her new found-friend, Therese, was missing. After their visit to the island no-one had seen her, nor had they noticed where she had gone during their visit. She had been ferried in on a different boat, otherwise Bedelia may have asked her to join them on their excursion and picnic.

"Surely she just strayed off the path and got herself lost," Bedelia said to the captain. She was mindful that Therese had been in low spirits since she had lost her companion Maureen. Added to that was the ostracism she had endured after her indiscretion during the Equator-crossing celebration. Despite that, Bedelia and Therese and more recently Isla had formed their own little private connection with each other. Their mischievous antics in order to pass the tedious yet challenging hours as the ship rose and fell with the huge swells of the Southern Ocean, waves crashing over the decks, had ignited and fuelled their friendship.

Bedelia recalled the past few weeks with considered attention. The weather had been harsh on their way to the penal colony, and Bedelia, Isla and Therese had been the only women passengers with good sea legs, who had not needed to take to their bunks. Even the matron had succumbed and been incapacitated as the overwhelming sickness overrode her duties to her women. Mrs Pentwick's beady, judgemental eyes had been mostly closed and she had no interest in anyone else's welfare as she moaned and groaned and vomited.

The whole vessel had shuddered as it fell to almost tipping point. Moving became almost impossible without being battered and thrown about, but the three women would collapse in hysterical laughter when they ended up entwined on the floor. The icy salt water and the cold air coming directly from the Antarctic had seeped through the ever-present cracks in the deck and the hatch, even though it was as tightly closed as it could be, but they hadn't let the difficulties and discomfort dampen their spirits.

During the long hours between their chores they had swapped stories, and despite being among the women who had previously shunned her, Isla soon warmed to Therese.

Bedelia, Therese and Isla had schemed and shared their hopes and dreams for their new life that would be only weeks away when they reached their new home. They had talked about when they would be able to get their feet on the sturdy, solid earth of the land that lay ahead. Despite making steady progress, the sails had been furled and the ship hoved to for safer sailing in the severe stormy weather.

"Maybe Therese just decided she'd enough of being on the ship. I know I've had those thoughts myself," Bedelia considered.

Bedelia had continued to work tirelessly to ease the discomfort of her ailing fellow passengers, and her two companions had taken her direction in tasks that needed to be done. After long hours without sleep, she often thought, *Wouldn't it be better to be the one being tended to?* That notion very soon passed as she wiped her sister's pale brow and watched her lose even more weight from her already slender body.

As the seas started to ease the welcome call, "Land ahoy," rang out from one of the crew above. On hearing this, even the sickest passengers had risen slowly in their bunks.

No one would miss being confined to this sodden hold, with the odours of animals, the stink of bodily wastes, the smell of salty water as it dripped through the crevasses and the dankness of mouldy straw-filled mattresses. Of that Bedelia had been certain. The thought of unswaying land seemed to have cheered everyone out of their malaise.

"Therese, more than everyone, seemed brighter," Bedelia reminded Isla.

Mrs Pentwick had behaved like a nicer person as she slowly regained some composure. Even the ill-feeling towards Therese had left most of the women, as their gratitude for her care had replaced their disdain.

When the seas had calmed enough to safely open the hatch, Therese, Isla and Bedelia had raced to the ladder to gasp in the fresh sea air they had been denied these last weeks, down in the bowels of this ship. Isla was first on deck, Bedelia and Therese close behind. The billowy clouds raced through the deep blue sky and Jimmy, hanging from the rigging, pointed to the subtle change of colour on the horizon that was a land of trees. "It be Van Diemen's land," he shouted.

As the day advanced and the sea settled even further, more passengers left their bunks to join the growing throng on the deck. The land was still in the distance, and the captain pointed out that it would stay so until the ship was ready to turn into the stretch of water leading portside up to Hobart town. He told the passengers, "This will be only a brief stop to give us time to unload the supplies for the convict colony."

The ship headed up the harbour with no signs of life on shore. Pointing out Port Arthur to starboard, a huge monolith of brick, stone and mortar, the captain told the passengers standing near him, "This is used as more strict confinement for troublesome convicts."

As the channel narrowed and the ship dropped its anchor in the paling sky of dusk, curious fellows lined the beach and waved their hats to those on board. This was the last time Bedelia remembered talking to Therese.

She had said to Bedelia, "I have been told the convicts' passage to the penal colony was much tougher than ours. They have been banished to the colonies for all kinds of wrongdoings, from stealing a loaf of bread in order to keep their family alive, to murderous acts. My friends in the brothel told me some of their families have been transported this way."

Bedelia had heard that the convicts' lot was a life of hard labour, and the probability of ever seeing their native country and families again was next to impossible.

Early the next morning, as the sun tipped over the island from the east, some passengers had readied for their outing. They had been warned that if they chose to have an excursion off the ship into Hobart town, it would be wise to travel in a larger group.

Bedelia had no idea whom Therese had gone with in her boat. She had only seen her at breakfast, and she looked as excited as Bedelia. One of the women who did go in the same boat as Therese, when questioned by the captain, remembered noticing she had stuffed her tote bag full. "It never occurred to me why," she said, as she described seeing her tucking the bag under her cape.

Veronica had chosen to remain on board due to her weakened state. Bedelia and Isla had joined Michael and Keenan. "We aren't going to miss a thing," they told the lads, who had fared better through the storms than many of their fellow single men. They all agreed that the walk around dry, unmoving land would be a treat.

When they alighted from their transport ashore, they heeded the captain's advice to stay together. It was easy to distinguish the convicts from the others. The soldiers, whom the group guessed were the jailers, wore red English military coats and white trousers, not quite as spick and span as those seen in Britain.

All the convicts, on the other hand, wore a plain cotton shirt of light orange and grey stripes, and a thick blue wool jacket. Some were wearing a yellow and grey waistcoat under the jacket. Long stockings covered their legs beneath the white canvas trousers, and on their feet were plain leather shoes - a change from the bare feet many would have been used to. Completing their garments were neckerchiefs, and they wore wool or leather caps on their heads.

The women wore a "uniform" also, consisting of a linen cap and shift with stockings and a petticoat peeping from underneath. A brown serge jacket, leather shoes and a neckerchief were added. The children, whom the group were told had accompanied their recalcitrant parents or were born here, wore a miniature version of the adult attire.

The small party from the ship was approached by a group of convicts asking for any news of home and wanting to know where the newcomers hailed from. It was difficult to ignore their pleas for titbits from their long-lost home. Bedelia and Isla conversed with the female convicts without reserve while Michael and Keenan spoke with the men. Bedelia wondered if Therese had received the same questions. She might have even known someone among the prisoners.

Trying to make some sense of her friend's disappearance, Bedelia recalled their encounters during their trip ashore.

"Now come along," a British officer had barked to the convicts, "and don't be bothering these fine people. They have better things to do than associating with the likes of you." He had been distracted by some activity going on with the ship's crew, who were offloading stores. Bedelia had heard him say to one of the crew from the *Catherine Mary*, "We're grateful you received our message. We were becoming desperate for food to keep us going until our own ships return from England. They are months late, and we fear they may have met with ill-fate." The captain had told the passengers, when they were pulling into port, that passing British ships were a lifeline for the colony and there was sometimes near starvation when months went by between shipments.

As Bedelia dredged her memory for more clues about where Therese may have gone missing, she recalled the pleasant outing.

The party had wandered to the edge of the small town to discover for themselves what nature had to show them in this strange new land. They were met by a cacophony of colourful birds in greens, reds and golds, not unlike the parrots they had seen in Tenerife. There was such a variety of birds in the lush, green canopy; too many to count. The forest was thick, with layer upon layer of different bushes leading up to smaller trees, culminating in trees with trunks so massive it would take many men joined fingertip to fingertip to get right around them. The foliage was "up to the heavens" Bedelia said, as the exploring party craned their necks to see to the top. This was flora they had never experienced in Ireland.

The animals that they encountered on their walk were just as numerous, varied and fascinating.

"We'd better be moving along. I know there are snakes in this country and it isn't that long since our last encounter with one of those creatures," Michael said.

Bedelia and Isla jumped back as they heard a rustle of grass close by. Bedelia thought she saw the slithery reptile coming towards them, but it was only another furry creature with a long fluffy tail dashing through the long grass before heading up a tree. It seemed more afraid of them than they should be of it. Michael jumped forward and grabbed Bedelia by her arm. She screamed. The fear in her eyes quickly turned to a glare when she noticed Michael's big grin.

"Is it a coddin' me you are, Michael Mahoney? You fair scared the bejasus out of me. I remember like it was yesterday that snake coming through the grass. I was sure it would climb up on that wagon and get me, so I was."

The lads laughed heartily, although Keenan picked up a long stick and was prodding the path in front as he took the lead.

"That long grass could easily hide a mass of snakes," Keenan said, looking to both sides as they retreated to a more open area.

"Come along, 'tis back to the ship we need to be heading." Michael led the way, offering Bedelia his looped elbow to bring her in closer.

As they were on the last boat ferried back to the ship, they were quizzed by the captain when they climbed on board as to the whereabouts of Therese. One of the passengers who shared her boat stirred some anger in Bedelia when she commented, "All I saw was the back of her skirts as she hot-footed it up the main street of Hobart town."

Bedelia shuddered as she said to Michael, "I hope that Therese hasn't been killed by a snake, entirely. She may be lying in the long grass where no one will find her."

As these ideas floated in and out of her mind, Bedelia became more afraid for Therese. If she hadn't been bitten by a snake and was stuck in the bush all alone, with God-knows-what other dangerous animals to contend with, what would be her fate? "Oh, I hope we can find her," she said to Michael.

"Mr Albert Hardy," the captain called. After being interrogated, the first class passenger hotly denied any knowledge as to the whereabouts of Therese, or of having any liaisons with her since they had been banned from any future contact.

Therese had confided in no one as to her intentions for the day's outing. She and Bedelia had spoken but a few words in the last two days, so Bedelia could not shed light on Therese's plans.

Mrs Pentwick said she had only noticed that she was less trouble. The matron spat out the words, "I needed eyes in the back of my head as far as that charge is concerned."

Even though she felt a strong urge to comment, Bedelia held herself in check. *You old bitch,* she thought, *You couldn't conceive of what Therese has been through, and you all poorly in your bunk for days, tended by her.*

Bedelia whispered to Michael, "Mrs Pentwick wouldn't have a clue even if it jumped out to bite her on her big fat arse."

Michael put his hand up to his mouth attempting, unsuccessfully, to suppress his mirth. Laughter spilled out the sides of his fingers, then quieted as he cleared his throat.

It was obvious the captain was fast becoming livid. "I cannot afford to be delayed any longer looking for some lady of ill repute absconding in this den of iniquity," he said.

"How could I have missed this happening?" Bedelia said to Isla. "I really thought we had formed a close friendship in the last few months, especially since the time we struggled to keep Desy alive."

When a party was organised to go back ashore in search of Therese, Bedelia begged the captain that she may go with them.

The captain and the doctor conferred out of earshot. All Bedelia could see was the captain shaking his head as the doctor talked in earnest. Eventually they returned to the milling crowd of passengers.

"Drama has been sparse on this voyage, and all of a sudden it's hotting up," Isla whispered, but Bedelia didn't reply, her eye's intent on the captain's face.

"I've decided," the captain said, "that this young lass would be helpful to the search party, being as she has spent some time with the runaway. That goes with the provision that she is accompanied by a gentleman, given the dangers of mixing with criminals on shore. The good doctor has kindly offered his services and I've agreed."

Bedelia's anxious face relaxed slightly as she readied to climb down into the tender once again, helped by the doctor and the for'ard hand. As they were rowed in, the doctor turned to Bedelia, "Now don't get your hopes up lass," he said, "it may be like looking for a needle in a haystack. If Therese doesn't wish to be found it will be that much more difficult."

They went straight to the governor. After some discussion and a plan having been set in place, the governor briefed the ship's search party. "If the woman has joined the prisoners she will not be far away. They are mostly free to wander as long as their assigned tasks are completed and they report for roll call every day."

Turning over some pages in the ledger on his desk he continued, "They also rely on supplies from the food store in this unforgiving land, and if they don't toe the line, they go hungry. Therefore, they don't go too far afield. Only the hardiest of men would survive in the wilderness of this vast island without a food supply, if they did try to escape."

Bedelia's brow furrowed as she looked into the distance.

When Bedelia told the governor and doctor about Therese's previous occupation, the governor said, "This woman will likely have been aided to disappear by any one of the convicts. She may even be known to several of them."

"Oh, I hope Therese hasn't got lost. I am so afeared for her; she really has a good heart," Bedelia said to the two men.

The governor released some of his men to assist in the search, but reiterated, "Take care. This is a wily bunch of blaggards who need to be ruled with an iron rod. Even then," he said, "they often get away with murder."

He went on to tell the doctor, "The convicts often band together, and there's nothing to be done but punish them all by cutting their rations. That can sometimes pull an informer from their ranks, but that's rare. Under these circumstances, and because we have such little time, I will not be attempting to do this."

Bedelia, the doctor and two of the British officers headed into the town while the rest of the search party combed the perimeter of the colony. The convicts had built their own little settlements dotted within walking distance of the officers' barracks.

Bedelia spotted the women she and Isla had spoken to earlier in the day and approached them without hesitation.

"Can I ask you ladies if you've seen our shipmate, Therese O'Hara? She's as tall as myself with the black hair and pretty blue eyes."

"Ladies, she says! Never been called such a thing," the spokeswoman for the group said. They all screamed with laughter. "No miss, we've not seen a dicky bird, but we'll be sure to tell her you called. Wot's yer name, sweet lassie?"

"Bedelia it is, but Therese calls me Delia."

"Well, you can be sure, Delia, you won't find her here." The woman looked to her companions with a wink. "Mind, she'll be in good hands, rest assured, if we do find her."

The crew searched until the daylight began to wane and they decided to give up the hunt. As they prepared to depart, the governor said, "This woman is not a convicted felon, so we cannot make her leave the colony. She will just have to make do among the convicts here. If we find her, the only thing we can do is try to send her on to Sydney. Ask the captain to leave her belongings in safe-keeping on the wharf there."

Bedelia and the doctor were rowed back to the *Catherine Mary* to impart the news. The message to the captain from the governor was to set sail with the hope that the woman would come to her senses and take the next ship bound for Sydney or New Zealand.

When the news reached the other passengers, Mrs Pentwick said, "Good riddance to bad rubbish," as others nodded.

Bedelia berated herself that she had not been able to spend more time helping Therese. She turned to Isla and said, "If only she had asked me. But I thought she was coming out of her blackness since the three of us spent so much time laughing together, and getting up to all kinds of mischief. I surely didn't notice she was getting ready to skip ship."

As the ship departed the harbour bound for Sydney, Bedelia and Isla stood at the ship's railings facing the penal colony, and waved their bonnets. Their hope was that their friend would see their gesture. It was with heavy hearts they were reminded that they had spent so many months on board ship with Therese, in such close confines, and yet knew so little about her.

Chapter 8

The captain told the passengers, who were disembarking in Australia, that it would be at least five or more days before they reached Sydney.

"My Archie will be waiting for me ever so soon if he received my note. I have quite missed the old boy. What will he have in store for us?" Mrs Pentwick said to Bedelia, who nodded in agreement without answering the question, despite having heard the same information so many times before.

The ship made good time on its way up the coast to Sydney. A week later it arrived at Port Jackson and sailed up though the heads to Sydney Cove and Darling Harbour. The day was glorious, with the cloudless sky and warmth from the sun welcoming half the occupants of the vessel to their final destination.

Mrs Pentwick stood at the railings. Bedelia was close by and couldn't help but notice as the older woman moved from foot to foot, wringing her hands, all of a-jitter. Her movements became more exaggerated as they sailed closer to the wharf. Bedelia was aware, that as for the others, it had been a long and arduous journey for the matron, with many challenges. She had freely told Bedelia that she was ready to relinquish her role and rest before she and her husband decided their future plans.

Many other ships dotted the harbour. Some could be seen loading horses, wooden crates and large sacking bales. Once the ship was safely at anchor, awaiting a berth at the wharf, the first mate joined Veronica and Bedelia at the rails. He pointed out to the sisters that these bales would be jam-packed with wool for the mother country. "The wooden crates are likely to contain anything from whale and vegetable oil to wine, tallow and some minerals," he said.

Another ship, tied up at the wharf, was loading buckets of coal into the hold. The first mate explained that the coal was found north of Sydney. It had been brought down to the port in wagons or on smaller ships, ready to be sent abroad.

A third ship was ready to load logs of wood, all of different lengths, some harvested from the hills surrounding the town. Many of these logs came from a place inland, which was being cleared in preparation for farming.

Michael was talking to his brother as he stood at the ship's rail. Bedelia saw them and moved over to stand beside Michael. They had hardly talked about it, but Bedelia was already feeling melancholic at the thought of parting from this man she had grown close to since their meeting several months ago.

"It's a hive of industry we are seeing," Patrick said. "It makes me certain we are doing the right thing settling here, so it does. This new country will have plenty of opportunities for setting up in business or working as a labourer if farming doesn't help us on our way. Although I'm mindful of what I've been told; that the menial tasks may have already been taken up by the convicts given ticket of leave."

"But there are sure to be more chances of work for others," Moira said as she turned to look at Michael.

They had been told that vast areas in the outback, where land could be farmed, lay waiting for settlers. Many of these holdings had already been taken up by some of the British officers and governors who had come to this country with the convicts. They were always happy to employ willing workers.

"Mind, I've heard tell that the conditions may be harsh in the hot, dry land, and feed for the stock scarce," Michael said.

After waiting for space at the port, when the tide was right, the whale boats prepared to tow the ship in alongside the wharf. All hands were on deck ready to throw ropes to men on shore. These ropes were then tied to the bollards. Watching the ship berth was a first for the passengers. "Unlike other ports of call, along our way, this bay can accommodate the larger ships without the risk of beaching the vessel," the captain told the nearby passengers.

Danny pointed out to Maggie the dark men in minimal clothing walking in the distance. Both were getting off in Australia with the families they had travelled with. "Jim, the cabin boy, told me they are aborigines and have lived here for thousands of years. Imagine that, Maggs. They really know how to survive in the bush," Danny said.

The trees they could see from the ship carried less foliage and seemed more sparce than in Van Diemen's land. The spindly trees reached high into the sky and there appeared to have been a recent fire on the hills behind the town. An unusual blue shimmer rose from the forest like steam rising from a distant, boiling pot.

Many buildings in the town were made of sand-stone, some more substantial than others. Built at intervals on both sides of a wide street, they sported ample verandas jutting out over a wooden promenade.

One of the sailors walking past Bedelia was talking to another younger sailor. "Them there taverns are a danger to seafaring men." He pointed to the road leading up a hill. "Many a tale has been told of the capture of inebriated sailors by hustlers to make up the crews for trading ships. Watch out young Harry, when you go ashore. Be sure you drink at the taverns closer to The Rocks."

Passengers who were disembarking in Australia were busy sorting through their trunks and boxes. The crew had brought them up from the hold and placed them on the deck. A hive of activity ensued and there was a rising sense of excitement from everyone.

Those continuing to New Zealand had been told they would have two nights in Sydney, and they could either sleep and eat on board ship and explore during the day, or stay in one of the taverns in town. The ship would sail at 0800 hours on Wednesday, to catch the outgoing tide, and not a moment later. If they were not back the ship would sail regardless. Their belongings would be deposited at the first port of call in New Zealand.

"We aren't going to have any of the delays the little harlot caused us in Hobart town," the captain said. Bedelia flinched when she heard these harsh words about her friend. Who was he to judge without knowing everything about Therese's past?

Bedelia and Veronica decided to take Michael and Keenan up on their offer of escorting them around the town. They planned to go to the outskirts where they could experience more of the country's wildlife. It appeared, from what they could see, that this could all be done on foot. Michael and Keenan would stay at a tavern in town and Bedelia and Veronica planned to return to the ship for the evening meal and their beds.

Because it was the first day and mid-morning, the group would stay within the vicinity of the harbour and explore on the fringes of the settlement. There was plenty to see with the activity of a bustling port and a busy town. Bedelia and Veronica allowed themselves a couple of pennies each to purchase necessities to help with their lives in New Zealand.

Provisions for making a light picnic had been set out on the wooden bench in the galley. Bedelia sandwiched the cold meat between bread slices spread with lard, wrapping them and placing the parcels in their utensil bags. The cook gave her an extra bag of sugar and tea and a small billy in case they had the chance to heat water somewhere.

"I be loving you for the care you've given others," the cook said. "You're surely a gem, and such a worker. These are for you as a thank you." With that he handed her a small bag of biscuits. "Now take care and mind those men folk of yours don't let ye outta their sight."

"We will, for sure," Bedelia nodded to the cook. "I am thanking you for your treats." She saw the cook's face light up as she pecked him on the cheek, picked up the bags and stepped out of the galley.

The others were waiting for her at the bottom of the gang plank. She handed them their bags of food as she skipped along beside them.

The men had taken their trunks to a nearby tavern after being processed through the immigration hall and spent the last hour assisting Patrick and his family to disembark with all their belongings. Patrick's family were to take up lodgings at a nearby boarding house until they could organise transport. He had already secured a position as a farm station hand. An agent acting for the farmer, had come to the port to recruit more immigrants arriving in Australia. They would be heading to the farm where the family were to settle.

The brothers had arranged to meet up the next day. They wished to spend a few hours together before bidding farewell. Michael and Keenan would wait until the *Catherine Mary* had departed before they started their search for work.

Dressed in their lightest clothing, the group set out for the rest of the day to explore. It was already steaming hot and the flies were sticking to their sweaty skin.

As they passed the immigration hall, they saw Mrs Pentwick slump into a seat beside her. A gentleman wearing an official uniform was tending to her. She held what appeared to be a letter.

Bedelia ran over to the matron, sensing that she was in some distress. She looked at the official questioningly. He turned to Mrs Pentwick, who was ashen as she continued to stare at the contents of the paper she held in her trembling hands.

"It's my Alfie," she told Bedelia. "He's met with an unfortunate accident and been killed in a bush fire where they were milling trees. The note, well, it's from his companion, who knew I was coming on this ship. Oh lassie, what am

I to do? We had such grand ideas for our life in the new country ... and now they've all been dashed, and me left quite alone."

Bedelia beckoned to the others and told them of the dilemma. "I'll just take Mrs Pentwick back to the ship, and the captain or the doctor will likely help her. I'll just be a jiffy if you care to wait in the shade over there."

"We're sorry for your troubles, missus," Michael said.

Bedelia supported the matron, whose knees were shaking. "What am I to do, what am I to do?" she muttered continuously until the two women reached the ship. They walked up the gangplank and onto the deck, where Bedelia spied the doctor and the captain in deep conversation.

"What ... " they both said in unison, but before they could get the question out, Mrs Pentwick wailed her news and showed the doctor the letter written in crude English by her dead husband's friend. "Oh, what will become of me?" she said, tears streaming down her cheeks. "There's nothing in this god-forsaken country for me now."

Bedelia excused herself. Her friends were waiting across the wharf. She promised the matron she would be back in the evening. The doctor gave her a reassuring nod and took Mrs Pentwick's arm as he steered her towards a place to sit.

As she walked to meet her companions, Bedelia felt Mrs Pentwick's despair. Bedelia's resilience in the face of bad news came with a numbing acceptance of life's tragedies. Sadness and emotion could never be denied, but she had learnt to just put one foot in front of the other. Her mother's reminder came back to her. *This too shall pass.*

Nothing more was mentioned about the interruption to their day. They set off up the hill to explore this infant town. Michael steered the ladies to the opposite side of the road as they passed the notorious taverns. There was loud, vulgar conversation and laughter spilling out from the open doors. Even at that early hour, a drunken sailor fell as he exited. He rolled over, picked himself up and waddled his way down the street. Every now and then he swayed to miss a tall lamppost. On top of each pole sat a lantern holding whale oil, ready to be lit come the evening. This was a familiar sight from home.

The streets were dusty. A gentle eddy whisked up the light red soil and carried it down the street as if following the inebriated sailor.

The sun streamed down, and the party stopped for a cool lemon drink. A stall had been set up beside the street and Michael spared one of his pennies to buy a cup for each of his companions. They all carried a flask of water, but this treat of fresh squeezed citrus was too tempting to pass by.

The shop behind the refreshment stand lured the men in. A large window displayed unusually wide-brimmed hats. They had seen many of the locals donning these and could see how this extra protection would serve them in the intense heat they were experiencing.

"Well, don't you look quite the thing in yer hats," Bedelia said as Michael and Keenan left the store with their new acquisitions.

As they carried on up the street Veronica said, "Many a head will turn when they spy you wandering by, so they will."

The houses and buildings started to thin out as they headed towards large stands of trees. As they looked up into these trees, Veronica pointed to the furry animals cradled in the crooks of the branches. On these creatures, large black leathery snouts protruded between two furry round ears. These append-ages sat on either side of rather substantial heads.

"What sweet fluffy pets they are," Veronica said, looking at the grey bear-like animals. Some had small babies clinging to their shoulders.

No one in the group had seen such an animal but, from what they had been told, they guessed these were the endearing little koala bears found only in Australia.

Bedelia had an overwhelming desire to cuddle one of them. There was nothing sinister about their appearance, unlike some of the other wild animals they had come across on their travels. "Oh my, but are they not the sweetest darlings ever to cross God's earth?" she said.

As they continued along the path, the men looked to the floor of the forest. Keenan picked up a fallen branch and used it in a sweeping motion, to part the grass ahead.

"What is it you're doing, Keenan?" Veronica said.

"Why, I'm just clearing a safe path, so I am. Yer can never know what surprises may be lurking."

Bedelia nodded.

The sisters scanned the branches above for another sight of the little bears. Every now and then they would hear thundering bounds, and a large kangaroo would cross their path at a safe distance. They agreed the kangaroos outnum-bered the koalas two for one.

Finding a log lying across the path in a shady clearing, they decided to stop. A magnificent view of the town and the expansive waters opened below. They could just make out the masts of the *Catherine Mary* surrounded by the other vessels in the harbour. She was distinctive because of her three masts, whereas many others had only two. Smaller boats required just one mast. Gathered in the harbour, they resembled matchsticks among the tinder box buildings.

Veronica laid down the cloth that Michael had brought from his trunk. They spread out the picnic from their bags.

"What of the biscuits, Dee? Where did they come from?" said Veronica.

"Cook gave me a small treat. He popped them in our bags. Only for us, mind," Bedelia smiled.

"We all know you've done yourself proud. The cook and everyone else on board think you're the bee's knees, Dee."

"Well, that's a hoot, Vonnie, you're a poet and didn't know it."

They all laughed.

They picked up their mugs and pretended they were ladies and gentlemen, like children at play. Keenan stuck out his little finger in elegant fashion as he drank his water, and the girls giggled at the gesture.

After lunch they all sat in introspective quiet. Bedelia wondered if the others were also imagining what lay ahead. *It will not be many more days before we reach our new home,* she thought. *Oh, but I am going to miss these lovely men. I may never see them again.* She turned away and wiped her eyes. She did not want to let anything spoil these last hours with Michael and his friend.

The afternoon sun spun shards of light down on the group as they rested in the long grass. The shady spot they had found was directly under three tall gum trees. The sisters lay back searching the high branches, while their escorts puffed away on their pipes.

The others didn't hear or see the stealthy serpent slither its way towards Bedelia. Its scales of grey and head of orange shimmered in the sun's rays. Bedelia tried to yell out as she turned her head and saw the snake opening his jaws, but the scream had stuck deep in her throat.

"Don't move, missus," said a man approaching from their right. In his hands, held above his shoulder and parallel to the ground, he carried a long stick with a sharp spear-head lashed tightly to its end.

The sisters froze, their eyes wide open, their mouths agape. Michael and Keenan slowly rose to defend their charges. Bedelia wondered if they would need to be saved from the snake or the native men who stood naked but for a small red cloth tied around their hips and through their groins. Their deep brown skin was artfully painted white and orange. A red band, of the same material as their loin cloths, was tied around their foreheads.

These were the aborigines they had been told about, but Bedelia felt more afraid of the long object still sliding silently through the grass, so close to her now. As the snake prepared to lunge at Bedelia's exposed ankle, the man threw his spear. It was over in a second, just inches from her. The snake's head was pinned to the hard earth, the rest of its body lashing this way and that in a final death throe.

Just as quickly as they had appeared, the aborigines disappeared into the undergrowth, but not before they had grabbed their prey and retrieved their weapon. They never said a word as they departed, the reptile hanging limply around the neck of the man who had so deftly killed it.

Veronica started sobbing. Bedelia hugged her sister tightly as tears trickled down her own dusty face. Both men rushed to comfort them. They appeared to be as relieved as the sisters.

Shaken but unharmed, they packed away their picnic and made their way back to the ship. They hardly spoke a word, the men walking protectively on either side of Veronica and Bedelia, their arms intertwined with those of the sisters.

When she was sufficiently recovered from her fright, Bedelia said, "That snake was so close. With its mouth wide open, I swear I could see what it had eaten for lunch." This broke the spell of serious contemplation, and the party of four sat down in uncontrollable laughter, tears cascading down their cheeks.

Bedelia and Veronica had chosen to spend the next day within safe range of the ship. They had settled under the shade of a gum tree.

Bedelia had been given a book to look at by the doctor. In it was information on all things concerning birth. Although she could manage to understand only some of the words on the many pages, she was fascinated by the diagrams. She vowed to herself that she would find some way to learn from the explanations.

Veronica turned the pen Mrs Pentwick had given her to another letter to their Uncle Paddy, in more than just simple words now. The matron had told her that she had a "lovely hand" during her tuition. A steel nib embraced the end of the wooden shaft. It was quite unlike the quill she had used at home. Veronica placed the small glass container of ink on the bench beside her. She carefully dipped the tip of the pen into the dark blue liquid and delicately formed the letters on the parchment, which was supported on a small wooden board positioned on her lap.

Cook had given them food for another picnic, and Michael had loaned them his tea cloth. "Let's just enjoy a quiet day on steady ground," Bedelia said to her sister.

While they were idling away the hours, Bedelia day-dreamed. Every now and then she turned to speak to her sister. "I'm thinking so much about what life in New Zealand will be like." Then she would browse through more pages of the medical book. "Where do you think we might live, Vonnie?" and before her sister had a chance to reply she said, "And do you image the countryside will be as pretty as our own Emerald Isles?"

Veronica's eyes had glazed over, but she seemed to nod in all the right places as her sister rambled on without waiting for any answers to the barrage of questions.

They made a pact that, no matter what, they would get work close to each other. "You're the only family I have left in this whole wide world," Veronica said, "and I will not lose you too."

Michael and Keenan had spent the day helping Patrick and his family ready themselves for their journey inland. They had spoken at length to the agent. Patrick was hoping this move would be a step towards ownership for the family. Life in this vast and arid country would likely be a huge contrast to farming life in Ireland. Patrick knew he had much to learn, experience to gain, stock and farming equipment and money to accumulate before the family would be ready to purchase a farm of their own. These considerations they readily shared with Michael and Bedelia as they ate their final meal together.

Veronica and Keenan had chosen to have an early night and had already said their farewells.

Bedelia and Michael held hands, but nothing was mentioned about their parting. The conversation during the meal centred around Patrick's family and dreams and hopes for their future. Michael walked Bedelia back to the ship. Not a word was said. They hugged, turned around and walked away from each other in silence. Bedelia walked up the gangplank, onto the ship and across the deck her eyes clouded over with tears. She didn't look around once; she just couldn't.

Chapter 9

Everyone was accounted for, and a few extras also, when the ship set sail on the last leg of the very long journey. Bedelia had taken her position at the railings, hoping to see a tall figure with a wide brimmed hat waving from the shore. She waited there until any features on the wharf were just dots in the distance.

Mrs Pentwick was included in those journeying on. She had decided to stay on the ship. She wanted to see what possibilities there may be available for her in New Zealand. She said to Bedelia, "There's nothing for me in Australia now. Just dashed promises of new beginnings and memories of a long, happily married life to my Alfie."

The captain had offered the matron free passage home on his ship if there were any passengers returning to the mother country needing a nursemaid or governess. First-class passengers sometimes went back to England for health, education or other reasons. Young women in steerage were few and far between on the return journey. This prospect was well beyond their means.

The other new passengers, who filled the places of those who had disembarked, were among some who had tried their hand at settling in Australia. For whatever reason, they had been unsuccessful. Some ex-convicts who joined them had served their time in the penal colony and were free to live wherever they chose. They only had to pay a minimal fee for their passage. Some had skills much sought-after in New Zealand.

Bedelia lingered on the deck. She had risen early to keep vigil, missing breakfast. As she stood there, looking into the distance, she was aware of someone approaching her from the right. She turned, expecting to see her sister she started to speak. Her bottom lip dropped, her mouth agape. Bedelia blinked twice trying to make sense of the person standing there. It was Michael.

"What? … When? … Why? Bedelia stuttered, her eyes brimming with tears.

"It was that last snake that made up our minds," Michael said. Keenan nodded. He and Veronica had been right behind Michael. " We are going to try our luck in the land of birds."

The original passengers had left England in June. It was now approaching December, and the women discussed the fact that this would be a very different Christmas from the cold and snowy one back home. "You can have a picnic by the sea," Bedelia said, with more excitement than she had shown in many years, about the festive season.

The women's quarters became a flurry of activity. They had all decided to make the most of their last weeks on board ship and to use up the materials donated for their handiwork.

"I know what I'm going to make for Michael; a handkerchief with his initials on it. I'm sure he'll use it and be quite the la-di-da gentleman with it peeking from his jacket pocket," Bedelia said to her sister.

Bedelia also had a plan to complete the shawl she had started for her sister. She knew this task would be more difficult to achieve as a surprise, especially due to the close quarters they lived in, so she pretended it was for Mrs Ashcroft's baby.

Buoyed along by Bedelia's enthusiasm, the atmosphere in the often dark and dingy quarters became vibrant with creativity. The musicians in their midst pulled out their instruments, striking up some lively Christmas carols familiar to all.

The excitement was contagious. It spread to the other areas of the ship along with the words to "Good King Wenceslas", "Silent Night" and "O come all ye faithful" as they wove their magical way to the other inhabitants on board through the cracks that had often been the reason for complaint with the unwanted odours, or sea-water. Now rays of sun shone though the apertures and the small portholes.

"It is altogether a splendid day, don't you think, Vonnie?" It was more a statement than a question.

The captain had even deemed it safe to have the hatchway open. The men and women were still kept to their allotted times on deck, although there was now more leniency.

The sisters had exhausted the "What ifs" and settled into a calm complacency, just waiting to see what the future would hold. But Bedelia's confidence that they would have no problem finding employment was not held by Veronica.

Between stitches, Bedelia leafed through the pages of the doctor's medical and obstetrics book, "The Science of Midwifery". She was sure that helping women give birth would be her future, although she still had doubts as to her capabilities.

Mrs Pentwick sat in the corner wringing her hands. Bedelia thought she had aged ten years in a week. "Vonnie, I feel helpless for the old duck," Bedelia whispered. Since the bad news, Bedelia had made sure she spent time with the matron despite the previous nastiness from the older woman.

She filled a mug of tea from the pot on the communal table. "This is for you, Mrs Pentwick; just how you like it." The matron continued to look at her hands and sigh deeply as she took the tea. All she could do was shake her head and tut her tongue as she stared into the depths of the mug, as if she would find her solution in the tea leaves floating below. She supped the brew with tears weaving their way down her pink, wrinkled face.

Veronica and Bedelia, who still had respect for this woman along with some foreboding, grew more and more concerned about the matron's melancholia. Bedelia even consulted the doctor, who reassured her that there was nothing to be done. He advised them to "just show her patience and compassion."

"Now, lass," the doctor said to Bedelia when they had a moment together, "I have been thinking about my plans for settling in New Zealand. I have offered Mrs Pentwick a position as my housekeeper until she can make a wise decision as to her future. This will give her time to know if she wishes to settle in New Zealand or take a ship home to the old country. Have you spared some thought as to what you intend to do?"

"If the good Lord is on my side, I wish to work in the service of mothers having their babies," Bedelia said. "I've thought often about your kind offer. I know I have much to learn, but I am willing to work hard, and I would like to work for you, so I would."

"Bedelia, that is good news. I know you have the aptitude to become a fine midwife."

"I'm not sure of that word, but I'm guessing it means you will employ me."

"Yes, you are quite correct. I believe you will be perfect in your role as my assistant."

By this stage of the journey the women were settled in their routine, and they all looked out for each other. They knew the rules, so the absence of the matron's authority, due to her grief, did not create any problems. Even the timing of the stroll the women took on deck was less rigid, and sometimes the men were up there at the same time. This pleased Bedelia, as she wished to share as many of her last days on the ship with Michael as possible.

As they stood together, watching the sea rush past in a foaming lather, a pod of dolphins entertained them as they gambolled through the wake. "They're truly a playful creature, aren't they just? I have the feeling that their presence is a good sign for our future," Michael said.

"They are playful for sure." Bedelia looked up to the man beside her and held his eyes for the longest time. "I'll be missing you. I've become quite fond of our little times together."

"Since we met, I've been as happy as the days are long. I feel sure that we will find each other again when we have ourselves all settled, *ceann milis*." Michael moved closer to touch her shoulder. "Keenan and I will be looking for work until we find our way. I don't imagine we'll be that far from you." Bedelia had shared the doctor's proposal of working as his assistant near the town of Nelson.

It had been a wrench for Michael to leave his brother and family in Australia. Bedelia was pleased he still had his companion, Keenan, with him. She knew that any meetings in the future were uncertain, for there was no surety that Bedelia and Michael would settle in the same area.

"You'll know where I'll be, and mind you don't let the grass grow too long under your feet until you return, Michael Mahoney," Bedelia said. "I may have learnt to write good and proper by then. Vonnie has the gift of the pen and I will too, of that I'm sure. We'll put a note in the local store so you'll know where we've hung our hat."

The week it took the ship to arrive in the harbour of Nelson flew by. The weather was kind to them. The wind rushed behind, pushing the ship on its way as if shooing them on to better prospects.

As they sailed from the west and rounded into the bay, Bedelia told her sister, "If I'm not mistaken, those mountains look like our mammy's huge embracing arms welcoming us to this new life. I'm thinking long about her these days. What would she say of this?"

A lick of snow remained on the tops of the mountains, which were more majestic than any the sisters had ever seen. Their first close encounter with the land was the forest that reached down to the golden sands. A near deafening orchestra of bird song blasted from the trees, a symphony of welcome for the newcomers.

Everyone on board was up on deck, some hanging precariously over the rails as if they were about to dive into the crystal-clear waters and swim to their new home without waiting for the ship to dock.

"Ahoy," the captain yelled, "we're not wanting a man overboard now. Not after getting this far with only a minor accident. Get yourselves back and safe."

"Aye, aye Cap'n," resounded from the passengers, along with wails of laughter.

The captain was in a heightened state of vigilance. Bedelia and Michael overheard much of the conversation at the wheel between the captain and the helmsman as the rest of the crew dropped the sails and the anchor.

"We must sail in with that large rock yonder to our starboard and the island to the portside." The captain was pointing to a huge rock, shaped like an arrow head, jutting from the water closest to the land. "We are fortunate with the weather, and if my calculations are correct, we will have the perfect tide and wind to safely navigate the narrow entrance on the morrow."

That night the captain gave permission for the passengers and crew to let their hair down and celebrate. Although some of the passengers were going on in other ships stopping further north, the last of the stores were used and there were some extra special treats for everyone from the cook's galley. The feast was quickly followed by a *ceilidh* that went on well into the night.

Molly and Siobhan took out their instruments and were joined by some of the men, who broke out their additions to the band. The musicians combined to produce a lively, foot-stomping celebration. Everyone joined in to sing the tunes they knew.

Laughter, singing and gaiety rang out to round off a long 148 days of journeying to this faraway place they would now make their home, although most would still call Ireland or England home for some time to come.

Bedelia danced every dance. She didn't wait to be asked, but boldly tapped every available man on the shoulder in turn. She whirled and tapped, twirled and clapped, but saved every alternate dance for Michael. When the makeshift band finally took a break for supper, she sat down with a gasp of relief next to her sister.

"That fair warmed the cockles of my heart, Vonnie. I saw yer dancing with the mate. Now tell me, how on earth did you coax the doctor up? I've only had one dance with him before and I surely haven't seen him let his hair down at all, at all."

Veronica answered Bedelia with a demure smile as the younger sister continued her chatter, not waiting for an answer.

"I'm all of a jitter worrying myself sick how tomorrow will be. I know our Mammy said to just put one foot in front of the other, but my mind doesn't care to listen to her right now," Bedelia said.

The ship stayed the night in the bay just out from Nelson. At 5.30 am they weighed anchor, setting minimal sails to power a safe passage into the sheltered area of water. Nelson Haven was almost completely enclosed by a shingle bar. There was just the narrowest of margins leading into the anchorage, which would be their last obstacle.

Veronica and Bedelia had joined Michael and Keenan in their favourite spot at the rails facing the settlement. It was just downwind from the wheel, where the captain took up his place again.

It was easy for the group to hear the captain as he said to the helmsman, "Ships have been blown onto those rocks with a lee shore and the wrong tide, but it's a safe anchorage once you pass through the gap."

Bedelia looked at Michael with wide eyes. "Glory be to God and Mother Mary, how many times on this voyage I was frightened out of my wits wondering if I was going to see the light of day," she said. "Now we're finally here, imagine being shipwrecked with the land in sight, let alone being killed by the sea entirely."

"Those poor shipwrecked souls may never have combed a grey hair," Michael said, the serious look on his face mirroring those of the others beside him.

They were heading towards the gap with the tide aiding their way and just the gentlest of breezes wafting the sails to push them forward. All hands were on deck, and the passengers had been warned to remain in their places. The crew were on tenterhooks as the ship slowly inched its way to their final destination.

Before any one of the passengers had time to realise what was happening, the captain was shouting orders to drop the remaining sails and lower the lifeboats. There were whale boats being launched from the shore and every single crewman appeared to know exactly what was happening and what was expected of them.

Michael grabbed Bedelia around her waist, as did Keenan with Veronica. It was only when they looked into the men's faces that the sisters knew they were in dire straits. Their brows were furrowed. Fear spilled out of their eyes.

Michael said to Keenan, "The wind has changed and turned on its heels. It'll be coming from the east and that doesn't bode well for staying clear of those rocks over there." He pointed to the jagged grey slabs just visible above the water at the edge of the little island.

Bedelia's knuckles turned white as she clung on to the rails. She looked at Veronica, whose teeth were biting down hard on her lip, wide eyes streaming tears.

Bedelia turned her hands back to hold on to Michael's huge fingers that encircled her tiny waist. She chanted over and over, "Jesus, Mary and Joseph, keep us safe in your arms. Holy Mary, Mother of God, pray for us sinners, now and at the hour of our death. Amen."

The crewmen in the lifeboats attached to the sides and bow were rowing for dear life, pulling the ship in the opposite direction to the gusts of wind coming from the land. The ship's progress had been completely powered down, with all the sails eased. Some of the crew were tending to these as they folded and harnessed them out of the way.

As occupied as the crew were in their individual tasks, they all kept one eye on the portside. The only noise was coming from the captain as he continued shouting orders to the crew in the boats below. They had now been joined by men in boats from the shore, who had grabbed the ropes thrown to them from the crew on the ship. Every muscle in those men's bodies was working to capacity. The strain was showing on the ligaments in their necks as they rowed and rowed, pulling the heavy ship towards safety.

With only inches to spare, the stern of the ship crept past the last grey obstacle. The captain's expression told it all. Bedelia and the other passengers, whose eyes were glued to his face, could now see that they were in the safety of the harbour.

It took some time for any words to come out, but Michael was the first to speak. "It's little wonder they have named this harbour Nelson Haven. I don't think I've been that scared in my entire life. I had us all quite dead and gone to Heaven in my mind's eye." Michael turned to Bedelia and without hesitation embraced and kissed her.

Part 2

"New Beginnings."

Chapter 10

As the passengers disembarked they were met by some official-looking gentlemen who directed them to a large landing hall. All the passengers lined up and were herded into rows. At a table there was a man with a large ledger book in which he was writing down what each immigrant was telling him. When it came to Bedelia's turn, he asked her in clipped tones, "Full name, age, nationality and occupation."

Bedelia said, "Bedelia Mary Maher."

"Spell it," said the man, without looking up.

She did, then added, "Sixteen years old."

The man, half-glasses perched precariously on the end of his purple, bulbous nose, turned to his assistant, saying, "Oh, for heaven's sake, we have yet another Mick. The whole boat's full of them."

Bedelia looked at Veronica, eyes fiery, lips pursed, hands on hips, ready to jump down the man's throat. Veronica shook her head and motioned with her hand below the desk. "Don't you dare, Dee," she whispered out of the side of her mouth, lips hardly moving. "He's not worth it."

"Nationality, as if I don't already know."

"I-R-I-S-H," Bedelia spelled the letters out loud and crisp. "And mighty proud to be."

At this the man finally looked up at the person he was registering.

"And I'm a midwife," Bedelia said. "And that is spelt M-I-D-W-I-F-E."

Veronica looked at her sister with a nod of approval.

"Next," the man said, peering over his spectacles.

Veronica stepped up to the table, gave her details and joined Bedelia.

Bedelia glanced around for Michael, and spied him at the other end of the building. Their eyes met, and a tip of his hat and a nod reassured Bedelia he would meet her as arranged before they went their separate ways.

Michael and Keenan were looking at a notice-board made of scrim. There were many pieces of paper flapping in the breeze coming in through an open door. Keenan was pointing to one of the notices, which was neatly pinned underneath a heading, and he appeared to be reading out what was written on it.

Veronica was claiming their trunk as Bedelia turned to tell her sister about the notice-board. "It may be helpful to find some work and a bed to lay our heads," she said.

The doctor and Mrs Pentwick came over to join them, followed by another gentleman Bedelia had never seen before. "Ah, just the young lady I've been looking for. Bedelia, this is Doctor Nation. He is my long-standing friend and colleague who has set up practice in this region. He has been telling me there's more than enough work for all of us. In fact, he told me there's a real shortage of workers in many trades, especially in the medical field. That then carries through to all other areas and people who are willing to set their energies to work, Veronica."

"My colleague tells me you have the gift of midwifery. A valuable vocation, especially in our rapidly expanding new world," Doctor Nation said to Bedelia.

"My sister here is going to look for a job as a nanny, or helping in the house of a family in need of her services. This looks like a fine place to live. I can't believe the beauty of the forest and the bird song. It fair warms the cockles of my heart," Bedelia said, the excitement brimming in her voice.

"I have a modest home on the hill over there," Doctor Nation said, pointing to his right, "and if you agree to sharing a room until you have some plans arranged, you are welcome to join Doctor Pattison and myself." He directed his offer to the sisters and Mrs Pentwick. "I know Mrs Nation won't mind. In fact, I'm sure she will be rather pleased for the company. No doubt some help in the house and with our four children would be gratefully accepted."

"I can get my man to carry your luggage to our wagon," he said to the three ladies, then turning to the ship's doctor he said, "It is such a blessing and relief to see you here, George. You will be a great asset and relief for my busy practice."

The sisters looked at each other in disbelief. Veronica turned to Bedelia, quietly saying, "How can we turn down such an offer?"

Turning to Doctor Nation, Bedelia said, "Please, sir, just give me a minute to catch my breath. Your offer is very generous, and I'd be obliged if I could take a little time to chat with our friends over there, so I would." Veronica and Bedelia walked over to where Michael and Keenan stood in intense discussion.

"Michael, we have fallen on good fortune and have had an offer of a bed. It will give us time to look for some employment, so it will. I can't believe how easy it all is," Bedelia said. "And what of you, is there anything there that draws your eye?"

"Well, Delia, it's looking like there are enough jobs for hard-working folk and for those with skills and trades. We might put our hand to farming with the view to buying some land, or we could help with some building. I'm thinking that's the way we'll go."

As they walked out of the building, the warm sun rained down on them through the branches of magnificent trees hugging the track's edge. Each tree was covered in brilliantly adorned brushes of scarlet. They looked up onto the nearby hill, where some cottages had been built. Dotted between native trees and shrubs, still more were under construction.

The ship's doctor joined them and introduced his colleague to the men. They exchanged pleasantries, then the doctor asked Bedelia if they would be joining them, so that their trunk could be collected and loaded on the wagon.

"We'd be delighted to take up your offer, Doctor Nation," Bedelia said, and Veronica nodded in agreement as she left with the doctors to point out their luggage.

Michael took Bedelia's hands. "We will leave a note in the local store when we know where we'll be laying our heads. We will also look out for a note from you." And as he squeezed her hands gently in his, he said, "May the road rise up to meet you and God bless you, *macushla*."

Bedelia thought they may never see each other again, but that one parting endearment put hope in her heart as she stood on tippy-toes and kissed Michael on his cheek.

By the time Bedelia joined Veronica, their box had been loaded onto the wagon by the driver. The sisters joined Mrs Pentwick. The women sat on the forms of timber along each side of the wagon with all the luggage in the middle.

The discussion was well above the heads of the women as Doctor Nation shared cases with the ship's doctor that he commonly dealt to in the small community. Bedelia was listening to words she was totally unfamiliar with. She hoped that one day these topics would be a natural part of her conversation. The doctors hardly drew breath as they took the seat beside the driver and continued talking. The women sat quietly. Bedelia was absorbing the beauty around her with awe and wonder, wrapped in her own thoughts.

The wagon rounded the base of the hill from the left as they approached the settlement recently named Nelson. Many small buildings made of materials from the surrounding land dotted the hillside to the right. A large timber-clad construction sat on a flat piece of land, halfway up the hill.

Pointing towards this building, Doctor Nation said, "Those barracks are to be some of the settlers' accommodation until they can find more permanent arrangements."

As they were moving slowly along the track, Bedelia noticed a group of settlers from the ship *Morgenfrue*. The passengers from both ships had been processed through the arrival hall at the same time. Doctor Nation stopped his conversation with the ship's doctor and said to the ladies, "These immigrants are from a third wave of Germans and are looking to settle in the valley to the south of Nelson alongside their countrymen."

There were several men rolling barrels and a few women and children. One of these women caught Bedelia's eye. She appeared to be having difficulty walking up the incline towards the barracks, stopping every few minutes to lean on her companion. Bedelia noticed how one hand attempted to support her pendulous belly while the other pressed on her back. Although the woman's garments were full and loose, Bedelia guessed this woman was with child and that her behaviour could be a sign of advanced pregnancy.

"Stop the wagon," Bedelia shouted.

The doctors had returned to their previous conversation, but when Bedelia said, "Look, she seems to be in trouble," pointing up the hill as she jumped down from the wagon, both of them followed her.

On reaching the procession, Bedelia intuitively knew that this woman was in labour, and the sooner she reached the shelter of the barracks, to which the group appeared to be heading, the better.

The track to the shelter was narrow and steep. The doctors nodded to each other as they took their positions on either side of the labouring woman.

"Wir sind Ärzte," Doctor Nation said, introducing himself and his colleague.

The labouring woman accepted their proffered arms for support. The German woman repeated, *"Veelen Dank!"* several times as they made their way up the hill.

Bedelia ascertained that the woman in labour was named Sophia and that her little boy, holding tightly to her skirt, was Henri. He reluctantly took a hold of Bedelia's proffered hand, but soon relaxed and skipped along beside her as the other little boys in the group gathered around them.

Doctor Nation spoke in his fluent German to the men, who were having some difficulty rolling the heavy barrels up the steep path. Bedelia noticed that the doctor was earnestly encouraging them to do something, and finally one of the men said, *"Ja, ja,"* leaving the barrels on the track at the side of the hill with one man remaining with them.

Re-joining the group, Doctor Nation said to Bedelia and the ship's doctor, "I will take the wagon on to my home with the other ladies, collect my medical bag and return forthwith." Bedelia and the ship's doctor continued with the German families.

On their arrival at the barracks, the families were ushered into the area set aside for sleeping. Several of the German women milled around the labouring woman and settled her onto a basic canvas cot that was lined up with others along one wall of a large room. There were four large poles at even spaces around the room, supporting the roof. Two of the women busied themselves with what Bedelia supposed was their birthing bag, as she recognised objects they were setting out on a cot beside them. The other women gathered the children together and took them outside to play.

The two women remaining seemed to be tending to Sophia. Although they had no common tongue, Bedelia could see as she watched that the women knew what they were about. Without need for direction, Bedelia moved closer, and as the waves of contractions overtook Sophia, Bedelia rubbed her lower back. It was no time at all before Doctor Nation returned with his medical bag. The doctors stood back watching the women work seamlessly.

Bedelia heard Doctor Nation say as he turned to his colleague, "My goodness, George, what are we here for? These women appear to have it all under control." With that, the two doctors stepped through the wide-open doorway into the sunshine.

As she watched them leave through the wide entrance, Bedelia noticed the bush-clad hills that surrounded the settlement forming a natural amphitheatre of bird song and children's laughter. *But there is work to do,* she thought, turning back to Sophia as another contraction overtook her.

She could see the doctors settling down on forms near the opening to the barracks, in relaxed conversation with the new arrivals.

The low hum of the men's conversation was interjected by moans and re-assuring platitudes of the attending women. Bedelia was aware that the men's dialogue would come to a halt, then resume when the noises inside ceased.

When the doctors and the group of German men moved over to the shade of nearby trees, Bedelia supposed they were attempting to escape the increasing intensity of heat powering down from the blazing sun, as well as the escalating sounds coming from Sophia as she rode another wave of pain.

As the labour progressed Bedelia continued to respond to Sophia's pains, rubbing her lower back with a firm hand. The other two women worked to-gether, the older woman appearing to give the younger one instruction.

A short while later the men stood up when Bedelia approached them from the barracks. "Oh, doctors, we have a situation." Bedelia rattled off in a volley of excited words. "What we thought was a lock of fine black hair coming with the baby's head is really a bit of the first dark *cac* from the baby's arse."

Doctor Nation looked at his colleague and raised his eyebrows, with the faintest grin he shrugged his shoulders while Bedelia carried on speaking.

"Maureen's little Desy came that way but he slipped out with no bother, he was so small. I've seen this kind of a birth in your medical book, doctor, they called it a breech presentation, but I have no idea the best way to assist a bigger baby coming the wrong way." She continued talking, "The German women appear a little bothered. They have Sophia standing beside a pole with her leg raised on a small box, it seems they're letting nature take its course. I'd appreciate your guidance here if you care to help."

The doctors and Bedelia made haste to the barracks. As they entered, they stopped two cots away and watched the two women encourage their country-woman. *"Utpressen!"* they said to Sophia as the baby was now displaying his gender. With the next push, first one then the other leg was released along with the umbilical cord, and the body hung between Sophia's splayed legs.

"Watch that cord, Bedelia. As long as you can see it pulsing, all's well," the ship's doctor said. The throbbing vessels running though the baby's lifeline were easily visible. Bedelia and the doctors continued to stand back. The doctor expanded on his explanation. "While that is happening the baby is still receiving oxygen from his mother."

As Bedelia and her companions observed the miracle of nature and the natural instinct of mother and baby to birth, the baby rotated a quarter circle, and out dropped one arm and then the other as it rotated the other way. The ship's doctor whispered to Bedelia, "Sometimes you need to assist the limbs out. As I said before, the cord is your best indicator. If it stops beating then you only have a short amount of time, for the baby needs to be out and breathing before you run into trouble."

The older woman had her arms below the baby ready to receive it. Bedelia noticed that the cord had stopped beating. The woman gently supported the hanging baby as he lay body down with his legs straddling the upper part of her lower arm like a child suspended over a tree's branch. With the next "*Utpressen!*" the baby's face started to move out. The woman placed the middle finger from the hand of her supporting arm in the baby's mouth, with the other two fingers placed along his cheekbones, avoiding the eyes. Then, with enough traction to bring the chin down, the rest of the head was born smoothly.

The woman had brought the baby's face and head through in a sweeping motion. It was a natural flow of ease and perfection. Bedelia was overcome.

The ship's doctor said to Bedelia, "See how the *Hebamme* allowed the head to come down and through. She flexed the baby's head with her finger in his mouth as she followed the natural arch of the mother's birth canal. That is one of the most perfect breech births I have ever witnessed. In some cases, if the mother's birth canal is too small or the birth attendant is unskilled, this stage of the birth can end in disaster."

"What is a *Hebamme*?" Bedelia asked.

"That's the German name for a midwife," Doctor Nation said.

With those words, the baby let out a hearty cry, and the older woman carried the baby to the mother's outstretched arms. The words "*Mien Baby, mien Baby,*" brought tears of sheer relief to Bedelia. She noticed the doctors quietly turn away as they retrieved handkerchiefs from their pockets.

Bedelia had carefully noted all the exacting manoeuvres in birthing this new arrival, much larger than Maureen's baby, but also coming in the less common way of bottom first. She could see how important Sophia's position helped in widening the birth canal, allowing the baby to manoeuvre itself through, although she was a little unsure about the safety of the baby left hanging in mid-air. One of her many thoughts was, *What if he drops to the ground?* But

Bedelia could see that the *Hebamme* had been poised ready to do what she needed to do when the moment came. The calmness and skill shown by these two women as they helped the baby into the world eased Bedelia's uncertainty.

"I don't know if I'd be able to do this and be as calm as those *Heba* … I mean midwives," Bedelia said to the doctors. Then, without one second's hesitation, she strode over to help the German women. The doctors turned to one another, smiled and nodded, then quietly slipped out the door.

The baby was wrapped in his mother's large flannel skirt. She cradled him in her arms while she was assisted onto the nearby cot to rest from her labours. United in purpose, the three women then carried out the necessary tasks following a successful birth.

The older *Hebamme* turned to Bedelia. *"Veelen Dank!"* she said. She waited, looking at the younger German woman. When there was no response she pushed her elbow into her side, nodding her head towards Bedelia. The younger *Hebamme* just turned and moved away, tidying some of the equipment into the open bag without saying a word.

Herr Brandt, Sophia's husband, was invited in to meet his new son. Holding his hand as they approached Sophia was Henri, wide-eyed with awe. *"Mien lütte Broder,"* Henri said as he placed a gentle kiss on the baby's forehead. As she watched the Brandt family welcome baby Jens into the world, into this new country, Bedelia smiled as she thought, *This is a land of infinite potential, where we will each make a new and better life for ourselves.*

Chapter 11.

Waking from her very first sleep on New Zealand soil, Bedelia turned to her sister lying beside her and said, "I feel so refreshed from a wonderful, comfortable night's sleep. What a difference our bed is from the bunks on the ship. We have endured them for so long. But still, Vonnie, I get the feeling of the rolling sea. Every time I go to walk it feels like the floor is falling away from me and I have to grab on to something to stay upright."

Even Mrs Pentwick's snoring hadn't bothered the sisters. In fact, Bedelia thought, it was a lot quieter sleeping in the room with her than on board the ship with all the other sounds they had to contend with. Mrs Pentwick had already left her smaller bed, dressed and disappeared from the room.

After they had risen and dressed, they tidied the bed and straightened the meticulously made quilt. On a small side table was a large ceramic jug sitting in a washbasin painted with matching flowers. Pointing to the bureau, Veronica said, "Look, Dee, these doilies make me feel at home. They are just like the one's our nan made for us."

Bedelia nodded, she felt so welcomed by the family living in the cottage on the hill. The dinner the previous evening and the way they had been treated like guests felt so foreign yet wonderful. "I have to pinch myself to make sure I'm not dreaming," Veronica said.

Following their evening meal, after the excitement of the birth, the doctors had taken Bedelia aside. They had discussed the experience in detail. She understood how important it was to learn from such a situation. This would help her when a breech birth presented itself again, so she could confidently and competently do what was needed.

"I am thanking you doctors from the bottom of my heart," Bedelia said, "but I'm thinking that I'm not really made for this work. I had the fear of God in me today. How am I to do what those German midwives did with the baby coming backside first? I wouldn't know where to put my hands, what to do and not do. What if the head got stuck like you said may happen, doctor? When little Desy came that way he was born in seconds with no time to think of what could go wrong."

Doctor Nation was about to speak but Bedelia continued. "I can't understand why those things happened to me on the voyage. Why are trials thrown my way? I surely don't look for the bother." Bedelia looked pleadingly for answers from the doctors. "It's after that I get the shakes," she said.

Both doctors shrugged their shoulders and the ship's doctor said, "Because you have the gift, Bedelia. You just need some assistance. There are so many things to learn and absorb. Doctor Nation and I needed to train for many years to become doctors, and we're still learning. It never stops. And as for birth, as I've told you before, there are so many possibilities for which we cannot always be prepared. All we can do is our best."

"You will have our guidance, and if we can find a skilled midwife for you to work alongside, that would be of great help for your learning," Dr Nation said.

Bedelia said, "I am truly fascinated in everything about birth. I know trust is needed in nature's processes. I thank you; it did help to have things explained simply."

She silently repeated to herself the valuable ditty the doctors gave her: *Hands off the breech, unless you must.* She had even chanted it to herself as she slumped into a deep sleep.

The day was a hive of activity as the sisters sorted through their meagre worldly possessions. Veronica seemed excited to have a roof over her head with such a kind family who had offered her employment. Bedelia was pleased for her sister, as she could see that Mrs Nation was thorough but patient and extremely grateful to have some help at last. It was very unlike previous interactions with the upper-class English. In this home Bedelia felt like they were treated as equals.

Veronica had agreed to help in the house until she found something more permanent. Mrs Pentwick said she could help with schooling the children and teaching Veronica so she could take over the matron's role when she found a ship returning to the mother country.

Up until now, Mrs Nation told her new helpers, she had managed to keep the house running in every aspect. Alongside these demands she had the four children whom she cared for and educated, she grew a comprehensive garden and tended hens, milked a house cow, and cooked all the meals. Due to the lack of young, single women in the colonies, she was expected to do all this unaided. Dr Nation was constantly away on house calls or seeing patients in the front room that doubled as a surgery.

Mrs Nation also assisted the doctor in his daily administrations if he needed another pair of hands. Bedelia could see all this was taking its toll on the slight woman. Her complexion was pasty. Her black-rimmed eyes betrayed the tiredness she endeavoured to keep hidden, and her hazel-coloured hair had lost its lustre.

The family were well provided for despite the fact that money exchanging hands was rare. Mrs Nation said that many of the patients could only afford to give a chicken, eggs, vegetables or some wild meat in exchange for the doctor's time. Most payments came in favours returned.

The Nations informed their guests that the community was in the very early stages of settlement. Many of the pioneers had arrived with what they stood up in and a few pieces of extra clothing and basic household items that were required on the voyage. Sometimes they brought the essential items of their trade, if they had one.

"The land they were promised," Doctor Nation explained after dinner one night, "does not meet the expectations of many of the settlers or the agents who have recruited them. Unfortunately, immigrant labourers who need work to establish themselves, far exceed benefactors expected to provide the capital to fund development. This has caused a financial deficit. Freedom has come from escaping the restraints of the class system so many have left behind in Europe, but gruelling work awaits them in this new country and money is in short supply."

Some of the earlier German settlers, to whom Doctor Nation had been talking to at length when they needed medical attention, had told him they had been warned about and anticipated the shortage of basic farming equipment in the new colony. "Building materials, tools, seeds for crops and animals, as well as household utensils and homemaking luxuries are in short supply here," he said.

"That is why I brought many more items with me than most of the passengers on the ship, on your advice. Thank you, Stephen," Doctor Pattison said.

The doctors also shared the conversation and information they had gleaned from the German settlers and the new arrivals at the barracks.

"The barrels of the German migrants from the *Morgenfrue* contained much of their worldly goods. Some established settlers arrived in the New Zealand spring, and they encouraged their fellow countrymen to get straight to their allotted land in order to till the soil and get the seeds sprouting as soon as they could. This would help them to get the crops growing and ready for harvest in preparation for their first winter.

"I am moved with the Germans' energetic and industrious plans, George. They appear to be united by their desire to make the most of their new lives. From what they told us, the country they have just left offered them no chance to improve their lot. Their work ethics appear to be the cornerstone of their culture and now they have a chance to reap the benefits of their hard labour."

"Very impressive indeed," Doctor Pattison nodded. "The new arrivals told us they plan to leave the women and children in town until they are able to erect suitable living arrangements for them on their allotted land. They will head out and begin working as soon as they are able," he told the ladies at the table.

"Doctor Nation, do you think I would be able to visit with Sophia some time?" Bedelia said.

"Why yes, of course. I will make inquiries as to where she may be staying."

Bedelia smiled and said, "I'm not quite sure what I will say to her, but the new baby and young Henri won't mind my lack of German, I am thinking."

"They speak low German, or Plattdeutsch, as they call it," Doctor Nation explained to the ladies. "It's the primary dialect spoken by the farmers and residents from Northern Germany, but they had no trouble understanding our German, as this is the language of their sponsor and benefactor."

The men had told the doctors that they had been enticed to cross the vast oceans, and leave many of their family and friends behind, in the hope of shedding the shackles of serfdom that kept them forever landless in their mother country.

Settlers from earlier migration had come to the harbour to meet the ship when it arrived. These families had endured much hardship. Many setbacks had come from the agent who had recruited them.

"I was told he is a fat, arrogant man only interested in his and his family's welfare," Dr Nation said. "I am also aware that he has proven a most unsuitable leader both on board the ship and since they arrived in Nelson. There is only one despicable character I have met around the town. I am sure he is the one they described. It is well-known among all who have come in contact with him that he is completely devoid of benevolence towards his fellow men. In my opinion he is out to feather his own nest, despite his assumed role of looking out for the interests of the settlers."

The evening meals were a great time to share and learn from the Nations, as they proved to be a wealth of information. The ladies at the table discussed the pioneering spirit of the women coming to this new country. There was no easy way to assist them with their tasks unless they had been fortunate enough to bring the items or domestic help with them from their home countries. The ability to purchase home aides or employ servants was next to impossible. They just had to make do with what they had.

Mrs Nation, who insisted the ladies call her Lilian, said, "These hardy women see their role as keeping the home fires burning, no matter how simple that home may appear. Their men-folk labour outside while the women labour mostly indoors."

As Veronica and Mrs Pentwick helped Lilian clear the table, the doctors included Bedelia in more discussion.

"As I said when I first met you, Bedelia, there is more than enough work for all three of us," Doctor Nation said. "Nelson and the areas south, east and west are ever-expanding, with many miles to traverse to minister to the communities settling in the surrounding districts."

"It's all going too fast," Bedelia told the doctors. "I'm only sixteen, with very little experience of life and its troubles and as green as the grass in my home valley. It fair scares the bejasus out of me thinking I will have two precious lives in my hands."

"Dee, mind yer mouth, will yer," Veronica chided from her place at the sink. "We are among gentle folk, so we are. Mammy would fair turn in her grave if she could hear you. If she were alive today it would be the soap treatment you'd be getting, and that's for sure."

Bedelia put her hand up to her mouth. "Pardon me for my blasphemy." The doctors waved their hands in dismissal.

Doctor Nation resumed the conversation. "Well, Bedelia, the only way you are to learn is with practice. Just remember, you will have guidance from Doctor Pattison, myself and possibly the *Hebammen* you worked alongside on your first day here."

The conversation changed tack as the doctors started to discuss where Doctor Pattison could best hang up his shingle.

"The main mode of transport at the moment is by horse-drawn wagon, George," Doctor Nation said. "Although some tracks are being formed, the roads are very much in their early stages of construction. The way to the east takes a coast road around, then over bush-clad hills. The road to the south is through swamps bordered by native bush of fern and *mānuka*, with only a few tracks passable. The passage west allows the use of transport by water to the nearest point to wherever your destination may be. That is often the most direct, and has the fewest obstacles."

Without disturbing the conversation, Lilian wiped the table with a damp dishcloth.

Doctor Nation continued, "From what they said, the newly-arrived German families are planning to roll their barrels of worldly goods along the crude tracks formed though these marshlands. They will be heading to their allotted land to the south, on the fringe of the hills and up a low-lying valley. If they choose to head west by boat, the landing sites are still very basic as the survey-ors are in high demand for the road construction and land allotments."

Doctor Nation spoke of the difficulty in reaching outlying communities and the hazardous journeys he had made in order to reach those in need of his services. "This leaves a void for the ailing town folk, with only myself in the whole district. I am so grateful for the reprieve your arrival will give me, George. Added to that is the bonus of your arrival, Bedelia."

Bedelia smiled.

"From what you have told me, George, this young lassie has proven herself to be beyond her years in wisdom and intuition," concluded Doctor Nation.

Bedelia's smile widened.

The other women joined Bedelia and the doctors after the dishes and cook-ing equipment had been washed and put away. The children had all gone to bed earlier and were sound asleep in their parents' large feather bed.

"An afternoon of play has quite worn the children out," their mother said. "It has been all very exciting to have new people to give them the attention they have so sadly lacked. Stephen and I have had no time to spare."

The three boys had been boisterous, wanting to play rough and tumble games and outdoor activities, while little Rosemary had been content to play house with her little wooden doll in its neatly stitched clothes.

Veronica and Bedelia were happy to play with the boys. They had a ball to pass around, but hide and seek proved to be the most popular game, with a whole acre around the house and some overgrown land beside it that remained uncleared and uninhabited. It was here that many little places could be found for suitable hidey-holes in order to remain undetected.

Mrs Pentwick had been happy to take the less exuberant task of playing pretend house with the wee girl, whose blonde ringlets dripped around her shoulders, a neat little blue ribbon attempting to tame the unruly curls.

Lilian fetched a tray of port for the gentlemen and some tea for the ladies. If they had owned a bigger house the men would have retired to another room for a cigar with their port and the ladies would have shared the time stitching or reading, but these traditions were mainly for the gentry and had been left behind in the old country. Instead, they all remained around the dining table discussing the future. The Nations asked many questions about England and shared familiar memories with Doctor Pattison.

Bedelia and Veronica discovered, through their conversation, that Doctor Pattison and Doctor Nation had been educated together in Oxford. They had joined up again at St Thomas' Hospital in London for their medical studies and practicum to become doctors.

The sisters were extremely interested to discover a whole different world to the one they had left behind in Scarriff. *Such a small and insignificant place compared to London,* Bedelia thought.

Bedelia and Veronica were just happy to listen. To dredge up their past, Bedelia thought, would be like scouring a weir full of sorrow and deprivation. It was hard to remember a time when they had been as happy and content as the Nation children were when outside playing, with not a care in the world.

Mrs Pentwick was still very quiet and appeared lost in her own sorrow, looking down at her hands clenched in her lap.

After their supper, Mrs Pentwick, Bedelia and Veronica excused themselves and retired to their beds.

"I don't know whether I can bring myself to call Mrs Nation Lilian. I feel quite uncomfortable being as I will be serving her, Dee."

"Well, just do what feels right for you. She seems like a lovely lady who appears to have dropped all pretences from the old country. I can see that many have thrown those overboard on their way, although you can be sure some haven't. Our toil is what is sorely needed here. We can't be done without, and that's for sure."

Bedelia lay awake. Over and over the doubts bobbed up, like apples in a barrel full of water, as to her abilities to care for women and babies during the birth process. Her youth, her lack of knowledge and experience and all the things that could go wrong flittered through her mind, denying her the refuge of the sleep she so craved.

Chapter 12

Just three weeks after their arrival, Bedelia and Veronica experienced their first summer Christmas. Although they were pleased to be celebrating the special holiday season with this lovely, welcoming family, the sweltering heat coming through the door and windows as they ate their festive meal felt oppressive and surreal. The children's delight at sharing the occasion with visitors made it more fun. Carols were sung around the family piano, brought by the Nations from England.

A rimu tree was decorated and the children's stockings hung above the hearth in expectation. Lilian explained that it was a custom from her German ancestors and her family in England had carried on the practice.

"My, how beautiful it is," Bedelia said. "Vonnie and I have never seen such a lovely sight at Yuletide. Why, we just attend midnight mass and exchange gifts. It's also a time for remembering the dead, at mass and by decorating loved ones' graves with wreaths made of holly and ivy."

When they had a quiet moment alone the sisters said a prayer for their entire family, dead and buried across the other side of the world. "At least Mammy and our baby sister went straight to heaven, being as they died just after Christmas," Veronica said, tears in her eyes.

After the children had emptied their stockings, Bedelia presented Veronica with the shawl she had completed. "That's so beautiful, Dee. I shall treasure it always, but I have nothing for you, so I haven't."

"Just to have you with me in this new life is gift enough for me, Vonnie. We have fallen on better times, we have, and it is all due to you being brave enough to take that step with me."

Bedelia had given Michael his gift before they left the ship. Very grateful for the care his friend had taken in embroidering his initials, he vowed to take good care of the handkerchief. She thought of Michael and Keenan now and hoped that all was well with them.

The week after Christmas, Bedelia and Veronica visited Sophia and some of the German families who had arrived in Nelson on the same day as the sisters.

Some spoke a little English and they were able to converse in simple words easy for Bedelia to understand.

Heading down country with their belongings, the men were keen to see to their land and planting. Other than the reports from the German settlers who had arrived in the previous years, they had only an inkling of the hard work ahead of them. There were fourteen families in all, made up by members of various ages. Some children were able to lend their fathers a hand while others remained in town with their mothers.

If they were able to, the men took a variety of farming implements, animals and seeds along with the carpentry tools needed to erect cob houses. "Their countrymen will likely join them in constructing their homes and farm buildings," Doctor Nation said.

They took enough basic food to last them some months as the men did not know when they would be able to get more supplies. Herr Brandt had a shotgun he had inherited from his father. Sophia told Bedelia that he had a sharp and sure eye and a good reputation for bringing wild animals and birds home for the pot.

Sophia and her two boys and the other new arrivals were staying in several basic houses, called whare by the Māori people. Doctor Nation had told Bedelia that these had been hastily built by local Māori, their payment coming in various treasures like blankets, articles of clothing both old and new, razors and other requested items.

Sophia explained that the families would stay in these makeshift houses as long as it took the men to build homes on their allotted land, after which time the women and children would be sent for.

Bedelia took an interest in the construction of the temporary dwellings. The whare were built from crudely cut small trees and vines making the framework. These were harvested from the surrounding forests as sawn timber was scarce. The hard but flexible stems of the vines were woven into a lattice between the frames, daubed with clay and stuck together with a strong yellow grass forming the walls. Glass for the windows or a fitting door were rare. The roof was thatched with another, unfamiliar plant. Bedelia thought this resembled the reeds that donned her cottage back in Ireland. The floor was of rammed earth, with a fireplace at one end of the single room made of stones joined together by clay, and constructed inside a timber framed chimney.

Bedelia could see how resourceful the families were in making do, and they had made these temporary houses comfortable enough, with their own bedding and cooking equipment. The Brandt family shared one large bed. The new baby slept safely in a little wooden drawer taken from the base of a cabin trunk. It was lined with a woollen blanket. Sophia told Bedelia it had been hand made in Germany by her great-grandmother and handed down through the generations. "It is very ... precious, is that a correct word?" Sophia asked. Bedelia nodded.

The cooking place was simply put together, with a large cauldron and kettle suspended from a cooking tripod inside the chimney. A basic table and bench seats, Bedelia could see, were fashioned from some of the wooden crates rescued from the wharf, which had carried merchandise to the new settlement.

"My Thomas, he made iron nails on the ship during our sea voyage," Sophia proudly said.

These families were pleased that their arrival time had coincided with summer and the promise of more settled weather. This hadn't been the case for the first ship from Germany, which had arrived at the beginning of winter. Unfortunately, that had proven disastrous in more ways than one for some of them, causing setbacks with inclement weather and flooding. Sophia told Bedelia she hoped their luck would be better.

As Bedelia and Veronica walked down the hill from the temporary homes, Veronica said, pointing to the west, "This view across the water to those mountains is so beautiful, so it is." The sun's rays were reflecting off the bay below. Two recently arrived ships anchored in the sheltered harbour with its protective boulder bank were busily disgorging their cargo onto smaller vessels.

From this vantage point the sisters could clearly see distant hills, a grey smudge to the north, where the other large island of this new land lay. Bedelia's spirits soared, "Oh, Vonnie, this is what I call paradise, so it is. I feel like I have died in the night and gone to heaven."

Lilian and Doctor Nation had gladly given approval for their children to accompany Bedelia on one of her visits to the Brandt family. Despite the lack of a common language, the barrier to communication melted away in no time, with the children's laughter reverberating from the scrub where they were playing.

Several days passed as the doctors made plans to explore the area to the south and west of Nelson. Doctor Nation wanted to show his colleague a likely place to build a house that would double as a surgery, in order to service the surrounding settlements.

The women settled into helping Lilian. Veronica set up a routine of chores to make life easier for the doctor's wife. Assisting Mrs Pentwick in schooling the young Nation family, Veronica was learning fast. Soon she was able to keep a few steps ahead of her charges in their reading, writing and arithmetic. It warmed Bedelia's heart to see her older sister find her niche as she listened to the lessons being taught at the kitchen table.

When there was a spare moment, Bedelia could be found at the same table, lost in the pages of her tome. Although she was still wading through Doctor Pattison's book, she had gladly accepted the loan of *The Art of Obstetrics, a Doctor's Handbook for Practice,* belonging to Doctor Nation. She struggled with the medical terminology and spent some hours in the evening in an earnest quest for understanding. Although the diagrams of abnormal outcomes of birth were graphic and sometimes disturbing, Bedelia was quick to grasp, when reassured by the doctors, that these incidents were rare and mostly beyond her control and expertise.

While the doctors were away, Lilian and Bedelia accepted calls from townsfolk who had various ailments and injuries. On the whole they were able to deal with the minor maladies.

One day a man came to the door of the doctor's surgery. His dusty shirt had a band collar with a placket opening in the front, his woollen trousers were held up by a crudely plaited rope in lieu of a belt and his sturdy boots were covered in mud. He also sported a flat cap, which he had taken off in a gesture of respect for the ladies present.

He demanded to see the doctor, and grew angry when Lilian told him he was away down country and would not be returning for several days. Lilian and Bedelia managed to calm the man enough to find out what the problem was.

"Me mate's sliced his leg real bad," the man said more calmly after he had gulped down the cup of water Lilian had offered him. "We're up there felling trees," he said as he pointed east towards the hill behind the town, covered in forest.

Lilian sat the man on the stool at the back door when he had refused to enter the house. He was still panting from his run down the hill. "My boots," he said, pointing to the thick coating of mud encasing his footwear.

Lilian nodded. "What is your name, young man?" she said.

"Colin, but me mates call me Col," he said in a more congenial voice.

"Be rest assured, Colin, my assistant Bedelia and I will come to help."

Both women went into the surgery to gather the first aid equipment they presumed would be needed to tend the injured man's leg. Bedelia was unsure how much help she could be with her limited knowledge and lack of experience of injuries, and expressed her doubts.

"I trust you will be of great assistance to me. Reading all the medical books in the world is never as good as learning by doing," Lilian said.

When they reached the accident site, they found the injured man sweaty and quite ashen. Bedelia turned to Lilian and said, "He looks like he's in much pain, and I'm certain, I am, that the loss of blood will not have helped."

Lilian nodded. His fellow workers had made him as comfortable as they could with a bed fashioned from mānuka cuttings.

The gash in the lower leg was deep and the bone was just visible through the gaping, bleeding wound. As she set to work, Lilian explained to Bedelia, "I'm tying this makeshift tourniquet above the wound to stem the bleeding; that will make it easier for us to see and deal to the damaged tissue." She secured the length of rope above the injured man's knee, winding it in the centre with a small carved stick to tighten it.

Between the two of them, the ladies were able to clean the wound using water fetched by a workmate from a nearby stream and some ethyl alcohol from the bag. The latter caused the injured man to gasp in pain and lash out. They continued as Col and another man held their mate's arms away from the women. Two more men pinned down the leg to stop him from fighting and hindering the work in progress. Guided by Lilian, Bedelia began to stitch up the wound with some catgut she had threaded into a curved needle from the well-stocked doctor's bag.

"Now, you start from the deepest tissue. See the cut ligament just above the bone?" Lilian said. "Be sure to catch a good chunk of the flesh, as this will keep it together while it heals. Go over and over like you're sewing up a blanket."

Lilian dabbed away the pooling blood inside the wound with clean linen then took over temporarily as she showed Bedelia the art of a finishing knot that would hold sure.

Lilian then handed the work back to Bedelia, who finished off the knot. "Very good," she said, "now continue up the layers to the skin where we finish by sewing intermittent stitches with a thicker thread. This will add some strength to hold the wound together, giving it time to heal completely before we remove them. The catgut we used in the deeper layers will dissolve by itself."

When she had finished putting the skin back together, Bedelia bandaged the leg neatly with a roll of clean rag under Lilian's direction.

A small crowd of workers had gathered around to watch these women perform the surgery on their work mate.

"Now Colin, make sure your mate rests up," Lilian said. "Keep the wound clean and dry and have him come to the doctor's house in a few days so we can check on the healing, then in two weeks' time to remove the stitches."

Bedelia put their equipment into the doctor's bag, with Col and several of the men saying, "We thank you, ma'ams, for your trouble."

As they departed, one of the men said in a booming voice to the man standing beside him, "Who would have thought these pretty ladies would get down and get dirty?" Then he turned to the others and said, "Well, that's our entertainment for the day, gentlemen. Now we'll be getting back to work. You two fellas," he said pointing to Col and another man, "help Bob back to camp. Cook can watch him for the rest of the day."

The crew of tree fellers watched from the ledge as the ladies scrambled down the steep track that would take them back home. Lilian congratulated Bedelia on a job well done.

Bedelia giggled. "I hope Bob doesn't know that the stitch I used on him was what I use to sew my frock seams together. I've never done that before on a man, so I haven't."

Lilian smiled. "You are born to care for others, Bedelia," she said. "I would have you as my assistant any day. Thank you for helping me."

"Do call me Delia," Bedelia said, smiling at the compliment.

The following day the doctors returned from their mission. They were happy to report that they had found an ideal location. Many small settlements were starting to grow between the base of the high mountains to the west and the new German village to the immediate south of Nelson.

The doctors described their findings with the ladies over dinner.

"Although there have been some difficulties with flooding for the German settlers, where they have lost their tilled land and crops more than once, there are several English and German families well on the way to establishing a community," Doctor Nation said.

"We have found an abandoned house, damaged in the floods, that is still in good enough condition to repair in order to establish a surgery. This will all depend on whether we can locate the previous tenant and come to some arrangement to lease the land," Doctor Pattison said.

After visiting the Lands Office to find the owner of the dwelling, Doctor Pattison discovered it had been abandoned completely. The clerk said, "It is believed that the owners left in despondent haste. No one knows where they've disappeared to. So, because more than two years have passed, it is deemed for sale."

The doctor bought the property forthwith.

"A father and son have set up a carting business, with two strong horses carrying the settlers' supplies brought in from town. I can see the area thriving with plenty of work and land for everyone," Doctor Pattison said. "I have asked the cartier to transport the materials I will need for the repairs."

The carting business also transported some of the settlers. They came to claim their land and prepare it for their waiting families. They came to build a more permanent home and establish a farm. They came to make a start planting crops and every-day food for consumption. Bedelia thought of Sophia's family with their plans.

Lilian told the doctors about their medical call-out. Doctor Pattison said, "Despite your misgivings, Bedelia, your skills and tenacity will be indispensable to me in setting up my practice."

Bedelia and Lilian glanced at each other. Lilian nodded, with Bedelia grinning from ear to ear.

The discussion carried on late into the evening about all that needed to happen before the doctor and Bedelia could move to the new home and surgery.

Doctor Pattison turned to Mrs Pentwick. "Would you please consider joining us to be our housekeeper? Your presence would be invaluable."

The widow looked relieved to be asked and included in the plans. "I'll think on it for a wee while before I decide one way or the other," she said, with a rare smile.

Bedelia and Veronica smiled too.

The hustle and bustle of gathering the stores needed for a new life down-country, excited the children. They were going to miss the full house that had been their life for the past few months, with some of the adults now making ready to leave. The boys said they would miss Bedelia, but at least they would have their own room back and still get to keep Veronica.

"There are schemes for labourers, who are working their allotted land one day a week," Doctor Pattison said over the dinner table. "In order for them to earn a meagre living and to give them money to develop their own land, they work the rest of the week on establishing roads from the landing on the harbour close by. I have already asked some of the men we met at the barracks if they might help me."

Doctor Pattison went ahead of Bedelia and Mrs Pentwick, who would await word on when they could join the doctor in their new home, as soon as it was habitable.

Pleased that they had agreed, the doctor employed the German immigrants to repair the building, some having skills in carpentry. He later told Bedelia how impressed he was with the men's work ethic and the speed and thorough nature of their renovations.

"These settlers are also working hard on building their own homes in order for their wives and children to finally join them. The workers told me that their first priority was their own land. After clearing the bracken and flax they set about tilling the soil, and will plant crops next spring for harvest in the autumn. They have already planted small gardens to get them through the winter."

While working on the damaged house, they used it as their shelter for six days then travelled on foot to their own holdings for a day of toil benefitting themselves.

The settlers were efficient with the timber used on the doctor's house, commandeering every scrap to use for their own buildings. They were extremely grateful for the chance to earn some money to pay for the supplies for their own farms. Other jobs working on the roads and bridges and felling trees were limited, as labourers were abundant and money was scarce.

When the some of the German families from town arrived, along with Bedelia and Mrs Pentwick, they were greeted with much joy and celebration. Sophia was there with Henri and her baby, who had grown into a chubby, bubbly little person.

"Our neighbours, they will come to help with the house on Saturday. Come, Bedelia and the doctor, and you, *bitte*," Sophia said as she turned to Mrs Pentwick.

Henri was bouncing on Bedelia's knee as they sat in the back of the wagon carrying them from the boat landing. "A jiggedy, jiggedy jig," Bedelia said. Henri was screaming with laughter as the rhyme progressed. "A hobbled hoi, a hobbled hoi."

Two wagons managed the load, each pulled by two draught horses and driven by the cartier and his son.

Mrs Pentwick had made up her mind to give life in New Zealand a trial. She said that she would feel useful in her future role as the doctor's housekeeper. "I'm not the best at cooking, but between Bedelia and myself, we could turn out a meal that may be satisfactory for you, Doctor, and for ourselves."

It didn't take the ladies long to make their new home inhabitable while the doctor made his surgery ready and suitable to administer to the sick or injured. Bedelia and Mrs Pentwick had purchased basic ingredients and utensils to set up a working kitchen before leaving town. They had bought just enough perishable food to make do for the time being, hearing that there would be ample supplies of fresh produce to purchase from the neighbouring farmers. The more established settlers were already churning butter, growing vegetables and had hens on the lay. The newly arriving German wives planned to start the cheese-making process.

Bedelia knew, like the Nations, that many of the payments for the doctor's services would be in produce. Anything they needed to purchase would put some well-needed money in the settlers' pockets for the extra farming materials they required. Bedelia could see it was an arrangement beneficial to all parties.

Bedelia and Mrs Pentwick shared a bedroom at the end of the hall, and the doctor slept in the lean-to added alongside the surgery. This had a sunny position facing north and sat to the left of the main entrance, which the prospective patients would use to access the surgery. A makeshift waiting room was formed on the veranda to the right.

Bedelia complimented Mrs Pentwick on her skills in turning a house into a home with the few materials she had at hand. Her stitchery was delicate and could be seen dotted throughout the kitchen, living room and bedrooms. She told Bedelia, "My job is to make this home a place where you and the good doctor can rest after the toils of the day. You will be working hard and I am here to take care of you."

Bedelia felt pleased to be nurtured, and that Mrs Pentwick now had a purpose in her new life. As she placed the linen runner on her bureau, the one she had swapped with Michael, it made her wonder what he was doing and where he would be laying his head on this warm evening. She had been too busy with her own excitement around her future plans to spare much more than a fleeting thought for this man, who had helped make life on board ship that much more tolerable. She wondered, also, how Patrick and his family were faring in Australia. Before leaving Nelson she had left a note in the general store for Michael.

When Bedelia informed the doctor of Sophia's invitation, he told Bedelia he was fascinated with the homes the German farmers were building and had spent many evenings discussing their construction with the men who were staying at his home during its renovation.

"Certainly. I would be most pleased to attend and help in any way I can," he said.

After they had finished their meal that night, the doctor said to Bedelia, "The cob houses are like their homes in North Germany. They are built with an interesting and simple technique. Affordable materials made up of clay, sand, straw, water and earth are used because they can be procured from the surrounding land."

"Cob," the doctor continued, "is fireproof and has the ability to give a little in the event of earthquakes, which are not an uncommon occurrence around here. Herr Brandt told me of several homes that were not even slightly damaged in the recent big quake that would have toppled many wooden houses."

On Friday Mrs Pentwick and Bedelia shared the task of making some food to take to the Brandts' home. Mrs Pentwick made two extra meat pies when cooking their evening meal. Bedelia baked oatmeal biscuits.

Mrs Pentwick decided to stay home. She said, "I just need some quiet time to myself. Besides, I have much difficulty understanding the language and would be happier here."

Work had commenced on the finishing stages of the living room. The rest of the house had been completed before Sophia had arrived.

"*Willkomen, Willkomen!*" she said, gesturing them into the house.

The doctor and Bedelia stood out of the way of the workers, watching carefully what they were doing.

"See Bedelia, the walls are thick with deep-set windows and doors, which make them ideal in all climates. Herr Brandt also said that cob is worked from the bottom up and is mixed together using a trampling method, either by human feet or the hooves of animals. The drying time for the cob is only two weeks, after which it is trimmed and more added. That is what they are now doing," the doctor said, pointing to the men at work. "Then a lintel, that large piece of wood over there, will be added for the door. Hopefully we will see that being erected today."

Bedelia looked around the room at each person carrying out different tasks.

"As you can see," he continued, "when men from several families join forces in a communal working party to erect the houses and farm buildings, it enables them to work so much more efficiently and effectively, for many hands definitely do make light work. Some of the men we saw as we arrived are completing the thatched roof, which is fashioned from whatever materials can be slashed and collected from the surrounding bush. In Germany it would have been with reeds, but Stephen told me here they use raupō from the local swamps, which is an ideal substitute. I would say that the man directing the operation is likely to have thatching as his trade. There is more skill to it than we realise, and he appears to know what he is doing."

Bedelia nodded. "I am remembering my da doing that on our cottage back home, and we had thatch on the roof. I had no idea how it was made, so I didn't."

"Then it's all finished off with a white-wash on the inside and outside walls. See, that man and woman over there are doing just that," the doctor said.

Laughter and smells of cooking food were drawing Bedelia into the kitchen next door. She left the doctor just as he picked up a brush and pot of whitewash and headed towards a wall needing attention.

Bedelia noticed the floor was mostly bare earth trampled into a flat surface. She knew from her childhood home that over time this would be moulded by many feet and brushing with brooms. One such broom, made from mānuka scrub, stood in the corner of the kitchen.

"*Moin, moin!*" said the trio of women tending to the food. Henri and some other little boys and a girl were eyeing up the fare.

Henri ran over to Bedelia. "*Mien Fründin, Dee,*" he said, patting the skirt of her dress as he turned to his little friends. Bedelia surreptitiously took five of her oatmeal biscuits and handed them to the milling children. She gave the children a wink, placed a finger to her lips and waved her free hand in the direction of the door. The other ladies smiled. The last thing they saw were ten little heels disappear as they watched the children run out the door hiding the booty behind their backs.

On their way home the doctor and Bedelia discussed their new neighbours and friends. They talked about the hierarchy and accepted poverty of the old ways back in their home countries giving way to a shared determination to work together in equality and mutual support in this new land.

"Back in the old country," Dr Pattison said, "despite my privileged upbringing and my parents' expectations of correct behaviour, I was ostracised by my peers for treating those poorer souls with respect. As a child I had a strong sense of justice and fairness but was mostly shot down in flames if I voiced my opinion."

"I really was so young and sheltered by my parents and family," Bedelia said, "but I did get a sense that we had to mind ourselves with any of the owners of our land and with those who weren't Catholics. I knew we were looked down upon, judging by the hurtful words said to us. I thank Jesus that I was so carefree in those days, I would just laugh when the mud got slung. Vonnie was less resilient and took the words and bad deeds to heart."

"And," Bedelia added, "I was pretty sharp and could give as good as I got. None of this 'turn the other cheek' for me," she laughed.

The doctor said, "Like you, these German settlers have only known suppression by the gentry because of the families they were born into. Now they have a chance to make life different for themselves and generations to come. It is such a huge opportunity, the scale and enormity of which is not lost on these pioneers. They really are showing grit and determination."

Bedelia could see they would take every opportunity to thrive and prosper in New Zealand, and she was excited to make a home in this new country also, and allow herself to be surprised by what lay ahead.

Chapter 13

Rat-a-tat-tat. The incessant door knocking startled Bedelia, the urgency apparent by its loud and rapid staccato rap. They had just sat down to lunch. Mrs Pentwick was carrying a tray of hot scones, steaming from the oven. She was tutting as the second wave of knocking reached a crescendo. "Where's the fire?" she growled.

Bedelia jumped up first. She reached the door and opened it. The man on the other side, arm in the air, fist raised ready to knock again, fell into the hallway, only just able to keep his balance and remain upright. He was flushed and sweaty and so were the two horses Bedelia could see, harnessed to a wagon outside the gate.

The doctor and Bedelia had just hung the shingle that very morning. The lettering was black on a whitewashed board and read:

DOCTOR PATTISON

MEDICAL DOCTOR/SURGEON

Bedelia had felt so excited as she held the pole while the doctor attached it firmly to the wooden fence beside the gate.

"I have come to fetch the doctor for my neighbour Mr MacMillan," the man said. "His wife, she is very poorly and bleeding, with still a while to go before the baby is expected."

"Sit yourself down, Mr Wright," Bedelia said, for she recognised the man who had transported her from the landing. "I will get Doctor Pattison."

Bedelia turned and nearly bumped into the doctor. She opened her mouth to relay the message but the doctor put his hand up. "No need, Bedelia, I heard everything."

"Hurry Doctor, for I fear Mrs MacMillan is in a bad way. I came as fast as I could and I will take you back in my wagon."

The doctor looked at Bedelia. She nodded, as she understood that both their services may be required. The doctor went into his surgery and grabbed the items in his medical kit he expected he may need, while Bedelia went to change into her shift-frock and pinny.

The trio sat on the front of the wagon. Bedelia and the doctor were silent. Mr Wright, intent on getting his horses to go faster than they seemed able to, was high-yupping and wielding his whip more than Bedelia thought was necessary.

As the wagon bounced along the rutted road, Bedelia, nibbling on one of the buttered scones Mrs Pentwick had wrapped in a tea cloth, was lost in her thoughts when the doctor said to her, "I have only a small idea of what we are about to encounter. Until you see the situation for yourself, the amount of bleeding can often appear different from one report to another."

Scenarios played out in Bedelia's mind from the books she had been absorbing. She was sure the doctor would be contemplating things in his own way. *What will we find? How can we help?* So many what ifs. Bedelia's head was swirling with thoughts.

Bedelia knew that she had not the years, nor the experience, to surmise what may greet them on arrival at their destination. She had lost Maureen and her mam to bleeding, she was thinking, but that was after the baby was born. *This may be different.*

It took about half an hour to reach Mr Wright's neighbour. The horses were spent and Mr Wright had run out of steam also as he pointed to the house up a short driveway.

Mr MacMillan met them at the door. "I am much afraid I am losing my wife and losing the bairn." Bedelia and the doctor were ushered into the house through the kitchen, with the remnants of a breakfast of porridge for five half-eaten on the table. On the floor of the hallway and into a dimly lit room, a trail of smudged blood, hastily wiped, led them on. A small lantern on a bed-side table barely divulged the occupant of the bed. A woman lay there, unmoving, brown hair hanging over her shoulders in disarray, skin the colour of the sheets.

As Bedelia's eyes adjusted to the darkness she pulled back the quilt, revealing the blood underneath the bed's occupant, soaking into the mattress through the ticking. Her eyes went straight to the pale face of the head on the pillow. "Is it that we may be too late to save mother or baby?" she said to the doctor, remembering her last encounter with this much blood loss.

The husband stood at the doorway, eyes wide, brow furrowed. "Will you do something to help us, Doctor. This is our fourth bairn. We've *nae* had trouble afore."

Bedelia placed her open palm on the protruding belly and was relieved to feel a movement deep within. She relayed this to the doctor, who smiled and nodded.

"How long has your wife been bleeding, and when are you expecting the baby to be born?" said the doctor.

"Young Jamie came to fetch me at breakfast time to tell me about his mam taking poorly. I was in the byre finishing milking the cow and the goat. I sent a message with him to the Wright house and his missus took the bairns while Mr Wright went for you. We weren't expecting the *wee bairn* to arrive for another month or so."

After performing an examination of the woman's abdomen and vaginally, the doctor shook his head slowly. "There is little I can do, Mr MacMillan. The baby has no way through to be born; the afterbirth is in the way."

Then, as if she already knew, Mrs MacMillan opened her eyes. She called out weakly, "My *bairn*, save my *bairn*!"

The doctor looked to Mr MacMillan, who had moved to the side of the bed and was holding his wife's slender hand, then turned to Bedelia. "Lassie, you are right. There is no time to lose. If we are to save the baby we have to act immediately, and if God is on our side, there may be a glimmer of hope for the mother."

The doctor explained to the husband that the only chance for the baby's survival was to cut it from the mother's womb.

Mr MacMillan, biting his lip, said, "I cannot make that decision. We are God-fearing folk, so do what you have to, Doctor. We will put our trust in Him and in your skills."

Directed by the doctor, Bedelia laid out the basic surgical equipment from his bag. She had been taken through each of the instruments and their use several times by Lilian as they had sterilised them in boiling water, along with the cloths they were wrapped in and the clouts needed to soak up the blood.

"There is no chance to reduce the pain for this woman; she is already so weak from her blood loss. I cannot use the new compound of ether I brought with me from England to put this woman to sleep. It is too dangerous for the baby if we are to get it out alive," the doctor told Bedelia. He told Mr MacMillan he would be needed to restrain his wife during the operation.

The doctor steadied his shaking hands and made the first incision with his scalpel. Then, cutting through layer by layer, he reached the womb. Bedelia followed his instructions precisely, wiping away the blood coming from the open blood vessels exposed with each slice of the blade. Careful not to cut the occupant, the doctor made the last cut through the thick wall of the uterus, narrowly avoiding the obstruction to this baby's passage out - the placenta, lying deep in the pelvis.

Reaching into the womb with both his hands, the doctor instructed Bedelia to hold the gaping wound open for easier access, and he delivered the baby's head. He then slipped both forefingers between the upper arms and body and lifted the baby boy out. Bedelia received him in the cloth she had warmed next to her chest, rubbing the blood, mucous and fluid off his body.

The baby was stunned and lay flaccid in her hands. He didn't move, his own body as pale as his mother's. Bedelia rubbed his body more firmly, praying for some reaction. There was no response. Everyone was silent, holding their breath as if in sympathy for this wee soul.

Without hesitation, Bedelia placed her mouth completely over the baby's mouth and nose and sucked and spat the blood and mucous out, then again sucked and spat. Still there was nothing. Again, covering his mouth and nose completely with her mouth, she gently puffed her breath from her cheeks into his airway several times. At last he let out a weak cry, then a more lusty cry followed. The doctor and Mr MacMillan took a deep, audible breath. His colour changed from white to a natural skin colour from his trunk out to his fingers and toes. Bedelia laid the baby on his mother's bare chest and covered him in the small blanket she had found, which she had also warmed close to her skin.

The mother, who had not uttered one sound through the whole gruelling procedure, opened her eyes and smiled at her newborn son, her arms weakly cradling him. With her husband kneeling beside her, she started to fit, shuddered and breathed her last.

"There was nothing more I could do, Bedelia; her blood loss was too great." The doctor looked at Mr MacMillan as he spoke.

Bedelia checked in a sewing basket by the bureau and found some sturdy wool and a pair of scissors. She tied the ropey cord tightly, in two places, about two inches from the baby's abdomen, releasing the wee bairn from his dead mother with a snip. She swaddled the baby in the blanket and placed him in his father's outstretched arms, tears rolling down her cheeks.

After he had removed the obstructing placenta, the doctor proceeded to stitch up the gaping wound in the dead woman's lower abdomen.

Bedelia found a bowl and cloths and proceeded to wash Mrs MacMillan's bloodstained limbs with water. Changing the water, she continued to wash the rest of the body. She took clothes from the wardrobe that looked like Mrs MacMillan's Sunday best, and with great respect, dressed the woman. Bedelia had cleaned and covered the blood-soaked mattress as best she could concealing the products of this mother-of-four's demise.

When the three MacMillan children were brought home by Mrs Wright, they ran into the bedroom to greet their mother. Getting no response, they turned to their father sitting in the chair holding their baby brother. He found room for them all on his broad lap as he told them, tears streaming down his cheeks, "Your mother has been taken from us, but she has left the gift of a wee brother we will call Brian. It will just be the five of us now."

The young boy and girl wailed as the reality dawned on them. The youngest girl, only just walking, looked around and started crying also. Bedelia cried alongside them. She cried for that brave new mother who would never grow to know her son. She cried for her own mother lost in a similar birth event. She cried because she had been given permission. She knew this way of grieving. She had done it more than most women her age. It, too, was the Irish way, and as she wept, she felt lighter.

The doctor checked the baby thoroughly, and looking at Mr MacMillan he said, "Despite being somewhat early and little, he appears to be a fighter. He needs to be kept warm, with only small amounts of, I suggest, goat's milk. It will be easier for him to digest than cow's milk." He gave Mr MacMillan more instructions and told him to bring the baby to his surgery or call for Bedelia if he needed any help.

"Aye, thank you Doctor Pattison, and of course you, lassie, for your care and attention to my Eileen. You did your best, and for that I am grateful."

Weariness from their long and eventful day didn't stop Bedelia and the doctor discussing the whole scenario as they trudged home along the track. They had turned down Mr Wright's offer to take them. They thought that he and his horses deserved a rest.

"As you saw, Bedelia, the placenta was covering the wee one's exit from the womb," the doctor said. "There was no way out, naturally, for the baby. The placenta is extremely vascular, as it's the garden from which the baby gets its nourishment and oxygen. The mother does the eating and the breathing and by doing so fertilises the garden. Do you understand?"

"Oh yes," Bedelia nodded, surprised by the doctor's simple yet lovely way of explaining something. "I have read and re-read both your and Doctor Nation's books. The pictures help, for sure. Mrs Nation has been wonderfully patient and has taken time to explain when I've asked her, and if it isn't too much for Mrs Pentwick, she helps me with some of the words I get stuck on. I'm hoping that this is something I don't ever see again."

The doctor went on, "When the womb starts to open at the beginning of the labour, the blood vessels in the placenta are exposed, and just as if you'd stabbed someone, the bleeding starts and won't stop until you get the placenta out. That means there is nothing to do but deliver the baby by Caesarean section. That surgery is extremely dangerous for both mother and baby and must be done as soon as possible after the bleeding has started, by a fully trained surgeon. It is well beyond what would be expected of you, Bedelia."

"Me mam's midwife told me about a Mary Donally, a midwife one hundred or so years ago, who saved a mother and her baby by performing a caesarean section. I'm surely hoping I'm never expected to do that. It fair scares the bejasus out of me it does." Bedelia put a hand to her lips. "Sorry for my mouth, Doctor."

The doctor smiled as they carried on their way. "Yes, we were taught about that in our training; the first successful caesarean section done in Great Britain. Quite a feat."

"Unfortunately," the doctor said, "when faced with this situation, especially as late as we encountered it, our hands are tied. There was no way, even if I had time, that I could have saved that woman's life. Her baby would normally have died already, so it was a great surprise to me that he lived. Without a satisfactory clean area to perform the surgery, the outcome for the mother was unlikely to be good, even if she hadn't lost so much blood."

The doctor stopped on the track and turned to Bedelia. "It's a sad and frustrating part of our work. There's nothing for a midwife to do but call a doctor for support, and really that's only a token gesture. Unless the doctor has surgical skills and lives close by, there's very little that can be done. Fortunately, this doesn't commonly occur, and hopefully you will experience this situation only a few times in your career as a midwife."

Bedelia was thinking deeply about the problem of an afterbirth that wanted to come through first and what that meant for the mother and the baby. Once again the memory was rekindled. "It may have been the problem for my mam when she died in childbirth." These things weren't spoken about, especially by her da to a child of twelve years. All she knew was that there was much bleeding, and neither mother nor baby alive in the end.

What multitudes more learning there is ahead of me, Bedelia thought. All she knew right down in her bones was that, through thick or thin, birthing was fraught with dangers for mother and babies. She was sure she was going to need much reserve to endure the good and the bad outcomes, let alone the ones that were beyond her expertise.

Upon returning home they were greeted by smells of cooking emanating from the kitchen. It had been a harrowing time for both of them.

While Mrs Pentwick busied herself boiling enough water on the stove for two baths, Bedelia and the doctor sat at the table engrossed in a book, particularly the pages concerning placenta praevia.

After dinner and the luxury of their leisurely soaks in the baths Mrs Pentwick had drawn for them, one after the other, Bedelia's head hit her pillow and she fell into a dreamless sleep. There was no more energy for thought.

Chapter 14

The days turned into weeks as the doctor and Bedelia continued improving the working operation of the surgery. Bedelia enjoyed the company of the people in her new life, and didn't even mind sharing her bedroom with a more docile and amiable Mrs Pentwick. Bedelia's intention was to fall asleep first. The older woman's snoring resembled a saw working a large knotty log. Bedelia and Veronica had often giggled as they lay in their shared bed at the Nations' home, listening to Mrs Pentwick rasp away in her sleep in the bed opposite. Most of the time it hadn't kept them awake long as their own tiredness overcame them.

The sisters had agreed, before they parted, to write to each other every week. The mail was intermittent, as it had to wait until someone in the area was making a journey to town. Although they had been sad to be parting for the first time in their lives, they knew they were each going to be provided for with work they enjoyed and a comfortable home with a roof over their heads.

"Besides," Bedelia had said, "we're only half a day's journey away from each other."

Life in the house settled into a comfortable rhythm. Their connection with others in the ever-expanding district grew. They met industrious settlers who had planted crops and carried on building homes. Although there was much more work required on the roads and bridges needing completion, movement within the small district was becoming easier.

Bedelia worked alongside the doctor in his surgery where she could. She was refining her suturing skills, cleaning and bandaging wounds and assisting the doctor in minor surgical tasks.

At the end of one day, as they were tidying up the surgery, the doctor said, "Have you thought about approaching the German midwives, the *Hebammen* we met on the day we arrived, to ask if you could join them for some of their births? It will be a good way to gain more experience."

"I know we've discussed this before, but I have almost no German. I barely understand the English medical words in your book. To learn without being able to speak the tongue ... Oh, I just don't know how that will be."

"Bedelia, you have surprised me more than once in your friendship with Sophia and how the two of you seem to have such an ease of understanding despite knowing little of each other's language. If you keep the words simple you will get by."

Through word of mouth, they had found out where the *Hebammen* lived. They were seeing to the needs of their kinfolk during their confinements in a district close by. Stories of their successful births were filtering through the small community.

A few days after this conversation a German farmer, Herr Schwass, was brought into the surgery by one of his sons. He had slashed his leg while harvesting fodder for his stock. Quite by chance, the doctor and Bedelia discovered it was his wife and daughter who were the *Hebammen* serving their German settler community.

Bedelia said, "I never guessed the Hebammen were mother and daughter. Although, now I think about it, they do look quite alike."

Bedelia helped the doctor by cleaning the wound carefully and as gently as she was able, ready for suturing. She was naming each ligament and layer of tissue as she put the cut skin back together again with neat stitches.

The doctor was quietly observing Bedelia's fine attention to detail in her work while he was in conversation with the men. Despite them having no English and the doctor having only a limited amount of German, they were able to set up a meeting with the man's wife and daughter.

The doctor later related this planned meeting to Bedelia. "I understand your misgivings about communication with the *Hebammen*, but their language of Plattdeutsch is closer to English than High German. Conversing becomes simpler due to the commonality with the Anglo-Saxon language, which is the root of both English and Plattdeutsch."

Bedelia looked bewildered. "I'm not quite sure what you are telling me."

The doctor said, "In simple terms, lassie, many of their words will just sound slightly different to ours, and in the situation they are being used, it will take you no time at all to work it out. So, for instance, their word for sheep is *Schoop*. brother is *Broder* and baby is *Baby*. I believe that is how you have been able to talk with Sophia so easily. I feel sure the younger *Hebamme* will be learning English. It will be the same as you learning Plattdeutsch, but in reverse."

The doctor put the instruments they had used in a dish ready for boiling and continued, "Your young brains are so ripe for learning a new language. Look at how many new words and procedures you have learnt already from the pictures in my medical book. Even though you have done very little schooling, that means nothing, young lady. You have a brain on you that would be the envy of many."

Two days later, when he visited Herr Schwass at home to check on the wound and Bedelia's stitching handiwork, Bedelia accompanied him. As they approached the farm, close to a small stream, the white cob home came into view through an area of tall trees. Behind the house was a barn of the same material. Several small fenced areas confined pigs, goats, poultry and two cows. The doctor stopped. "Look at this fence, Bedelia. I am continually impressed by the versatility of the German settlers. The men helping me with the repair of the house and surgery told me that with minimal equipment they are making do with what they can procure from the surrounding land. To buy the items needed is almost impossible due to scarcity and expense. What doesn't require secure fixing with their precious hand-made nails is bound together with the sturdy flax that the men work into plaiting when they sit to rest at night. I was shown how to do this and tried my hand at it but, I can tell you, my hands are much too soft."

Bedelia nodded in agreement.

Pointing to the encroaching bush close by, the doctor said, "The fences are needed to keep the livestock out of the crops and from wandering off into the surrounding bush. They are also required to keep more lax farmers' livestock out of their crops. Apparently, these breaches happen often and, from what I've been told, became a bone of contention between some of the English settlers and the German farmers."

As they walked up the path they could see the rest of the ground was neatly laid out in planted crops and vegetables. Not an inch of land lay idle.

The son who had brought his father into the surgery greeted them with a crisp *"Moin, moin!"* The doctor and Bedelia returned the greeting and followed him into the cottage. The welcome was palpable, with firm handshakes from the adult members of the family. The farmer was shushed to his seat as he tried to rise, so the doctor and Bedelia went over to the chair he was seated on and shook his large, calloused hand.

The kitchen was cosy, with delicious smells emanating from the hearth. Whitewashed walls displayed paintings and small shelves holding ornaments. Bedelia thought that these looked to be treasures from their home country. In a corner by the fire was a spinning wheel made of a dark wood; a spool of grey spun wool sat on the spindle.

Taking centre-stage was the kitchen table, with two delicately lathed chairs at either end and two long forms extending down both sides. The table was adorned with a simple yet intricately stitched cloth. The finely embroidered flowers were those found in the Northern European countryside: crocuses, tulips and cherry blossoms, with an array of other wild flowers Bedelia did not recognise.

A shot-gun was mounted on the wall above the hearth. Beside it hung an ornate clock, its persistent *tick tock* barely audible above the chatter. Bedelia jumped in fright the first time the cuckoo sprung out of its little house above the clock-face with a resounding *cuckoo, cuckoo*. The family all laughed at her surprise.

Bedelia and the doctor were seated on the chairs. Bedelia felt honoured to be given what she knew were the best seats at the table. The family filtered in to take their designated positions on the forms. There were two older lads who looked to be in their early twenties, Bedelia guessed, two girls between fourteen and sixteen and three other smaller children of varying ages, including a smaller child only just walking.

With a smile on his face, the doctor raised his nostrils, taking a large inhale as the fresh coffee pot was placed in the centre of the table. "It seems like a long time since I've tasted this strong, alluring brew." The doctor nodded to Frau Schwass as he took his first sip. "*Dankeschön! das ist sehr gut,*" he said.

Bedelia had only ever taken tea and was a little reticent about trying this new assault on her taste buds.

A long loaf had been pulled from the oven minutes before they had arrived. Bedelia could feel the saliva in her mouth increase. The sweet and spicey German bread looked and smelled so delicious. The currants embedded in the dough looked like flies crawling out of the crevices, but even that didn't put Bedelia off. She decided to have a second slice if it was offered. The finely ground sugar, lightly sprinkled on top made the treat that much more enticing.

As Bedelia was dressing Herr Schwass's wound, the doctor talked with the *Hebamme. He's right*, Bedelia thought. *I can guess a little of what he's saying to her.* Bedelia wondered where the younger *Hebamme* was. Maybe she was visiting or off on an errand.

Despite her initial shyness and trepidation about the language barrier, Bedelia soon realised that this could be overcome. With the age-old traditions of midwifery and intuition that went unsaid, the budding midwife was feeling more confident.

The *Hebamme* nodded enthusiastically as she smiled, turning to include Bedelia in her answer. *"Ja, dat is bannig good."*

The doctor recommended that Herr Schwass remain resting for the rest of the week before attempting any farm work. He asked the lads if they were managing all the chores. They nodded in unison, and then he made arrangements to return in a week to remove the sutures and to check on the wound.

Frau Schwass insisted that they both come again next time. Bedelia looked with deep longing at the happy family, which brought back fond memories of when her family had lived like that.

The *Hebamme* and as many of the family who could fit in the doorway stood and waved goodbye. As they were walking away Bedelia caught a glimpse of movement from one of the windows. Bedelia started to raise her hand to wave as she recognised the face, but the figure turned swiftly and moved out of sight.

Several weeks passed before another loud rap on the door in the middle of the night brought the doctor out of his bed. When the door was opened, Christian Schwass stood on the other side. Before the young man asked for her, the doctor knew that this call would be for Bedelia. He showed Christian into the waiting room and went to fetch her.

Christian had come on foot. Having a new horse in their stable, the doctor insisted the pair take it. He had seen the need to purchase a reliable mode of transport to cover the vast area he would be expected to travel to serve this expanding community. Christian climbed up on the front and Bedelia rode at the back. Both riders were slender, so the horse got along at a good pace. Bedelia tried at first to hold on by the back of the saddle, but realised after a few near misses that she would need to hold on to Christian's waist to keep herself from falling off.

There was no conversation between them as Christian navigated his way along the rough roads in the dark. The sliver of moon in the sky was only enough to allow for a small amount of visibility in an otherwise black landscape, but Christian seemed to know where he was going as he negotiated the terrain with ease. The weather was still mild, so the old woollen blanket Bedelia had fashioned into a crude cape kept her warm enough over her simple calico dress. She wore small brown leather boots, a little worse for wear, laced with string. Real shoe-laces were among the many luxuries in this new settlement that were hard to purchase.

Christian didn't take her to his own home, but rode a little further towards the foot hills in the valley. There they reached another cob house slightly bigger than the Schwass home. It had a veranda and a second storey.

As the dawn was slowly bringing light to the countryside, Bedelia could make out fruit trees surrounding the house. They appeared to have been newly planted. From what Bedelia could make out in the dim light emanating from the lanterns on the veranda, there were some vines covering single runs of fences erected in rows. She recognised the bunches of small fruit, which she had only seen in a painting. *Grapes*, she said to herself.

The younger of the two *Hebammen* beckoned Bedelia into the house as she passed a cup of water to her brother. "*Dank!* Magdalena," Christian said.

What a pretty name, Bedelia thought.

Removing her boots, she took the slippers Magdalena shook in front of her nose. She was grateful for the warm and comfortable feeling of the felt, from which they were made. She quietly stepped up the narrow staircase to the upper storey, following Magdalena in the half-light. As they approached one of the two rooms at the top of the stairs, a low moan came from the bedroom straight ahead. A lamp was placed behind the door to give just enough light for the *Hebamme* to see what she needed. Bedelia immediately sensed an atmosphere of calm.

Bedelia saw Magdalena's mother with her pinny on, a bowl of water on the floor beside her and a cloth in her hand, with which she was patting the labouring woman's brow. The woman was kneeling beside the bed on a cushion. In the middle of the exposed floor lay a mat of plaited scraps of material, neatly spiralling into a large round floor covering. Roughly sawn timber floorboards were held down with cast-iron nails. Bedelia remembered what Sophia had told her about these handmade nails and how proud she was of her husband for crafting them.

The *Hebamme* stayed kneeling beside the woman, quietly anticipating her needs. She looked up with a welcoming smile and pointed to the floor on the other side of the woman and said something to Magdalena, who threw a cushion down. Bedelia retrieved it from under the bed and knelt down. After the next pain had subsided, she pointed to herself as she said, "*Guten tag! ich bin* Bedelia." It was a simple greeting the doctor had taught her.

Frau Schwass said "*Dat is Fru* Hamkens." The women smiled and nodded to each other.

"*Ik bün Jutta*," Frau Hamkens said.

As the labour progressed Bedelia noticed that the *Hebamme* would often press her fingers lightly on Jutta's pendulous abdomen. Then she would quietly say to the woman, "*Dat is good*, Jutta," in a tone Bedelia of praise and reassurance. She knew that this was a way to check the baby was moving, and worthy of that positive reassuring response for both mother and midwife.

As the woman's contractions became closer together and more intense, Jutta was becoming more vocal and her body movements were changing. Bedelia was thinking, *Each birthing woman has a different way in how they behave, but the noises they make during labour and birth surely tell us a story about their progress.*

Jutta was hot and sweaty. Even the cold cloths were not quite enough to cool her down. Without any sense of shyness or need for privacy, she began to shed her calico shift and undergarments. The curtains were drawn, but even if they weren't, Bedelia thought, they were on the second storey with no nearby neighbours. There was nobody but the women in the room to witness Jutta's nude, pregnant body. The *Hebammen* carried on their care paying no attention to Jutta's appearance.

"How wonderful is this natural process," Bedelia thought, smiling to herself.

With Jutta squatting forward, the *Hebamme* drew Bedelia's attention to the ever-increasing protrusion at the back of Jutta's pelvis. She also pointed to the crease that ran between both buttocks, which was now starting to flatten out saying, "*Dat is good*."

Bedelia smiled and nodded. She could already sense the baby's arrival was close. She understood and was grateful to the *Hebamme* for the wise tutelage.

Frau Schwass pointed to another sign, which was a blood-stained mucous discharge coming from between the woman's legs.

Jutta was becoming more vocal as the contractions changed, distress showing in her voice. She was saying, "*Nee, nee*" as she shook her head.

Magdalena and her mother were replying to her, "*Ja, ja*," nodding their heads. Bedelia joined the chorus and the "*ja*" drowned out the "*nee*."

It was no time at all before Jutta was making long grunting noises with each contraction and the *Hebammen* were saying in unison, "utpressen." Directed by her mother, Magdalena had taken her position opposite the woman, at the other side of the bed. She was supporting Jutta's elbows as she bore down.

Scraps of linen covering a large mat of canvas were placed under the woman in a timely fashion just as a large gush of green-stained fluid flooded the cloths. The *Hebammen* looked at each other and Bedelia realised that things may not be quite as they had expected. She had read in the doctor's book that green mixed in the fluid from around the baby meant it may be in some distress.

With each encouraging *"utpressen"* uttered by the Hebammen Jutta bore down, the exertion showing on her red, sweaty face. Bedelia could see that Jutta's abdomen was rigid, and when she ventured to touch it, encouraged by the older *Hebamme*, it felt like a rock. This rigidity lasted about one minute as Jutta pushed down at the same time. With her hand still on Jutta's pregnant belly, Bedelia was delighted to feel the flurry of movement from within. Bedelia copied the *Hebamme*, saying *"Dat is good*, Jutta."

After about an hour of this intense exertion, Frau Schwass directed Bedelia to look between Jutta's legs. A small peek of black hair could be seen. With each push thereafter, more and more of the baby's head presented itself. Jutta's skin at the exit of the vagina was stretching as the baby's head advanced. Bedelia was reciting the anatomical names of the woman's genitalia under her breath. She was visualising the baby's descent through the birth canal. The diagrams that Bedelia had soaked up while perusing the doctor's book were all starting to make sense.

Frau Schwass took Bedelia's hand and cupped it inside her own. She pushed it with reasonable pressure onto the advancing head and said "Ni pressen! Jutta." The *Hebamme* panted, Bedelia panted, and Jutta mimicked the shallow panting of the two women directing her.

Then, when Bedelia felt the skin holding the head in was stretched to its maximum, Jutta screamed as first a brow appeared, then two eyes and a nose and lastly the chin. The baby's head was born facing its mother's rear. Throughout the birth of the baby's head the two women were still applying strong reverse pressure on the crown.

Magdalena had fetched a piece of apparatus. It was a small rubber tube that bulged out for about an inch, halfway down. She handed the device to her mother, who placed it in the baby's mouth and sucked the other end of the tube and spat out several times. At the same time, she positioned Bedelia's hands at either side of the baby's head ready to receive the body.

Magdalena held two towels that had been warmed by the fire. It was no time at all before the baby's head rotated to face Jutta's leg and one, then the other shoulder moved down and out like a cork-screw unwinding. Bedelia's hands naturally went to secure a firm grip around the shoulders and arms of the baby. With one last push, the little boy's body slipped out entirely. The *Hebamme* guided Bedelia as she handed the ecstatic mother her newborn through her legs. He was still attached to her by his cord. Jutta reached down and gently took her son in her arms. He was pink and wiggling as he let out his first vocal response in a loud bellow.

Tears were tracking down Jutta's cheeks and love spilling from her eyes. Bedelia looked up through her own blurry eyes and saw Magdalena sniffing as she used her sleeve to wipe her own nose. The elder *Hebamme* proceeded with the task at hand. She continued tending to the confinement and Bedelia watched as she skilfully delivered the afterbirth.

Overjoyed to be working alongside such a wise woman, Bedelia thought, *So much to learn, so many difficulties to deal with, yet so much knowledge and wisdom. I can do this.*

When all the necessary cleaning up was done, Jutta and her new son were tucked up together in bed. He breast-fed for some time before Herr Hamkens was introduced to his son. The new father had been waiting downstairs in the kitchen, and when he had heard the loud cry from the newborn he had hovered outside the bedroom door until Magdalena invited him in.

After a while Magdalena and Bedelia went down to fetch some sustenance for the new mother, who had not eaten for many hours. Several women were in the kitchen waiting to serve the food they had brought with them. They made up a large tray of freshly baked rolls, cheese and thinly sliced ham, with a pot of steaming fresh coffee placed alongside a jug of cream and a bowl of sugar.

Food enough for everyone was brought upstairs. Seeing the new family needed time alone together, Bedelia and the *Hebammen* took their food and coffee cups back downstairs to join the ladies in the kitchen.

The room was cosy and warm, with a hint of the fire as it peeked through the slightly open slats in front of the cast iron range. The coffeepot was placed back on top of the stove and continued to bubble. Clouts, linen and a bundle of baby clothes had been placed on the wire-woven shelf above, taking the benefit of the rising heat.

The comradery of the women in the room took Bedelia back to days long ago when her parents' family would join her family at these special times of arrivals to and departures from life. Bedelia thought, *No matter where you come from, companionship, assistance and the sharing of food and stories at these times are the essence of family and a community. Language is the same in the joy and elation of a birth gone well.*

She wished she could talk in more detail about the event with the two *Hebammen*, to make the most of her learning. She knew she had experienced more than her share of challenges in her short career, and was learning fast that midwifery kept you forever humble. *My will is not always God's will*, she said to herself.

It was time for Bedelia to leave, and she naturally went to embrace her companions. They each proffered their hands to shake instead. It felt strange and a little distant.

Although, she thought, *their handshakes feel warm and friendly.*

Maybe open displays of affection are not comfortable for them, Bedelia thought as she turned to Magdalena with her hand out. The younger Hebamme huffed and turned her back on Bedelia as she walked away. Magdalena's mother cuffed her around her ear, saying something that Bedelia could only guess the meaning of by the sharp snap of the words.

Christian delivered Bedelia back home. He had waited for her on the veranda. From the crumbs of food left on a plate and empty glass beside, she could see he had been well fed by the ladies in the kitchen.

Once again Christian said nothing throughout the homebound trek, but sat easily guiding the horse as they travelled at a more leisurely pace.

The doctor came to the front door and helped Bedelia down from the horse. "*Dankeschön!*" he said to Christian as he dismounted. They waved the young lad on his way, and as Bedelia followed the doctor and his horse into the stable she moved straight into her free-flowing dialogue, hardly drawing breath.

"Doctor, it was a truly beautiful birth. I was fair jumping out of my skin, so I was. I can't believe how wonderfully Frau Schwass works. For sure it's the best time I've ever had watching a baby being born. Oh, that's not counting my mammy's birth of Moira, the first one I was let to see being born. Actually, the frau and I delivered the wean together, so we did. She was so calm, there was no fuss. My heart is soaring; it feels like it's going to jump out of my chest. And it was I who handed the sweet baby to his mam. We all cried. Oh, not Frau Schwass, she was too busy finishing the job."

She followed the doctor inside. The words kept bubbling out as Bedelia continued to relate the whole event in fine detail.

"Now slow down, lassie. I am having difficulty keeping up with you."

Bedelia continued talking so fast that even Mrs Pentwick shook her head as she lost the sense of the story.

"Oh my," Bedelia spilled out, "I can't believe how composed the *Hebamme* was, even with the wee stranger doing a *cac* in his waters. I saw everything she did with her apparatus to suck out the baby's mouth before he took a breath. I followed every guiding hand to bring the little man into the world safely. It lifted my spirits to be sure what to do and to stay calm when there are troubles with a birth. I couldn't speak to the *Hebammen* after, but I had so many questions to ask. Do you think you can explain it, Doctor, and show me in your book how it is?"

"Of course, but later, after you have eaten and rested," the doctor said.

"Oh, and the young *Hebamme* was there also, well she seemed a bit poorly. I found out that she's called Magdalena. I'm thinking she is close to my age."

The doctor looked at Mrs Pentwick, wiped his brow and rubbed his ears as he retired from the kitchen. The housekeeper went about her tasks with exaggerated concentration. Bedelia sat down and leafed through the doctor's medical book for a short time, put her head down on her hands and promptly fell asleep at the table.

Chapter 15

It was several days later, when Bedelia was sitting at the kitchen table reading the doctor's book, that she read aloud a passage about miscarriages before three months of pregnancy. She only stalled on two words: endometrium and hydatidiform mole. Although she sounded them both out, Mrs Pentwick came over from the bench to look at where Bedelia had placed her fingers.

"My goodness, lassie, you've come a long way from that time on the ship when you threw the book I gave you onto the floor, frustrated that you couldn't read a whole sentence of easy words." Seeing the illustration beside the words, Mrs Pentwick said, "Oh, that is certainly grotesque," and quickly returned to her task of tidying up the kitchen and packing the food to take with them.

Every other month the doctor, Mrs Pentwick and Bedelia would make the journey by boat to Nelson. They had supplies to obtain, business to do and people to visit. They were accommodated at the Nation family home. Veronica was always so pleased to see her sister; they had so much news to catch up on. The Nation children were excited for their visits as it meant some treats and someone else to entertain them with stories and play.

The doctors would lose themselves in conversation in the surgery, and if there were patients to tend to, the pair would work amicably together sharing skills and knowledge. Doctor Nation would have a pile of journals, recently arrived from the old country, to share and discuss. The ones he had read many times, from cover to cover, would be given to Doctor Pattison to take home. Bedelia hoped there would be some interesting new articles pertaining to birth that she could read and learn from.

The ladies would take an outing to town, and although there were only a few shops, these were slowly starting to fill with more stock from the many ships that were coming to Nelson from England, Australia and Port Nicholson, just across the strait.

Today was going to be an exciting outing for all the ladies, as the sisters now had a little money saved from their respective employers; payment for work done. Other than when they were embarking on their long journey to the colonies and had purchased the essentials from the shipping company's list with the help of their Uncle Paddy, the sisters had never bought new clothes or shoes.

Their first stop was the draper's store. This was a real treat, and they carefully selected durable yet pretty fabric for two outfits each, including cloth and trimming for their undergarments. They felt extremely fortunate to be able to choose the colour of the garments, let alone have the luxury of patterned material or some pretty lace with which to embellish them.

Mrs Pentwick helped them decide how much material they would require and what type of thread, buttons and needles were needed. They could even afford a little decorated thimble to protect their fingers when they sewed the garments.

"Well, aren't we just the luckiest girls in the world, Dee," Veronica said as the two of them skipped out of the shop heading to the cobblers for their shoes.

Just as they reached the street where the Nation children were happily playing with some other children they had encountered on their walk into town, an angry commotion arose. Bedelia recognised the language coming from three of the men, dressed simply in blue labourers' clothing, as Plattdeutsch. Another stout gentleman's attire consisted of a smart pair of breeches and matching taupe jacket of wool. His gold-embossed waistcoat made of silk attempted, unsuccessfully, to cover his rotund belly. He was speaking a similar language but with an accent that sounded like he had a bone in the back of his throat. Bedelia thought it sounded more like the German that Doctor Nation spoke. It was difficult to make out what the argument was about, although Lilian could pick up some words from her knowledge of German and relayed them, as best she could, to the other women.

The heated argument continued until the constable came from the direction of the newly constructed quarters doubling as his home. "Now, now gentlemen," he said, looking at the men in blue, "we've been over this before, and the Magistrate has already ruled on the matter. You will be getting your recompense before this man leaves the country at the end of the week." The constable turned to the other, well-dressed man. "Isn't that correct, Herr Krause? Now get on with you, and keep out of each other's way before I lock the lot of you up together, and that wouldn't be good for any of you."

The three men slapped each other on the back in the spirit of good fellowship. As he walked away, the finely clothed man made some remark that jerked one of the three around so quickly, his fists poised ready to hit out, that the constable had to jump back to miss being bowled over. The man's fist connected with Herr Krause's chin and dropped him into a puddle left by the heavy shower from the night before. Laughter rained down on the man from the accumulating crowd.

"So, Herr Krause, you cannot help yourself but have the last word, can you? You have created such a bad reputation for yourself since you've been in this country, and no doubt for a long time before. Your presence will not be missed, and if you don't behave yourself I will lock you up until you and your family leave town on the next available ship. Now begone with you all. That's enough entertainment for the day." The constable directed this to the men involved in the scuffle as well as the growing crowd of spectators.

The sisters were about to take themselves into the cobbler's shop when they bumped into Sophia and Thomas Brandt with their two boys, who had been among the bystanders witnessing this spectacle.

"Oh, how nice to see you. *Moin, moin*! Thomas, *meine Schwester*, Veronica," Bedelia said, gesturing towards her sister, "*und meine Freunde*, Lilian … *und Frau* Pentwick." She was rather pleased with herself as she practised a little of her limited German.

Lilian told Sophia that they were going in to have some new shoes made, Bedelia made a beeline for baby Jens. He smiled and put his arms out mirroring Bedelia's, almost launching himself from his mother. "*Moin klein* Jens, my, haven't you grown," Bedelia said, as she caught the baby.

While Bedelia cuddled the baby, Lilian and Sophia had a short conversation in German as they pointed to the array of leather shoes and boots in the window of the shop. Lilian translated to her companions that Jutta, the lady whom Bedelia had attended recently with the *Hebammen* in her confinement, had a father who was a cobbler by trade. He had offered to make Bedelia and the *Hebammen* a pair of shoes or boots each as a thank you for their care of his daughter and the safe arrival of his first grandson. Sophia gestured towards Veronica; she had told Lilian that the German community got Mr Piehl to make all their footwear for a very reasonable sum.

Lilian also told Bedelia that Jutta's father lived close to the doctor's surgery, and gave them the directions to his shop. Sophia would send a message to Mr Piehl so he would be expecting them for a fitting.

Bedelia stood speechless. Never before had she worn new shoes specially made for her, nor had she ever been given something as valuable.

Mrs Pentwick said, "Well that's most unusual, lassie. I've never seen you at a loss for words." This caused an outburst of laughter all round. Sophia joined in and the infectious laughter drew smiles from some of the townsfolk who had been watching the previous fracas.

Lilian translated to the other women that she had asked the Brandt family for tea. Henri and the Nation boys had already struck up a friendship and were sloshing in the puddles. Sophia had declined because their group were returning home on the afternoon boat and they still had more supplies to purchase.

"*Veelen Dank! Tschüüs!*" the couple said in unison as they set off to the general store, collecting a muddy-legged Henri on their way.

As they walked away, Mrs Pentwick asked Lilian, "What was that commotion about?"

"That old scoundrel. He was the sponsor of the first German ship to arrive here in Nelson," Lilian said. "I have heard many stories about his cruelty on board, and it has carried on since they disembarked. He has created such a problem for his countrymen who travelled under him, that many made plans to turn back to Australia and join family and friends in Adelaide. Alongside this came the floods and other setbacks. Many of the families have had a most difficult start to their life in the colonies, most of all those under Herr Krause's sponsorship."

Lilian continued, "He has been charged by the courts to pay what he owes the settlers. He was meant to sponsor these settlers into good land here. He failed to do so. In fact, he has committed some despicable injustices and has finally been ordered to leave the country. And good riddance, I say."

Bedelia looked at Veronica, eyebrows raised, eyes wide. They were such strong words coming from a genteel lady. Herr Krause must have been very bad to have evoked such criticism from Lilian, Bedelia thought.

"I'm very pleased he was not on our ship. Imagine six months stuck on a sailing ship with that carry-on," Mrs Pentwick said.

"It was bad enough, the weeks of illness when the seas were rough, let alone having to deal with bad times in the good weather as well," Veronica said.

"Wait just a tick," Bedelia interrupted, saying, "I've just been reminded of my other task in town." She headed to the general store pulling a letter out of the new purse she had purchased. It wasn't long before she returned waving a folded piece of paper in one hand, her smile as broad as the purse she carried in the other.

"'Tis a letter from Michael, 'tis a letter from Michael," she squealed, pass-ers-by turning to watch as she skipped back to her waiting companions. The Nation children ran back from their play, followed by several of their playmates, eager faces looking to Bedelia.

She stood there for the longest time holding the paper closely to her breast as if letting it go would cause it to disappear into thin air.

"Oh, for goodness' sake Dee, will you open it or not," her sister said.

Bedelia sat down on a bench beside the butcher's shop, turning the letter round and round in her hands. Finally, hands on hips, Rosemary echoed Veronica's plea in the same tone, eliciting laughter from the expectant group. "Goodness' sake Dee, yer open a not!"

The little girl helped Bedelia break the seal that had been crudely placed on one of the open ends of the note in an attempt at privacy.

Bedelia read the words silently to herself first, then flapped the paper in an official display and read aloud, all eyes on her:
MY DEAREST DELIA,

"My dearest Delia, he says." Bedelia's eyes shone.
I HAVE KEENAN PENNING THIS NOTE AS HE HAS A FINE HAND. I HAVE RECEIVED YOUR LETTER.
WE ARE WELL AND HAVE WORK ON THE ROADS TO THE SOUTH.
YOURS,
MICHAEL.

Bedelia wished there had been more news, but for the meantime that small note would do. She folded the paper reverently and placed it in her purse, patting the latch reassuringly.

The visit to the German cobbler's shop stirred up some excitement for the sisters. It was easy to follow Sophia's directions and find the tidy little cob house with a small barn behind, which sat on the corner of intersecting roads. Fields of wheat, corn and cabbages were growing behind the house. A neatly fenced area for the mother pig, who had recently farrowed ten squabbling pig-lets vying for the best teat, sat beside the barn. Bedelia could see that the swine family were well-cared for, with a deep bed of clean straw in their covered box. A long wooden trough at the other end of the run held the meagre evidence of scraps they had gobbled up.

Three goats and one cow stood in their own enclosure, while less constrained hens and cockerels pecked here and there in the dirt and grass with the occasional scratching exposing a grub or insect.

The sisters rounded the path leading to the back of the whitewashed house and were greeted by Herr Piehl, clad in his leather apron and wearing the blue shirt and trousers Bedelia had identified as the uniform of a workingman. "*Schöön, dat do dor büst!*" he said as he gently shook the sisters' hands with his large, powerful ones. Their tiny hands seemed to disappear inside those of the strong, upright man. Bedelia remembered these work-enhanced hands, so like those of her da and Michael.

The person peering from the window beside the back door, Bedelia guessed, was Frau Piehl, for her head popped up with a beaming smile just as they were welcomed by Herr Piehl. A smell of leather and oil came from the lean-to room to the right, which stood with its door ajar as Herr Piehl beckoned Veronica and Bedelia inside. In one corner was a wooden last and a Strobel machine on a wooden bench. Several leather items, in various stages of completion, lay scattered on the bench at the back of the room.

After the cobbler had measured the sisters' feet and shown them the styles of ladies' boots he could make, they accepted the invitation for coffee and strudel in the Piehl home. Frau Piehl was a motherly figure with voluptuous breasts tucked behind a neat blue pinafore. Her hair was of several shades of grey as if, Bedelia thought, she had been sprinkled with pepper and salt. This sat loosely tied back in a roll, with strands escaping here and there.

The cooking smells of sweet apple and cinnamon wafting from under the covered plate on the table. The girls took the proffered bench. As Bedelia discovered again, coffee, not tea, was the hot drink served.

"Vonnie, it is rather strong to the taste, so it is," Bedelia said. "Cream and sugar are what you need with it. I am liking it more and more with the drinking." Mixed with the mouth-watering taste of apple strudel, the coffee was delicious, and it was impossible to turn down the offer of another piece and a refill of the coffee cup.

Veronica had returned from Nelson with her sister, at Lilian's suggestion. Veronica had said, "Why, I haven't laid my eyes on your new home yet, Dee, and the surgery you and the doctor have. It will be a treat to spend more time with you."

Mrs Pentwick was happy with the swap. She wanted to remain in town in order to look into the possibility of a return passage to England. She had found it difficult to settle to any firm plans of remaining in New Zealand, and said her heart was still grieving.

The sisters had so much to catch up on. During dinner the doctor hovered, eating his meal much slower than usual. The sisters were prattling on, sharing memories from home.

"Why Vonnie, you've got that recipe off pat, you have. It's so much like the one Mammy made us. It surely is the best stew I've eaten since we were little girls."

"I'm rather pleased with myself, so I am. It took some time to taste just right. Lilian was so patient with me. I was able to use the produce the patients brought us and I only made two mistakes. The pigs thanked me kindly for those, they did."

"It was a most delicious meal. Thank you, Veronica," the doctor said.

"Oh, do call me Vonnie."

"I would be happy to do so as long as you call me George, and only 'Doctor' in front of the patients."

"George it is, then," the sisters said in unison.

"Tell me a little about your home, if you please." The doctor directed his request to both women.

The doctor listened intently as they shared about the deaths of all their family members. They had buried their loved ones one after the other, in quick succession. They told him about their years in the workhouse, rescued from an inevitable life on the streets by the chance for free passage to the colonies.

"Now Doctor I mean George, what's good for the goose is good for the gander. Your turn," Bedelia said.

The doctor hesitated. His face coloured up as he stuttered, "Oh, oh, you do not need to be bored with my life so far. Moving here to the colonies, I believe, is where my life begins. No need to retrace the past."

"Now, now, George. You don't get away that easily, you don't," Bedelia laughed.

The doctor told them of his privileged upbringing, born to a surgeon of high standing with a practice in London, and a mother with parents in the aristocracy. He and his only brother were shunted off to boarding school, he at the tender age of seven, without ever really getting to know their family. The doctor told how he detested the bullying he encountered at school, and when his younger brother died of an infection at the age of ten, he felt very much alone. He determined that he would make the most of his situation and spent all his waking hours studying in order to follow in his father's footsteps, to gain a place in medical school.

"It was at Oxford that I first met Stephen Nation, and we became life-long friends, my first and only since my brother had died. We both had a burning desire to travel and experience the world and to become the best doctors in our field. We were very fortunate that understanding and knowledge came easily, but we did study hard. We had no difficulties with our exam results and our reputation as hard workers enabled us to find positions in medicine."

The doctor shifted in his seat, and taking a sip of his whiskey he continued. "Stephen met Lilian in his last year at medical school. I have never been so fortunate as to find someone whom I'd wish to spend the rest of my days with, or who would want to do so with me." The doctor looked down at his hands then quickly moved on. "Now that's quite enough about me. I warned you it was all extremely uninteresting."

The sisters resumed their familiar sisterly banter. They reminisced about their life back in Ireland when all was well and they didn't have a care in the world. They giggled like the young colleens they were as they made tentative plans for their future.

Remaining quiet for the rest of the evening, the doctor smiled as Bedelia and Veronica included him in their conversation and humour. "I will retire to my surgery," he said, rising from the table. "I have much to attend to, so I will bid you young ladies goodnight."

The doctor's formal words set the girls off on another bout of laughter as they rose to clear the dinner dishes. "*Moin, moin!*" Bedelia said.

"*Guten Nacht!*" said the doctor, with a rare grin.

The next week sailed by between the work around the house, Bedelia's work as the doctor's assistant and some exploring in the new community building up around them.

By the end of the week Bedelia and Veronica had each completed one of their two new dresses, and the boots had been delivered by the cobbler. Herr Piehl had also made each of them a pair of pretty black calfskin slippers, the first ones they had ever possessed. The fit was perfect, each finished with some unique fancy stitching on top. Herr Piehl only allowed them to pay for

Veronica's new footwear, and even then, for much less than the prices at the cobblers in town.

The sisters were so excited. They had spent some time that afternoon carefully seeing to each other's hair, and when they donned their new dresses they glowed with happiness.

Bedelia and Veronica had no memory of the experience of new garments, particularly not ones in which they felt so lady-like. They paraded through the house like princesses bound for a ball, and as they did a turn of the living room they imitated a spin around the dance floor.

Drawn down the hallway by the laughter, the doctor looked on from the doorway. His eyes were glued to the older sister as he watched her mimic the elegant, confident movements of a lady at a grand occasion. Bedelia and Veronica pranced around the room, dancing together with gay abandon.

The doctor could hold himself back no longer as he joined Veronica and Bedelia. He danced with each sister in turn as he deftly guided them around the small room, negotiating the few items of furniture and smiling from ear to ear. Bedelia was overjoyed to witness such a transformation. She had not seen the joy and laughter that now spilled from the doctor; he was normally so serious.

If there had been music to accompany their frivolity the dancing may have gone on for much longer, but the girls finally collapsed on the settee and the doctor in his chair as they caught their breath. They finished the night with a supper of cold cuts and potato along with a few of Mrs Pentwick's pickles.

The doctor sat watching the sisters interact as they cleared the dishes away and tidied the small kitchen. They were both singing some songs they recalled from their childhood. "Mammy used to sing these while doing the chores," Veronica said. Normally he would have retired to his room and his own company by now, but tonight the doctor lingered.

As they sat around the table smiling and laughing, Bedelia thought it worth savouring the moment and delaying bed, as this would be Veronica's last night with them. Tomorrow she would be taking the boat back to Nelson.

Chapter 16

The patients had come in steadily over the month, with all the usual ailments and injuries of young families and working men. Neither the doctor nor Bedelia had time to talk about their time with Veronica.

Mrs Pentwick had come home on the boat that had taken Veronica back to town. She had had no luck finding a suitable ship to take her home, so would have to wait until another chance arose in the springtime. She brought with her materials to make new clothes for the Nation children, whom she had become rather fond of. Winter was fast descending on them and there would be some long days indoors and even longer nights, so she wanted to have enough to keep herself occupied. She had also purchased a large container of candles and stronger eyeglasses to help her see the fine stitches.

The knocking on the door that night, as they had just finished eating, was loud and insistent. It was Christian again, and he beckoned for Bedelia to follow him. There was no explanation. He said to the doctor that he had been told by his mother to collect the young Irish midwife and take her to a German family to the west. Bedelia had no idea what she would find and what she would need, although she assumed Frau Schwass would have all that was required.

On one of their quieter days, the doctor, with Bedelia alongside him, had spent some time collecting all the essential items for birthing, in case she may need them. He handed her the brown leather satchel with the equipment inside as she followed Christian out into the dark.

"Why do babies decide to come at night?" Bedelia said, not expecting a reply.

The doctor said, "Now Delia, if my services are required you must send Christian back for me, but Frau Schwass is such a competent midwife that I don't expect to be needed."

"Of course, Doctor. I mean Geo ... Doctor," Bedelia said, putting her hand to her mouth.

Snow had fallen in the last few days. Bedelia felt grateful for the new woollen cloak the doctor had bought her for such an occasion. Historically, the red garment, with a lining of satin from hood to hem, was the symbol of the midwife in England. It had three large wooden buttons placed at intervals from under the chin to enclose the occupant in its warmth. Two slits on either side were positioned to enable the hands to protrude when needed. Bedelia felt most grown-up and very proud to be wearing it, and to be carrying the birthing bag the doctor said was now hers.

Moonlight shone down illuminating the path they were taking, while highlighting the range of mountains with snow on their tops, like icing on a bun. Bedelia could sense they were headed west, but into the valley. They travelled along a roughly cut track wide enough for one wagon, the ruts a hazard for their horse's sturdy legs. Bedelia realised why Christian had brought a draught horse used for farm work: it would be easier to ride, making better time than if it had been pulling a wagon. Besides, Bedelia could see a wagon may have become stuck in the muddy tracks.

Finally, they reached a farmhouse. As soon as they had tethered the horse they were greeted by the farmer, who introduced himself as Herr Fischer, "Nils," he added. Taking her cloak, he showed Bedelia to the back of the house, where the frau was in full labour. Magdalena was standing beside the woman, who was reclined on the bed. The young *Hebamme's* brow was furrowed and she was gazing anywhere but at Bedelia.

"*Mein Mudder geiht dat nich good,*" Magdalena said timidly, shaking her head forlornly as she folded her hands in and out of the sides of her apron.

Bedelia could see that Frau Schwass was not present so she guessed Magdalena's mother would not be coming. She took a pinny out of her bag and placed it over her dress. She looked at Magdalena with an expression of inquiry, opening her arms as if to gather in vital information. Between the broken English Magdalena had and the understanding of Plattdeutsch that Bedelia was developing, the two apprentice midwives communicated.

Bedelia found out that this was Frau Fischer's first baby, and she had been well so far during her confinement. The pains had commenced earlier in the day. Now they were coming closer together and were getting stronger by the hour.

From the behaviour and noises that the frau was making, Bedelia deduced that the birth was not far away.

"*Ich bin* Bedelia, Frau Fischer," Bedelia said.

"*Ik bün* Alina," Frau Fischer pointed to herself. She was not much older than Bedelia and Magdalena.

It seemed, from Bedelia's questioning, that Magdalena had not examined the labouring woman. Remembering the description of the procedure in the doctor's book, with Alina lying on the bed Bedelia ran her finger tips and hands up and down the vast belly searching for the baby's back, feet and head. She felt a firm shape under Alina's ribs. Bedelia sensed there was something unusual in what she was feeling. Alina's belly was very large for the size of her stature, and there seemed to be more limbs than Bedelia would have anticipated, wiggling and squirming under Bedelia's nimble fingers. After discovering the ball shape at the top of the womb, and one just detectable entering Alina's bony birth canal, she stopped to ponder her findings. She visualised the diagrams in the doctor's book, turning the pages over in her mind to find the answer. She wished she had brought the book with her.

Bedelia stopped and said, under her breath, "Oh Jesus, Mary and Joseph," and stared at Magdalena as she realised there was one more baby than she was expecting.

"*Bitte?*" Magdalena said, clearly asking what Bedelia meant.

Bedelia thought, *Two babies wrapped around and facing one another*.

"A perfect twin presentation." She quoted out loud words she had read in the book.

Magdalena looked at her bewildered, shaking her head.

Bedelia held up her two forefingers then sketched her findings of the twins' positions on the bed in front of her: a comma hugging an inverted comma.

Magdalena's eyes grew ever wider, her expression of concern intensifying. Bedelia's fellow apprentice nodded and shrugged her shoulders. She stepped away from Alina, indicating with one hand for Bedelia to move in. Bedelia realised she was being given the leading role and the responsibility to make the decisions. A look of relief washed over Magdalena's face when Bedelia reluctantly moved forward.

"Why me?" she said under her breath.

The way the babies were lying, Bedelia assumed there would be no problem with the first baby being born. The difficulty would lie with the gaping cavity left by the first twin, leaving the second twin to decide which way it would arrive. Bedelia had read that there was a way of manipulating this for a better outcome, but lacking the practical experience to do this, she would just have to take her chance when the time came.

Even though she was aware of the distance he would need to travel and the possibility of him not reaching the house in time to help, Bedelia decided to send Christian to fetch the doctor.

In order for Magdalena to understand better, Bedelia drew another picture with her finger on the bed sheet. With gesticulations and a few common words, she explained as best she could the difficulties they may encounter once the first twin was born. The finger diagram remained imbedded for a short time on the sheets, plainly laid out for the two young midwives to absorb the enormity of the problems they may encounter.

Taking a deep breath and telling herself *I can do this, I can*, Bedelia knew to act as if she had everything in hand. Only she knew this was not true and that what lay ahead would be a new experience for her. The knot in her tummy went unseen. Her relaxed demeanour gave neither the expectant mother nor Magdalena the true extent of Bedelia's uncertainty, lack of knowledge and dread.

Alina was standing at the end of the bed holding onto the bed end. Another hour of raging pains ensued, each becoming more intense and closer together. All of a sudden there was a large gush of clear fluid as Alina gave a huge grunt. For Bedelia there was no doubt the babies were ready to make their appearance.

Pulling up her sleeves, Bedelia nodded to Magdalena, who pulled up her sleeves also. "Ready?" she said.

"Ready," Magdalena said, returning the nod.

Magdalena had built up the fire. Many clouts had been prepared and more linen, which had been added to receive the babies, was warming on a chair in front of the glowing flames. She sopped up the clear fluid from the floor with some spare rags.

With encouraging words and hot water on the clouts to ease the stretching between Alina's thighs, Bedelia prepared to receive the first twin.

Alina was now squatting beside the bed. Bedelia knew both she and Magdalena were needed to attend to the births and to the two babies when they were born, so she indicated to Magdalena to call Alina's husband, Nils, to come in.

Bedelia thought the less worry for the new parents the better until they had the first baby in their arms. She looked at Magdalena with one finger to her lips shaking her head, hoping Magdalena would understand not to alarm the father with the news just yet.

Magdalena said "*Ja, ja,*" nodding her head and looking directly at Bedelia as she communicated her understanding.

With direction from Magdalena, Nils positioned himself on the other side of the small marital bed. Holding Alina's arms behind the elbows while she grasped his upper arms would give her more leverage to push. Two pillows were placed in such a way as to support her large belly so it was not pressing too firmly against the side of the bed.

Gravity enabled the first baby to descend through the birth canal and it wasn't long before a small peek of the head could be seen by the midwives. With each "*utpressen*" the midwives said and the effort of Alina's pushing, the head advanced towards where Bedelia held the warm, wet clout.

More and more of the head was visible as Alina pushed. Bedelia spared a thought of gratitude for Magdalena's mother, guiding her with hands-on experience to manage the birthing of the head in a slow and controlled manner. After the crown of the head had slowly stretched the exit completely, the face revealed itself: brow, eyes, nose then chin, completing the most painful part of the birth. Alina let out a loud, primordial scream and the rest of the baby slid out into Bedelia's waiting arms. She placed the baby girl in the warm wrap that Magdalena had passed from the fireside chair.

The baby let out a lusty cry, filling her lungs and breathing air for the first time. She put the baby in Magdalena's arms and tied the cord with two separate pieces of twine to separate the baby from her lifeline that she no longer required. Bedelia cut the cord with the scissors she had taken from her bag. Discarding the wet wrap, Magdalena swaddled the baby in a clean, dry cloth and took her to the other side of the bed where her parents could hold her. With a look and a nod from Bedelia, Magdalena explained to Alina and Nils that there would be another baby about to join the family.

With the rest of the first baby's cord hanging between Alina's legs, Bedelia indicated that she needed to examine Alina internally. She knew it was important to find out what part of its body the second baby would present first. Knowing this would hopefully enable Bedelia to determine what to do next. She positioned Alina, seated on the edge of the bed facing her, with Nils supporting her from behind, his arms coming from under the armpits and meeting across her chest. When Alina leaned back onto her husband, Bedelia put her two fingers in the birth canal, she could only tip the bag of waters with her outstretched fingers. No tell-tale body parts could be reached.

As Alina's pains continued, her new baby lay safely on top of the quilt on the bed beside her parents. Bedelia went to work to deal with the yet unknown events that lay ahead of her. She positioned herself, kneeling on the floor in front of the new mother, raised her voice a level and said *"utpressen,* Alina." Magdalena joined in.

"*Utpressen,*" the midwives said in unison.

The bag of fluid encapsulating the second twin could be seen between Alina's thighs, with still no hint of what lay behind.

With the next *"utpressen"*, two little feet and the new baby's cord could be seen. Bedelia already knew the implications of this presentation. She caught Magdalena's eye who nodded, showing she also knew. The cord was still pulsing, delivering all the baby needed to survive. At this stage, what flowed through it continued to do so unhindered. Bedelia recalled reading, that if the bag of protective waters stayed whole, the baby would have a better chance, as it would cushion the lifeline from obstruction by bony body parts.

Bedelia knew there would need to be a gentler descent of the baby on this perilous journey. She spoke firmly, hoping Alina would understand the importance of giving her full co-operation. "*Nein utpressen,* Alina." She shook her head as she mimicked panting.

"*Ni pressen!*" Magdalena said copying Bedelia's panting.

Despite the pain she was enduring, after absorbing the tone of Bedelia's voice, Alina appeared to understand. She cooperated completely with the midwives' instructions.

The lifeline was cushioned in the caul as the little legs peddled their appearance. The baby boy revealed himself and still the bag stayed whole. Bedelia realised that she was holding her breath, clenching her thighs and readying herself for the worst outcome.

Then, as the body came down, the feet penetrated the bag of waters. Bedelia's lap was drenched with the clear fluid flowing from the gaping hole. The baby's body descended completely. The baby was limp, hanging from between his mother's legs.

Bedelia knew time was running out and she had only a few minutes to get the baby out. She ignored the voice in her head that was saying, *Hands off the breech until you must;* this was a time for action.

Bedelia recalled what Magdalena's mother had done at the first birth they had attended together. She took a firm hold around the baby's trunk and rotated him first one way, then the other, releasing both his arms in turn. Positioning his body along her arm, she placed her middle finger in the baby's mouth and the other two fingers along his cheekbones. With a downward pull of the lower jaw with her finger, the baby's head flexed as Bedelia assisted his face out. The cord lay alongside Bedelia's bare arm, she could tell it had stopped doing its important job. She pictured it locked between the baby's head and the mother's pelvis.

"*Utpressen*!" she shouted to Alina, and at the same time, keeping the pressure on her middle finger, brought the smallest diameter of the baby's head through, following the natural curve of the birth canal. With the mother's help, the baby completed its journey.

Laying the flaccid baby on a warm cloth Magdalena had placed in her wet lap, Bedelia tied the cord twice with the twine and cut the cord between the two knots. She took the proffered warm, dry wrap and brusquely stimulated the unbreathing soul. She carried the baby boy to the chair by the fire and covered his tiny mouth and nose completely with her own mouth, sucked and spat, sucked and spat into the hearth. Again Bedelia covered the baby's mouth and nose completely with her mouth and this time she gently puffed, transferring a small breath into the baby's airways, inflating his lungs for their first fill of air. She continued doing this until the baby let out a resounding cry.

Just at that moment the doctor arrived to a room full of tears of joy and two new additions to the world. Bedelia cradled the little boy in her trembling arms. The enormity of the situation had caught up with her. She was spent.

Magdalena and the doctor completed the birth, with Alina pushing both afterbirths out. Magdalena watched as the doctor vigorously massaged the womb. He told her in simple German, while Bedelia listened from the chair, that there was a much higher chance of a mother bleeding when the uterus had been stretched with a twin pregnancy.

"Alina is young and healthy. Both babies feeding from the breast will help also," he said.

He started to translate all the instructions he had given to Magdalena into English, for Bedelia's sake.

"There's no need," Bedelia said, "I was able to understand, completely."

The doctor smiled as he concluded his examinations of the twins, and handed them back to their parents, one each.

"*Glückwunsch!*" The doctor congratulated the new parents.

With a summary of their healthy babies' checks, he gave them advice they may require for their care, in a mixture of English and German. The doctor looked at Bedelia with surprise, after Magdalena had finished translating his instructions to Alina and Nils, into Plattdeutsch, with no hesitation. Magdalena reassured the doctor that she would be staying on to help the young family for as long as she was needed.

As Bedelia readied to be taken home, the doctor praised both the young midwives for their professional handling of a difficult situation.

Bedelia said, "*Danke*, Magdalena. *Dankeschön*," as she put her hand out to shake in the German way she had learnt.

Magdalena gave a gulp and embraced Bedelia, sobbing. "*Dank, Dank, Veelen dank!* Bedelia," she spluttered out.

On the homeward journey, in her usual non-stop chatter Bedelia shared the whole birth event with the doctor. "Maybe you have some more valuable suggestions about what else I could have done to make the outcome better."

"Better? *Better?*" the doctor said in crescendo, smiling at the cascade of words that had flown from Bedelia's mouth. "There is no better. What you young ladies have achieved today is truly commendable. Why, even the most well-trained obstetrician couldn't have done better than you. And look at what you left behind for those new parents. Two of the loveliest little creatures God ever produced."

Bedelia smiled as they negotiated the ruts in the road, aching with the tiredness that was consuming her whole being after such a long and challenging event. It was a very satisfying tiredness after a task well done. *Yes*, she said to herself.

Chapter 17

When Magdalena's mother was well enough, she and her daughter visited the doctor's home. It was more of a social visit than anything. Young Christian brought them in the new surrey that their friend, a cartwright, had built for them. It was in payment for the *Hebamme* delivering his last two children, one on board ship and the other one just recently.

"It is rather grand," Bedelia said as she saw it had a canopy to cover the front seat in case of inclement weather. A bridge had been newly built over the river that once posed an obstacle to travel, and the roads were now in better condition for a lighter wagon.

For once Christian accepted the invitation to join in the afternoon tea. He seemed more relaxed than Bedelia had ever seen him and was talking with the doctor comfortably in his native tongue with a smattering of English. Bedelia picked up enough of their conversation to understand that the men working on the roads and bridges were strong men and their comradery and willingness to work together in every way lightened the toil. German, English and Irish worked together, employing the language of simple words and common understanding of men of the land.

Bedelia had heard that Magdalena's two older brothers were employed on the roads. "Have you heard your brothers speak of a couple of Irish lads, the one tall with black hair, a red beard and brown eyes, and his companion with the red hair and green eyes, standing about up to here?" She indicated a couple of inches above her own head. "Handsome fellows they are, to be sure, and very lovely too." She directed her question to Christian with the doctor translating.

"He says there are a couple of men fitting the description working alongside the road gang," the doctor said. "They're staying up the road from the Schwass home in a makeshift shanty. His brothers told him that the pair are hoping to get better paying work at the new timber mill. They plan to earn enough money to move on and purchase some land over the hills, towards the east, next spring."

Bedelia's heart skipped a beat and her face coloured up. "Can you please ask Christian's brothers to pass on my kind wishes to the men when they see them next. Tell them we are almost neighbours, closer than where we lived back in the Emerald Isles." She couldn't believe Michael and Keenan could be just a few short miles from where she had settled. Her head was full of schemes in case they may visit, but she stopped herself blurting out her thoughts. The visitors and Bedelia's companions looked at each other, smiling at her overt reaction to this news.

When they had devoured the scones with cream and jam and the tea set out for the guests by Mrs Pentwick, the elder *Hebamme* took Bedelia by both hands. With a display of gratitude, needing no translation, she looked at Bedelia and Magdalena in turn and thanked them for what they had done with the twin birth. "*Veelen Dank!*," she said, with such feeling that no other words were needed. The two young apprentice midwives looked at each other, faces beaming.

Magdalena's mother gave Bedelia the most exquisitely embroidered cloth with lace trim as fine as cobweb. The cross stitches in the centre depicted a whitewashed house with a hay roof and golden fields of wheat surrounding it. Bedelia was so overcome with the gift, the wee sob that slipped from her mouth and the tears that came from her eyes could not be stifled. Her new-found friend, Magdalena, embraced her and they both wept.

There was more discussion between the doctor and the *Hebamme* as Bedelia and Magdalena chatted in what little language they had in common. The German family left in their new transport, waving enthusiastically as they headed down the road. It wasn't until they got inside that the doctor told Bedelia what the older woman had said.

"Delia, I must tell you that Frau Schwass has asked if you will go and join her and Magdalena in their practice. I told her that your assistance is of great value to me right here. I said you have much to learn working with me in my surgery, while helping me with the increasing numbers of patients, including those with growing families. I also explained that she may call on you for your help whenever she needs to, if you are free and eager to do so.

"Of course," he continued, "it is completely for you to decide, and I will not stand in your way if you wish to take her offer. You will learn so much from the *Hebamme*. Take your time and make the best decision for yourself. I will support you in your choice whatever that may be."

Bedelia retired early that night, soon after helping Mrs Pentwick clear the dinner dishes. She had remained uncharacteristically quiet since the German family's visit, hardly saying a word at the dinner table. Her mind was a turmoil of thoughts around the decisions laid before her. So much to consider, so much change, so many possibilities. She was swimming in the "What ifs".

That night she tossed and turned until she fell into a fitful sleep with dreams of German words and babies being born, all with a man looking over her shoulder, whom she recognised as Michael. *What to do, where to go, where will my future lie? So many choices,* she said to her dreaming self.

In the morning she was no closer to an answer than she had been the night before. In fact, she felt further from the goal with her chattering mind. She washed and dressed, had her breakfast in her continued silence and readied the surgery for the doctor's pending day. Mrs Pentwick had glanced at the doctor across the breakfast table and said, "The cat has really got your tongue, missy."

The day looked quiet to begin with. The doctor had just two patients to see. One man needed minor surgery to repair a gash in his leg received from the horn of a rutting goat. The wound was dirty and ragged. Bedelia cleaned it thoroughly and readied it for the doctor to insert some stitches to hold the wound together until the healing was complete. She was reluctant to tackle the suturing, the opening was so jagged.

The doctor said, "Bedelia, this is a good opportunity to practise your skills on difficult wounds."

The farmer pricked up his ears and looked wide-eyed between the doctor and Bedelia. Noticing this, the doctor said, "Oh, have no concerns here, Mr Fairbright, this young lassie does the best and most gentle repairs of wounds in the district. That is one thing I can assure you of."

Turning to Bedelia, he said, "I would recommend a stronger thread on the outer layer because of the site of the wound. Mr Fairbright is a farmer, and I know it will be impossible to ask him to rest up, am I not correct?" The doctor directed the question to the patient.

Mr Fairbright nodded.

"This man has work to do and a wound on his leg will hardly stop him," the doctor said.

After completing the repair with only one question for the doctor, Bedelia placed a dressing over the wound and bandaged it firmly in place. She asked the farmer to come back if there was any excessive redness, swelling, pain or pus, and made an appointment for him to return in ten days to have the stitches removed. She also gave two extra bandages and dressings to his wife to use when this one got dirty, which Bedelia had no doubt it would. The wife had watched carefully when Bedelia had shown her how to bandage in such a way that it would stay firmly on the leg and keep dirt out of the lesion.

At lunch Bedelia continued in her quiet contemplation. She nibbled away at her bread and cheese with her eyes glazed over. Her companions did not try to coax any conversation out of her. They left her in peace after they had finished eating.

The doorbell roused her and she jumped up to answer it, bumping into the doctor coming out into the hall on the same quest. "Oh, mind me," Bedelia apologised. They reached the front door at the same time and were greeted by a little lad, no taller than the door handle.

"How can I help you, young man?" the doctor said.

"Me mam's taken poorly and I didn't know what to do so I came by here."

"What name have you? Is there anyone with her?" Bedelia said.

"Danny it is. No one is with mam, just my wee sister Isy, but she's just small and in her cot. Da's out bush. He won't be home 'til dark."

"Is it far to your home?" the doctor asked as he turned to Bedelia. "I am wondering if you and Danny should go ahead on the horse and I will follow on foot." They were yet to purchase a wagon, and in this case Bedelia thought it would have been very convenient to have one.

"No sir, it just be along the road and over the hill." The boy pointed in the direction of the south-west.

Mrs Pentwick took Danny into the kitchen for a glass of milk and a fresh scone with jam left over from lunch.

The doctor and Bedelia went into the surgery and discussed what they would possibly need to deal with the unknown situation they were about to encounter. "I think it's better not to ask too many questions about what's happening with Danny's mother, Delia. The lad appears to be no older than five. We will just have to wait and see what we find when we reach his home," the doctor said.

The doctor collected his bag and Bedelia put on her cloak. The days were still crisp with a heavy layer of snow on the surrounding mountains

Their horse, Sandy, was a sturdy mount, and she could handle a short ride with two and a half passengers, so they decided to travel together.

"Besides, if I send you and the lad ahead, I may lose sight of where you've gone."

They reached the small cottage within the hour. The door was ajar and a small child's distraught crying greeted them as they dismounted. Danny ran in calling, "Here they are Mammy, I got the doctor and his lady."

Following Danny through to the kitchen, the doctor and Bedelia found his mother collapsed on the floor, lying in a pool of blood, her skirt drenched.

With a nod Bedelia left the doctor and took Danny through to the small bedroom, where his little sister was sobbing with the hiccups of a child left distraught too long. Bedelia closed the door quietly so as not to alarm the children. She lifted the little girl, who appeared to be about one year old, and held her firmly to her bosom to settle her distress. Isy's clout was soaking and oozing a smell that called for immediate attention.

She cuddled the little girl and distracted Danny with conversation about his da and what he liked to do; anything to draw them away from the grim reality of what she could only guess was presenting itself to the doctor in the other room.

"My word, Danny, I'm sure you are a great little helper. So clever you are, for sure. Where might I find a clean clout for your sister?"

Danny was enthusiastic about being "Dee's big helper," as she put it, knowing she would eventually have to join the doctor to assist him.

After Bedelia had finished cleaning up Isy, the doctor called from the other room and Bedelia turned to Danny. "You're such a brave little warrior, you are for sure. I need to help the doctor now. I need you to look after Isy here while we fix your mam. Mind you watch her carefully and we'll be back to you in no time at all, so we will."

"I'll be coming now, Doctor. Danny is in charge in here, such a courageous soldier he is," Bedelia said as she slipped back into the kitchen where the doctor was bent over Danny's mam. As she closed the door, she gave a tentative glance back to the two little ones on the floor beside their parents' bed, giving Danny a salute.

"She is still bleeding, Delia. In the clout," the doctor said, pointing to a bundle on the hearth bricks, "there's a lost soul I've set aside, not much bigger than a mouse. Danny's mother has lost so much blood, there's nothing more to do. Her pulse is thready, her sclera is pale, and I cannot rouse her. If we can get her onto her bed, I believe it will only be a short time before she slips away. Much better for the wee ones to see their mam for the final time in her bed and not lying here."

"Help me wrap her skirt in this old blanket I found on the chair by the hearth, then we will get her to the bed. I'll take her shoulders and you take her under her knees. We can clean her later. We need to get her covered for the children's sake," the doctor said.

Once their mam had been tucked into her bed, Bedelia sat with Isy on her knee and held Danny's hand. "Now Danny, you were so grand coming for the doctor and myself, you surely were. Your mam is very poorly and you brought us to your home to help her, all by yourself. Very soon your mam will be going to the angels in Heaven. Hold her hand now and say goodbye. She will know it's her brave soldier beside her." After saying a prayer for the repose of the soul of the dying woman, Bedelia picked up Isy and left the doctor with Danny and his mam.

She went into the kitchen and prepared some food for the little girl. It would have been hours since she had eaten. While Isy was stuffing the food into her mouth, Bedelia took the time to mop up the pool of blood in the centre of the floor with the rags she had found in a bucket by the door.

She saw the makings of the stew Danny's mam had been preparing when she had collapsed, and proceeded to complete the task. The fire in the hearth still had enough embers to boost it into life again. Before Isy had finished her meal Bedelia had the mutton stew bubbling away.

With Isy on her hip, Bedelia returned to join Danny and the doctor, who raised his eyes and shook his head slightly, a silent but pertinent message to Bedelia. He gestured to Bedelia that his fingers had lost the feel of the weak pulse and he put his arm around Danny's shoulder to break the news to the wee fellow. Bedelia prayed silently.

Nothing could prepare the two adults for the ear-piercing scream as Danny fell on his mam's chest, wailing, "No Mam, No Mam, don't leave us." That set Isy off into a crying frenzy. She quietened as soon as her big brother had stopped crying.

"What's Da to say when he gets home?" Danny sobbed.

"We will stay with you until he comes, young man. You won't be left alone," the doctor said.

Darkness was well settled over the valley when they heard the wagon approaching. Isy had gone to sleep, exhausted from her ordeal, but Danny, despite drooping eyelids, fought sleep stubbornly. He was intent on being awake when his da arrived home.

Scrapings on the doorstep as his da removed his boots took Danny rushing to greet him as the door opened. "Da, Da, the angels came for Mam. She's in your bed, but she's gone to Heaven."

Danny's da dropped his jaw as he looked at the strangers at his kitchen table with suspicion. The doctor got in fast, introducing himself and Bedelia and telling the burly man what had happened to his wife.

The news of his wife's death took some time to sink in, and it wasn't until he went into the bedroom and saw her lifeless body lying on their bed that comprehension of the enormity of their situation dawned on him. Like his son before, he collapsed, weeping on her chest. "She's the love of my life, the mother of my children. What am I to do?"

After they had coaxed Danny into bed with a few bites of stew in his tummy, the three adults sat around and discussed immediate plans.

"I am feeling so very alone I can't think. Mary did all that for me, so she did."

"Surely there is someone you can call who would help?" the doctor said.

"I can call my wife's sister to come tomorrow. It's a pity there's no priest in the area."

The doctor and Bedelia offered to do anything they could, and it was agreed that they would contact the sister-in-law. "This," Bedelia said, "will give you time to spend with Danny and Isy and put the house in order for the wake."

Bedelia and the doctor set off for home well into the night. Bedelia had done all she could to clean the house. Before his da arrived home she had washed and prepared Danny's mam's body. Danny had chosen her Sunday best for her to be dressed in. He and Isy helped to brush their mam's locks "so she would look beautiful for Da to see," as Danny had said.

On the way home Bedelia told the doctor she would not be taking the *Hebamme* up on her offer. "If it's fine with you, doctor, I have the feeling that I would be of much better service and learn much from you," she said. "And besides, I can still help the *Hebammen* when and if I am needed, so I can."

The doctor smiled, and continued to do so as he listened to Bedelia prattle on about what this young family would do without a wife and mother, and about Danny and Isy, and how brave and sweet they both were, and all the things she had learnt today, and all the things she would learn tomorrow and, and, and. The doctor's eyes glazed over as he held the reins while the horse took them home, with the lovely lilt of Bedelia's accent in her ramblings ringing in his ears.

Chapter 18

Much to the doctor and Bedelia's relief, the next few weeks proceeded in a quiet, manageable way. They had attended the wake. It was an emotional gathering as they witnessed the grief of Danny, Isy and their da.

What amazed Bedelia was the resilience of young children and their ability to switch from an open display of grief to unbridled joy. She shared her thoughts with the doctor. "One minute they're crying fit to burst and in a hair's breadth they're laughing and squealing as they play tag with their cousins."

The doctor agreed. "They really are oblivious to the adult social norms of mourning."

Bedelia found it hard to recollect the same innocence, as she and her sister had endured so much loss and hardship in the last ten years of their young lives. "I am so blessed to have Vonnie," she said to herself.

Danny and Isy's aunt, who had only two children of her own, had taken her nephew and niece home with her so their father could continue working until he could find another solution for the care of his family.

Bedelia felt satisfied with her choice to stay working with the doctor. Since her decision she had returned to her usual exuberant self.

One Sunday Bedelia, the doctor and Mrs Pentwick set out for church in the new building for the German Lutheran families. With no Catholic church built, nor one for any other denomination, the large community of Lutherans were welcoming all Christians to share their place of worship. The priests and clergymen from the other faiths were itinerant, and they travelled around the new settlements surrounding the greater Nelson area, conducting intermittent services whenever and wherever they could.

When Bedelia and her companions reached the small church, they were greeted by the German families they had encountered and had grown close to. As they approached a small group outside the entrance, Bedelia let out an excited whoop. Despite the fact that the two young men had their backs to her, she recognised Michael's stance, the tall figure with the shiny black hair, Keenan's red hair a beacon beside him.

She skipped up to Michael from behind, and in a girlish gesture reached up on her tiptoes, using her little hands as a blindfold, saying, "Guess who?"

Michael whipped around and picked up his friend. His large hands seemed to reach right around her waist as they danced an exuberant kind of jig on the spot. The others in the group stopped their conversation as they watched this joyful reunion, smiling in that infectious way that happy laughter can incite.

Mrs Pentwick smiled. The doctor spoke to one of the men standing beside them enjoying the spectacle. "After six months in the close quarters of a sailing ship, it is difficult not to get to know the other passengers. These two men were always considered real gentlemen."

The pastor and the priest invited the congregation in. The Lutheran minister addressed the congregation, saying, "This is a rare occasion, when two clergymen from different denominations come together to preach and stand alongside each other. Both of us teach the word of God, we speak from the same Holy book, the Bible. I welcome my brother and all those who worship today under the same roof."

After the service, the German families invited the others to their shared meal. The feast had been set up under the large native trees left standing after much of the bush had been cleared for the buildings. The makeshift table was brimming with the products of their farms. Sliced black bread, freshly baked, was placed beside the churned butter. Various cheeses from cow and goat milk sat on wooden serving boards, with small knives to cut the portions. Pickled cabbage and cucumber in jars in the centre of the table gave off the astringent acidic odour of the vinegar and brine in which they had been preserved. Thinly sliced and minced smoked pork were on other wooden boards. At the end of the table all the delicious strudels and rich berry and cream cakes were placed in a row, as if in a competition for the best baker.

During the meal Bedelia and Michael took their plates of food and wandered away. They sat on a small wooden bench under some trees in the corner of the churchyard. They had so much news to catch up on, there was almost no break in conversation. When one was talking the other was eating and listening intently. Bedelia was so excited to share all she had learnt and the babies she had helped arrive safely into the world, and also to relate, sadly, the stories of those who hadn't made it. She told Michael all about where she was living and her connection with the German families.

When Michael got a rare break in Bedelia's dialogue, he told her that he and Keenan had found work on the many roads that needed to be constructed in the surrounding districts, including bridges. They had worked alongside many German men and others from the home country who were trying to earn as much money as they could while establishing land to farm.

"I heard from the *Hebamme's* son a little about your situation," Bedelia said. "His two elder brothers have worked with you. Their names are Freidrick and Hans. I just couldn't believe we were just over the valley from where you may be working."

Michael told Bedelia that with help from some local Māori men they had built temporary accommodation made from mānuka, flax and bracken fern. They squatted on a small area of cleared land unclaimed by settlers and built these dwellings, turning the site into a makeshift work camp. The group of men took it in turns to be camp cook, while the men with families, who lived too far away from their homes to go home every night, joined in the community.

Michael said that he and Keenan were considering moving to somewhere with warmer accommodation and more permanent work, in anticipation of avoiding the bitter cold of the previous winter. When work on the roads or money to pay them ran out, they got some work saw milling. That was only piecemeal work at the moment, as the land was slowly being cleared and the timber logged. They had heard of job opportunities to the north-east of the island.

Bedelia and Michael were reluctant to say their farewells but promised to meet again before the men moved out of the area.

Bedelia didn't stop talking all the way home. "I am lost for words to explain how much I have enjoyed the day, so I am," Bedelia said.

The doctor and Mrs Pentwick looked at each other, raising their eyebrows.

"Today has been so fun, filled with friendship, sharing of food, conversation and reuniting. Michael had so much to tell me I could hardly get a word in edgeways."

Mrs Pentwick had difficulty restraining herself, putting her kerchief to her mouth as her laughter spluttered into the embroidered cloth.

Bedelia was unaffected by the mirth. She prattled on, so absorbed in Michael's news that she didn't realise her companions were yards behind her, almost out of earshot.

As another autumn approached, Bedelia saw that there wasn't the stark shift from summer greens to vibrant orange, yellow and red shades like back in the home country. A light smattering of snow could be seen on the mountains surrounding the plains to the south and west.

To keep the home warm, piles of ready-cut wood was brought from here and there, recompense from the settlers who had used the doctor's services but had no means to pay in cash. These payments also included preserved pork turned into hams, assortments of pickles and ground flour from the mill just over the hill.

The household had a continuing supply of milk, butter and cheese from grateful patients. Any other items the doctor's household needed that could not be acquired in the small community was sent for. The general storekeeper in Nelson was happy to give credit to the doctor, such was the esteem Bedelia and the doctor's services had earnt. News and reputations spread through the whole community. There was little that went unnoticed.

A steady demand for the skills of both the midwife and the doctor meant their small surgery was rarely without someone needing tending to in one way or another.

One of the boats that travelled from the landing twice a week always carried someone from the area. Mr Wright and his son were the messengers and knew if anyone was going to town. The doctor just needed to write a note for that person, with a list of what was required, and it would be returned by the next boat if it had been obtainable.

Two more babies were born in the district, with Bedelia's assistance. All was well with both mothers and their new babies, and Bedelia stayed on in their homes for a few more days to care for the families while the mothers concentrated on the babies.

The person from the community going into Nelson, whoever that may be, would register a baby's birth on behalf of the family. The father would write the name of the baby, the date of the birth, his name and occupation at the time of the birth and his wife's name and details he wanted put on the registration. If he was not literate, especially in English, he would ask the doctor or Mrs Pentwick to write the note. It was always a proud day as a new addition to a family was officially registered and added to the New Zealand population records.

It had been months since Bedelia had spent those precious hours with Michael and Keenan. Despite having sent a message to Veronica to check in the general store in Nelson, she had received no news as to whether they had taken the trek over the eastern hills, on the rough track through to Marlborough, in search of work. She had often thought about how these men were faring and hoped she would hear from them soon.

The urgent rap on the door startled the household. They had just finished their evening meal. The day had only produced routine medical cases and there had been no emergency since little Danny's visit months ago. Bedelia jumped from her seat and was the first to reach the door. She was shocked to see her friends, and in such a state. Keenan's anxious look and Michael's pale face warned Bedelia of a dire situation. One of Michael's arms was draped over Keenan's shoulder as his friend supported him, his other arm was swathed in blood-soaked clothing.

"Doctor, come quickly," Bedelia called down the hallway.

As the doctor approached the front door, Keenan said, "We've been working in the saw mill over the hill, and Michael tripped with one of the logs and fell onto the blade. I fear it's not too good. I just wrapped it all up tight, got him onto the mill's cart and rode here like the clappers of a bell, so I did."

The doctor helped Keenan get his friend into the surgery, and he and Bedelia carefully removed the makeshift bandages to reveal the damage. The two middle fingers of the left hand were gone and the little finger was hanging by a thread. As the doctor dabbed the stumps there was a new wave of bleeding.

"Get the whiskey out of the cabinet, Delia," he said as he quickly wrapped the blood-soaked cloths back over the wound. "We'll need to get everything ready for cleaning and suturing. I don't want Michael to lose much more blood."

He told Bedelia that he estimated the amount he had already lost was significant judging by Michael's ashen face and his semi-consciousness.

Bedelia rushed back with the whiskey bottle and a clean cloth ready to bathe the hand. "A glass, dear girl," the doctor admonished with half a smile, "we don't want to waste a fine drop of Old Bushmill on the wound. We'll just use boiled water for the cleaning."

"The whiskey will help our friend endure the repair we need to perform and the workers will enjoy a dram after we finish the job," he said as he gave Keenan a wink.

Michael was lying on the table the doctor had set up for the repair of the injury. Bedelia had fluffed up the pillow, powerless to conceal her anxiety behind the usual straight face she had been able to keep in past emergencies.

She prepared all the instruments and clean clouts they would need. Mrs Pentwick brought in the bowl of clean, boiled water as requested. When the doctor exposed the wound the housekeeper made a hasty retreat.

As the doctor worked away, he told Bedelia that his first priority was to stem the bleeding. He praised Keenan for wrapping the wound tightly on the journey. "If you hadn't done that, my man, Michael would have been in a lot worse condition when you arrived."

Michael was still feeling some pain, but it had been greatly reduced with the help of three good drams of whiskey. Bedelia held his other hand when her help wasn't needed.

Keenen sat in the corner of the room looking at anything but the procedure going on. He was almost as pale as his friend. He had declined the doctor's suggestion to join the housekeeper in the kitchen.

"I won't leave Michael's side now, so I won't. I've made it this far after the accident and I won't be going away now," Keenan said.

The doctor surveyed the damaged hand with the hope that the little finger could be saved. As soon as the severed bone, blood vessels and nerves were exposed, he looked at Bedelia with a face that plainly said repairing the finger was not going to be possible.

"Michael," the doctor said, "there is no way I can save that finger. I have looked at every possibility and there is nothing for it but to remove it."

"It is equal to me then, Doctor, for I have no use for it hanging on a thread like that, more's the pity," Michael had slurred in his whiskey stupor.

Tears slid down Bedelia's cheeks as she watched Michael wince and react to the pain. She felt every stab of the needle and every slice of the scalpel as the third damaged finger was removed completely from its tenuous hold.

Many wood chip splinters had to be removed from the exposed tissue and dirt cleaned out of the wound. It was an exacting task, but necessary to avoid any problems with healing, the doctor explained. Completing his work, the doctor stitched the skin over the clean tissue and left Bedelia to finish by bandaging up the hand and immobilising it in a sling.

The doctor insisted the two men stay the night to see how Michael fared. Bedelia would not be persuaded to leave her friend through the whole night.

She remained on the chair beside him while he was made more comfortable on the table he had been operated on, with cushions and the quilt from her bed.

Keenan took his place on the floor of the veranda, with a spare blanket from Bedelia's bed. He told the concerned residents, "Why, myself and Michael, well we are used to hard ground with only canvas overhead. The floor of a warm house is a treat for us, so it is."

Michael slept fitfully through the night, and every time the pain got too much for him Bedelia would offer him another dram of the doctor's whiskey. Raising the hand lessened the throbbing, so she was constantly readjusting Michael's arm on the cushion she had positioned on his chest. The sling helped when seated, but was of little use when its wearer was lying down.

The doctor looked in to his surgery at first light and found Michael fevered and thrashing about. Bedelia was frantically trying to keep him covered. The noise had startled Keenan awake, and he had come in from the veranda to help Bedelia keep his friend from throwing himself off the table in his fits of delirium.

The doctor and Bedelia decided to get Michael into the doctor's bed, and with Keenan's help they managed to assist the big man to a safer place. Mrs Pentwick had quickly changed the linen on the bed "so it's clean and crispy for the special patient," she said.

Bedelia could not be dissuaded from keeping vigil. She once again sat herself on a chair beside the bed and ministered to Michael's needs through the following three days and nights. She quietly sang him the songs of Ireland that told of the beautiful green hills and valleys she had played on as a child. She described the Shannon River, passing through her village after wending its way through all the counties as it shared itself with the people of Ireland. Sometimes it ballooned into a wide lough, sometimes an insignificant stream would feed into it, but mostly it was a broad passageway for the river folk. Those watching from the shore would often wave to the passing barges.

Bedelia's heart lay bare on that bed. It lay alongside that big, beautiful man with the rich black hair and the fiery auburn beard. She could deny it no longer. She wished for this man to be the man she would spend the rest of her life with. Her only hope was, if he recovered, that he would feel the same.

Michael's fever persisted and the doctor wondered if he had left some debris in the wound that might be causing it. The doctor and Bedelia checked the wound. Besides the swelling of a healing hand and arm there was also an area of purulent ooze, which the doctor reopened to find a piece of wood splinter he had missed. The pus oozed out once the offending object had been removed. After giving Michael another dram of whiskey, Bedelia squeezed then irrigated the wound with boiled water to clean it out thoroughly.

The doctor said to Bedelia, "I'm pleased to find no red streaks travelling up Michael's arm, and there were no lumps under his armpit that may mean a more serious infection. The tissue around the rest of the stitches has remained a healthy colour also, so I am hoping I have removed the cause of Michael's ague in time."

On the fourth night, as Bedelia was nodding off to sleep, she was stirred from her half-slumber by a quiet request from her patient to sing again. "My darling Delia, your voice is so sweet and has kept me going, so it has. At times I could see you as my guardian angel and your songs were like those of cherubs from Heaven."

Bedelia jumped up and went closer. "Oh, Michael, I am overjoyed to hear you speak to me again and not in that delirious, fevered state. I was so afeared for you, I was. You appeared to be breathing for all like a corpse entirely. In my mind's eye I had you dead and buried and not a grey hair in your head."

The past few days had elicited all those memories and emotions that she had for so long suppressed. The good times had seemed beyond her reach, and she had been surprised when they had resurfaced as she prayed to the Holy Mother that her friend would recover from his ordeal.

Bedelia and Michael spent the rest of the night reliving all those special times in their lives before their innocence had been snatched from them, before they were forced to grow up and fend for themselves. They shared the feelings that were still there, the deep love for their mother country, their families now long-gone and that rich depth of culture embedded in who they truly were.

It was reliving the past and re-igniting their deep connection with Ireland that revealed the love that was blossoming between them. By the morning they could hardly imagine being apart. The bond was set, and they knew this was the first day of their new life together, however that would look.

When they arose that morning, the doctor and Mrs Pentwick looked in. "My goodness me," the doctor said, "look at you. It's hard to believe you're the same young man we left for dead last night."

Later in the day Keenan arrived back at the surgery. He had left his friend to return the horse and cart belonging to the mill. He expressed his surprise to see the change in his friend, from being close to death to only having eyes for Bedelia. Their relationship had been a slow movement in a melody, culminating in a love song crescendo overnight.

Chapter 19.

Michael could wait not a moment longer, and Bedelia was too smitten with overwhelming love for this man to do anything else but say, "Yes, oh yes," to his request to marry him.

There was a flurry of activity as plans were made. A message was sent to the Nations and to Veronica concerning the engagement of her younger sister. Finding a priest who would be willing to post the banns would be a difficult task, as Catholic priests were still itinerant, and there was no Catholic church in Nelson yet. The doctor was aware that Bedelia had no parents and therefore permission to marry would be needed from a legal guardian of which neither sister had here in their new country. The doctor offered to take on that role and Bedelia happily agreed.

The betrothed couple had now known each other for over two years. They had endured many peaks and troughs in their lives. Their friendship so far had been an enduring one, then in the blink of an eye it had become so much more.

Michael was still very weak, so he sent Keenan off on his behalf to search for a house and work that he could manage with his mutilated hand. The doctor felt he would be able to use his thumb and the remaining forefinger in such a way that it would not inhibit his ability to carry out most manual work, as long as the healing continued as well as it had up until now. In the meantime, the doctor insisted he rest and recover while remaining with them.

Once the message got through to Veronica, she returned on the next ferry. She stepped off the boat with a radiant face, excitement beaming from her eyes. Bedelia, who had walked down to the boat landing, flew into her sister's arms. "What good fortune is raining down on us, but two waifs from the workhouse in Scarriff," she said, when she finally released herself from their embrace.

They didn't bother taking the wagon up to the settlement. Bedelia decided they had far too much to tell each other. "The time it will take us to walk to the house will hardly be enough to allow us to share our news, and besides, I would rather avoid busybodies listening in," she said. "Oh, Vonnie, I never knew I could be so happy, I didn't. My heart surely feels like it could burst out of me bodice."

The sisters giggled.

"I can't believe I've known that man for all that time and, yes, I liked him, but marriage, who would have imagined?"

"Me," Veronica said with a glint in her eye.

"No, you never did." Bedelia looked aghast.

"Oh yes I did, and me being just a tiny bit jealous, so I was."

"Never," Bedelia said.

"Every time you spent time with Michael you were always going on with 'Michael this, Michael that'. It fair got my bile up."

Bedelia crossed her arms, raised her chin with a supercilious look and gave a little *humph*. "Well, I can tell you for certain, nothing but a friendship ever crossed my mind, it didn't." She lowered her arms and wrapped them around herself, twisting slowly this way and that, a dreamy look crossing her face as she told her sister, "I swear he is much more handsome than he ever was on that ship."

"I'm that pleased for you, Dee. There are no young gentlemen who take my fancy in Nelson, of that I'm sure."

"What do the Nations say? Do you think they approve?"

"They're a bit unsure as to whether you're too young, but they've seen what you're capable of and your ability as a midwife has given you the reputation of being responsible and proficient. At least, those are the very words they used at dinner time when the news got through of your betrothal."

"What would Mammy and Da say, Vonnie? Do you think they would agree to the marriage? And what would crusty old Father Doogan have to say about it, when he took time out from picking his nose with that old door key of his?"

That set the sisters off. They stood in the middle of the dirt track, hands on knees, rolling forward and back while they swung between hilarity and tears.

They clasped hands and continued up the road swinging their arms and skipping along freely. It felt to Bedelia like they were heading into the rest of their lives. She knew it would be a time of responsibility, of adulthood. Their lives would never be the same again. The sun was shining down, but the chilly wind reminded them that winter was still here.

When the sisters reached the house, they found Michael eagerly awaiting their return. "My, you're a canny one, Michael. I'm sure you didn't need to create quite such a mishap to sweep my sister off her feet, so you didn't,"

Veronica said with a wink and a smile. "I'm happy for you both and not a tad surprised."

There was much to do to prepare for the coming event. At Bedelia's request, Veronica bought some fabric for the dress the sisters would sew together for the wedding ceremony. Mrs Pentwick felt honoured to be asked to contribute to this task and help the young ladies with their creation. "Oh, how exciting it is for sure," Bedelia said as the women cut and stitched the gown.

The doctor and Bedelia continued to carry out their clinics as patients arrived on their doorstep with ailments and injuries. The maladies were mostly minor in nature, not requiring much more than some medicine, and the mishaps only a stitch or two and a dressing.

There were no more babies expected. The little community had grown so much that information as to the inhabitants' comings and goings was impossible to keep private. Even the plans for the upcoming marriage quickly spread.

The household eagerly awaited Keenan's return with news of work and possible accommodation for the soon-to-be newlyweds. When he did return, the news was not good. There was no work in the area, especially for a man with injuries to the vital hands that would prove his worth as a manual labourer. Houses were also in very short supply as more boats arrived with hopeful immigrants. Michael was determined that he would not be able to marry and provide for a wife until he could obtain a steady job and a roof over their heads.

Over dinner the discussion ensued. Bedelia talked about her abilities as a midwife that would at least bring them food to their table and a few minor necessities.

The doctor rose first as if to leave the table. "Let us go and enjoy the sunset with a whiskey, Keenan. Veronica and Mrs Pentwick, would you care to join us? We don't want to miss it. The clouds looked so spectacular last evening."

The four hastily withdrew and went to the other end of the house, shutting the kitchen door quietly as they went. Bedelia and Michael, so intent on their conversation, were oblivious to the others departing.

Michael said, "I do not want my wife's occupation to be what holds the family together, Delia. In my limited knowledge of a marriage, children will pop into our lives fairly soon after we start sharing a bed, and it would not do to have you working if you are in the condition. I will not have it." He banged the table firmly with his good hand. "I must be the one who provides for our family. Whatever it takes, I will find a way to do just that."

There was nothing more that Bedelia could say that would convince Michael otherwise. "No Delia, Keenan and I will be off to travel further afield to look for work and a home for us to live in."

A week later the sisters watched with heavy hearts as the ferry slipped away from the landing carrying Keenan and Bedelia's betrothed.

It was several days before Bedelia could even hold a needle to resume sewing the dress in which she would be wed. No amount of coaxing would lift her spirits, no matter what Veronica or Mrs Pentwick tried. She was in her own little world, imagining her newly found love dwindling away.

A visit from Magdalena and her mother finally pulled Bedelia out of her melancholy. They had heard of the betrothal and came to share in the excitement. When confronted with Bedelia's sad face they took from the container the black forest cake they had brought with them, filled with berry preserves and fresh cream from their house cow.

It was no time before the five women were chatting away in broken English and Plattdeutsch. Magdalena's English had improved so much, she even translated for her mother. Bedelia and Veronica had also gained more German words.

After only a short time Bedelia was sharing with her German friends the design she and Veronica had made for the dress. The older midwife offered her some of the homemade lace she had brought from Germany for a small veil. In fact, after some discussion, Frau Schwass offered to make the head-dress herself.

"*Ja, dat is good. Danke*, what kindness," Bedelia said to Frau Schwass. "I am truly humbled by the offer."

The lively afternoon tea lifted the spirits of everyone in the household. Later, after the *Hebammen* had left, the doctor sat at the table with the three women, enjoying the chatter about the visit while they ate their dinner. He wasn't at all inclined to retire to the other room. He sat back and listened to the banter between the sisters, saying very little himself. Mrs Pentwick seemed very much at home, often joining in the conversation.

The next Sunday the preacher, who was taking the service in the Lutheran church, approached Bedelia. He had heard of her betrothal and asked her about the reading of the banns, which he was aware was a custom of the Catholic church. "Father McGillivray only comes across from Wellington twice a year," he said.

The Christian denominations continued to work together amicably to share resources and provide meeting places. There was a Catholic family who opened their home in Nelson for prayers and rosary, but the rural areas worshipped together wherever they could.

Bedelia explained that reading of the banns would need to wait until Michael returned. In the meantime they would send a message to the priest with any further news as soon as they had made firmer plans.

The others in the congregation, who had come to know Bedelia, gathered to give her congratulations. She was quite the centre of attention, although she felt an uncertainty as to the success of Michael's search and their future plans.

As with other services, the settlers gathered to share a lunch. The conversations were mainly about the raising of a meeting place beside the church. Shelter was needed during inclement weather, as well as for large gatherings. This group of settlers had formed the community, and with many hands they toiled together on projects that would benefit all.

Bedelia hoped to settle with Michael in this area. It was so much like the community she recalled in her village in Ireland. She did understand that this hope may not be realised now, although she was certain she would choose life with Michael whatever that future may hold.

Chapter 20

Veronica had decided to stay on, with the doctor's permission. Mrs Pentwick's offer to go back to Nelson to help the Nations was gratefully accepted and so the temporary swap was once again made.

Bedelia noticed the doctor continued the habit of lingering at the meal table while the sisters' frivolity filled the kitchen. He would sometimes join in, but mostly he sat quietly, taking his time eating while Veronica and Bedelia chattered away.

Bedelia found that having her sister there was a great distraction from her worries concerning Michael. Veronica bolstered her with tasks in preparation for the coming nuptials and a future life together.

"Dee, we must get your hope chest filled while you have time. Let's be starting with some blankets. I've bought some fine wool, so let's get ourselves to it."

The newly spun wool was in hanks, so the doctor's hands were employed to hold the yarn while Veronica wound it into a large ball. They had their own wooden needles to do their knitting, brought all the way from home; one of the family treasures in their sea chest.

"Now, doctor, we've been rabbiting on about the old country and our clan and when we were young. We'd be wondering what you were up to as a lad," Veronica said with a glint of mischief in her eye.

"There's not much to tell that would interest you," the doctor said. "My childhood was very regimented, with my parents either working or at social events. Besides, children in my house were rarely seen and never heard."

Veronica chided the doctor. "Now be gone with you doctor, you cannot be telling me you and your brother never got up to any kind of mischief, can you?"

"Please call me George, Vonnie."

"I'm sorry, George, it's just the habit I have since we've called you doctor for so long."

"Yes," the doctor said, "we were normal little boys together, but our main activities were in the nursery and rooms above. Hide and seek was so much fun through all the big hallways, nooks and crannies and hidden rooms in the attic. Nanny was opposed to us getting our clothes dirty in case Mother or Father called for us to go downstairs to visit with them. We only had fun outside when we went to our country estate in the summer. We had this overgrown garden that was ideal for great imagined play of dragons, knights and highwaymen. Of course, we were off to boarding school so young and came home for only a short time in the holidays and at Yuletide."

The doctor came to an abrupt halt and Bedelia recognised the sadness in his eyes. His embarrassment evident on his face, he promptly made his excuses to retire for the night.

Veronica and Bedelia looked at each other in a short spell of stunned silence. Bedelia could only imagine being born into gentry and the culture of distance and propriety, when all she knew was the open, loving nature of her own parents. They had owned so very little, yet her mam and da had so much love to offer their family.

Bedelia was aware that the doctor had left the doors between the kitchen and his room ajar.

It wasn't long before the sisters were back to their shared memories of their childhood, roaming free through the countryside. The neighbours and family around were the community who watched out for them, kept them safe and out of too much trouble. Even the local garda, despite being a seemingly foreboding figure to be watched out for, would "just kick you up your arse and send you on your way," Bedelia reminded her sister, "with the threat of telling Father Doogan if he caught us up to any more mischief."

The sisters giggled at this memory, even remembering the feeling of the heavy leather boot skimming their bloomers as they fled through the hedge-row and across the fields. Bedelia recalled that at least they had something to confess when they saw the priest that Friday afternoon for their weekly penance of Hail Marys and Our Fathers.

Veronica and Bedelia made ready for bed. It had been a lively conversation, and they schemed to get more information out of the doctor about his life prior to emigrating.

Several days later Christian called for Bedelia to help at another birth. She collected her bag, donned her red cloak and headed out the door on her way to the stable, saying to Veronica, "Every time I'm called for, I get bubbles of excitement in my tummy. I don't quite know whether I have the nerves, the joy or the dread of something amiss. It's all mixed up, for sure."

She approached the stable door just as the doctor led the horse out, fully saddled and ready to go. Since the doctor had purchased the horse Bedelia had become more confident riding it. She took the mare and trotted off, following the young German lad on his gelding.

When they arrived at their destination, Bedelia was a little disappointed to find only the older *Hebamme* at the woman's side, as she was hoping to see her friend Magdalena as well. She had noticed the numerous moccasins in the cubby holes at the door and guessed that the woman had birthed many other babies. The small house was neat and tidy, with no children in sight. As she passed through the kitchen Bedelia recognised two women from the church gatherings who were busy preparing food.

"*Moin!*" they both said, pointing to a hallway and a room beyond.

"*Willkomen!* Bedelia, *dat is Fru Schmidt*," the *Hebamme* said as Bedelia entered the bedroom.

"*Moin, moin!*" said Frau Schmidt, weary lines across her brow and tired eyes looking back at Bedelia.

Bedelia took her place on the other side of Frau Schmidt. After some time, Bedelia realised that for someone who had birthed multiple times, the woman's labour pains were spread out and she was making slow progress. The *Hebamme* touched the woman's bulging abdomen and said "*slaap*" as she mimed a person yawning. Bedelia understood instantly what she meant.

"*Twölf Kinner.*" The *Hebamme* indicated with her ten fingers plus another two, as she shook her head slowly, looking tired herself. "*Slaap, slaap*," she said as she rubbed her own belly.

The *Hebamme* took out a vial. Bedelia could see what looked like a herb swimming in the tube of fluid. She did not recognise the floating sprig, but when the top was removed the liquid smelt like pickle juice. Bedelia was fascinated, recognising what she had been told was a herbal remedy used by the woman who attended her mother's births. She had asked her about it at the time, but this was the first time she had seen the like since.

The *Hebamme* carefully placed two drops of the liquid in a glass of water and encouraged the woman to drink it, then massaged the woman's belly in a firm circular motion. Round and round she went until Bedelia was beckoned to touch the protruding belly. Immediately she recognised the hard, contracting womb under the woman's skin, which remained like that for about a minute.

The *Hebamme* waited for three such tightenings, watching as Frau Schmidt worked hard to breathe through them. Bedelia noticed the attention the *Hebamme* was taking as to the frequency of these pains. She then put four drops in water for the woman to swallow.

The *Hebamme* went through the same procedure, rubbing, watching, waiting, timing, then doubling the drops again until she was satisfied that the pains had increased and were what Bedelia recognised as being more regular and predictable, like other confinements she had attended.

Frau Schmidt was standing beside the bed and the *Hebamme* was kneeling on it, supporting her from behind, encircling her arms above the bulge. The *Hebamme* indicated for Bedelia to kneel below the woman and be ready to receive the baby.

The *Hebamme* put downward pressure on the bulging abdomen from above. The waters broke and Bedelia's lap was drenched in the liquid that had protected the baby. The mother gave a loud grunt, and the next moment the new baby arrived in Bedelia's outstretched arms. The baby boy was stunned with the rapidity of his entrance into world, his eyes wide open and his mouth pursed, gulping like a fish out of water. Bedelia rubbed him down briskly with a warm clout, ready to assist him to breathe, but he let out a loud cry on his own. Realising she had been holding her breath for some time, Bedelia exhaled. She wrapped the baby in a clean, dry cloth then handed him up to his mother, who had slumped on the bed.

The *Hebamme* got to work straight away, using the herbal infusion in greater, but still carefully measured quantities. A large gush of blood followed the afterbirth, and the *Hebamme* vigorously rubbed the top of the womb, which Bedelia could see, by the placement of the *Hebamme's* hand, had reduced to the level of the woman's belly button. There were some clots expelled and the bleeding appeared to be reducing. Bedelia felt relief as she understood from the *Hebamme's* smile that, for now, the danger of bleeding was reduced.

Within the half hour the *Hebamme* took Bedelia's hand, laid it in a cupped shape high on the woman's belly and encouraged the young midwife to assess the state of the womb. There wasn't the hard ball shape she was expecting; just a spongy feeling akin to the dough of a large cob loaf ready to be kneaded down. It was situated a hand's width above Frau Schmidt's belly button.

"Rub, rub," said the *Hebamme*, mimicking the action Bedelia needed to do. "*Doller, doller,*" she said as she pushed Bedelia's hand harder into the boggy womb. A large gush of blood, along with two big clots, spurted out.

"*Nee!*" Frau Schmidt screamed as she grabbed Bedelia's wrist, trying to stop her from inflicting more pain on her.

"*Ja, Silke,*" the *Hebamme* said in a firm and authoritative voice as she unclasped the frau's fingers.

"*Doller, twee Hannen,*" the *Hebamme* said to Bedelia, "*doller.*"

Two more large clots were expelled with the deep massaging Bedelia was performing right into the woman's belly. She could feel the womb becoming rigid and reducing to the line of Frau Schmidt's belly button once again. Bedelia was surprised at the effort and strength required to carry out what she now knew was a life-saving procedure.

From what Bedelia had read in the doctor's book and already learnt for herself, she knew a woman bleeding in childbirth was of grave concern. She was now experiencing that a tired womb could continue to fill up with blood. Bedelia sensed that the danger for Frau Schmidt was not over yet.

She already knew the value of breast feeding in reducing the bleeding, and helped latch the baby to Frau Schmidt's nipple, holding him in place while the exhausted woman lay sleeping on her bed. The baby took no persuading and was suckling from his mother in no time at all while she snored, oblivious to her son's first feed.

On the way home, escorted by Christian once again as she was unfamiliar with the route they had taken, Bedelia pondered the events of the day. She believed, from reading and her limited experience, that Frau Schmidt would not have survived an unassisted birth this time. She was thinking that women's bodies were not built to endure so many assaults on it, run a busy home, farm and family. Frau Schmidt may have died of haemorrhage following her son's birth. There was a good chance the baby may not have survived either if the labour had been prolonged due to ineffective contractions. What a future for her surviving family without a mother.

Bedelia arrived home to find Veronica busy in the small kitchen. She had adeptly taken over Mrs Pentwick's role as cook. The doctor was completing his day in the surgery, therefore leaving the sisters to share their day.

"I took a wander up to the hill where I could look out over the bay. I do miss home, yet this land is creeping under my skin and into my bones. The sun is getting warm once again, so I'm thankful I wore my bonnet," Veronica said.

Bedelia related all that had transpired with the birth. She was expressing a maelstrom of emotions: in one breath she was brimming over with excitement, yet in the next, the seriousness of the situation was exposed. "It was touch and go. Yer know, Vonnie, it really is the mam who keeps the house humming along, for sure. That baby was her thirteenth." Bedelia said with great emphasis, "and twelve other children would have been left to care for themselves. The da would never have been able to work and keep that household running by himself. I kept thinking of Danny and Isy's da and our own da, when Mammy was taken with her baby. Da found it hard to manage our family. Maybe life would have been different for us if she hadn't had that last baby."

Veronica nodded as she turned to stir the gravy. Not soon enough, as Bedelia noticed the tears trickling down her sister's cheeks.

Quickly Bedelia said, "Vonnie, my heart surely soars when I see the little baby do what it needs to do to live, yet it skips a beat when trouble shows itself. Is there no way to stop popping those little ones out? I fear Frau Schmidt will be lost if she has another baby, and that's for sure.

"Do yer know," she continued, "for the love of Mary, mother of Jesus, I swear Mammy must have just been worn out when she went to Heaven with her baby. What with all the troubles, there must be another way to stop having babies other than leaving this earth, I feel sure there must."

"Now stop all that swearing, Dee. I am thinking your manners have all gone to the devil for sure."

Bedelia ignored the chastisement. "As much as I love helping babies come into this world safe and sound, I feel bound to help the mother know when enough is enough."

Looking at her younger sister, Veronica went over to where she sat at the table, putting her arms around her from behind in a tight embrace.

Veronica had resumed her preparations when the doctor entered, the smell of the cooked roast mutton and vegetables filling the room. Veronica stirred the brown liquid in the dish as it bubbled and thickened from the edges in.

Bedelia was laying the table and the doctor sensed he had intruded on an intense and intimate conversation. "Tell me all about the birth," he said. "I hope it wasn't as dire as your face betrays."

"I can't say it was dandy, but I did learn so much from Frau Schwass. I was very concerned about the woman; she is past having babies. Is there something we can do? I was telling Vonnie, I swear, for Christ's sake, if there's another baby that mammy will be done. Oh, pardon me doc … I mean George, for my mouth," Bedelia spurted out, looking at her sister in a contrite manner.

The doctor hesitated as he watched for Veronica's response. When she smiled, unreactive, as she continued her meal preparation he said, "It is something that I feel would be beneficial for us to discuss later. It is important for your ongoing knowledge in caring for mothers after their confinement, but it is a delicate subject best left until we have more time."

Bedelia rattled on. "The *Hebamme* gave a special concoction to … to make the womb work better to get the baby out and to help stop the bleeding, and alongside the rubbing of the womb that you have shown me, we managed to save the mammy. Mind, the rubbing we had to do was a tad more serious and brutal. It brought back nasty memories of that poor soul Maureen. I felt so helpless on the ship when you were poorly and I had to deal with it all by meself. It was the loneliest feeling caring for her that night, without help. Maybe it would have ended differently if only I'd known what to do."

Just as quickly as she had shared her sad moment, Bedelia changed tack and said, "What on earth was the herb I saw in her vial? Do yer think it may have helped Maureen?" Bedelia described the wheat-like twig floating in the sharp-smelling liquid.

"That, my dear, I believe may have been ergot. It is a fungus that grows on rye and has been used for many years by midwives. It is mostly used to stem childbirth bleeding, but it can be used to abort an unwanted baby."

Veronica looked shocked, but it didn't stop Bedelia interrupting. "The *Hebamme* used it very carefully. It worked a treat. Then with the help of her firm and downward pressure at the top of the womb the baby plopped out to meet us. It was grand.

"I don't know if Maureen's death could have been avoided; I believe her afterbirth was stuck firm, which was the cause of her bleeding. It appears that the *Hebamme* is proficient with the use of the herb. I have some in my bag," the doctor said, "although many of my colleagues do not carry it. I rarely have need of it, but it has to be used very carefully. In the wrong hands, without full knowledge as to its properties and what it can do, it can cause more harm than good."

The doctor looked towards Veronica. She was stirring the gravy pot vigorously, with a frown on her face. "We will spend some time discussing this soon," he said. "Right now, my mind is on the taste of that meal your sister is preparing, it smells so delicious."

Bedelia pondered the information about the ergot and decided to ask the *Hebamme* for the recipe and correct use for this valuable medicine.

"Dinner's on the table and getting cold," Veronica said with a look directed towards Bedelia. "I'm not sure I need to hear any more of this talk." The doctor smiled and nodded.

After dinner Bedelia couldn't help but have the final word on the affair. "You have to hear this, Vonnie, it'll surely make you giggle. It's nothing too gory, that I promise."

Bedelia proceeded to tell the doctor and her sister that after the birth the *Hebamme* and Bedelia had stayed on for some time to make sure that the bleeding was not going to recur. They passed the hours by discussing, in their limited understanding of each other's language, how Frau Schmidt had birthed all her other babies with no assistance from a *Hebamme*. Ten had been born in Germany, one on the ship to New Zealand and the last one was caught by her eldest daughter.

"The story was quite the talk of the community," Bedelia recounted. "I had already heard something about it from Sophia, so I had. Well, the young girl, the daughter, had been asked by Frau Schmidt, her mother of course, to come into her bedroom when she called. This is true, I'm sure, for Frau Schwass said so. By the by, she was told to put her hands between her mother's legs to catch the baby and hand it to her. When this was done the daughter was told she could leave. Can you imagine, Vonnie, the daughter up until then had no idea where babies came from, let alone that her mother was about to produce another family member." Bedelia laughed, while Veronica and the doctor looked at each other and smiled.

The discussion changed to a more congenial nature. They shared favourite meals from their childhood, Sunday activities and the Catholic culture. The doctor had been raised in the Church of England, but boarding school rituals had taken the religious fervour from his life. He still named his religion on official documents, but he seldom darkened the door of any of God's houses but the friendly Lutheran church he had attended with Bedelia.

The sisters had fun explaining the Catholic faith to the doctor. They told him that the priests were an object of mirth intermingled with fear as they preached their Hell, fire and damnation from the altar. Bedelia related the special days of the first holy communion and confirmation and the lies she told in the confessional because she didn't have any sins to confess.

"Forgive me Father for I have sinned. It has been one week since my last confession." The girls went off in peals of laughter as they gave a snippet of some of the sins they had invented.

" 'Impure thoughts' was often a good one to use, with most of us not even knowing what impure thoughts were," Bedelia said. "Mary O'Halloran, our old school friend, spent many hours in the playground sharing the list of the sins her older brother had taught her. The best one, that really happened, was when he looked under the door of the girl's toilet. That really got him the works for penance. Twenty Hail Marys, twenty Our Fathers and ten Glory Be's, and he got the cane from the nuns and a thrashing from his da when he got home." Bedelia threw her head back in wails so prolonged and infectious that all three were laughing with tears of mirth dribbling down their cheeks.

The mood was set, and many more hilarious memories were shared. The doctor looked embarrassed by some of the conversation, yet he remained at the table, smiling and listening as Bedelia and Veronica relived the happy memories from their childhood.

It was time to clear the table and head to bed. Bedelia noticed that the doctor seemed a little sad that the evening had ended. She had never seen him laugh so much in all the time she had known him.

Chapter 21

As the weeks passed with no news from Michael, Bedelia became quieter and quieter. Veronica and the doctor could not coax much interaction out of the usually effervescent young lady. Bedelia picked at her food, hardly joined in the conversations around the table and carried out her tasks in silence. Her gloom seemed to be seeping into the hearts of her sister and the doctor as their conversations waned.

The weather had become very warm, so Veronica planned a picnic on the beach. She made a bacon and egg pie and some sandwiches and baked some oat biscuits. She packed it all in a basket wrapped in an embroidered linen cloth; one of the treasures she had of her nan's. She also rolled up a blanket to place on the ground. She told Bedelia she was rather excited to get out of the house.

Despite some opposition from Bedelia, the three set off in the surrey that had been made for the doctor in part-payment for services rendered to the German community. It had been delivered to them the previous week. The doctor had made up the difference in the cost as the wagon would be extremely useful for attending patients at their homes.

The horse was able to pull the load with all of them on board. The sun was out to greet them with only a few white, fluffy clouds passing overhead. Teasing the sisters about having a swim, the doctor got the first reaction from Bedelia in days. "I have my bathers on already, under my tunic," she grinned at Veronica with a nod. "Just wait, if you don't come in with us you'll be swimming in your suit, George, and that's for sure. It is such a lovely day it's quite impossible to be gloomy, so it is." Veronica and the doctor smiled to each other.

After the doctor had tied the horse to a shady tree with a little grazing underneath, they found a spot on the shore where they could enjoy the vista of the bay. The golden sand spread out before them, fringed by the gently lapping sea as if a painting had been cut out and pasted in front of them. There was even a small sailing yacht catching the gentle breeze as it wafted across the water.

"It's just the tonic I needed," Bedelia said.

The party of three made the most of their day out. They set off to travel home, damp, sandy and a little weary from their playful frolics in the water. Before they had gone far Bedelia spotted two familiar figures hiking up the road. The taller man had an unmistakeable gait that set Bedelia's heart into a flutter. As they drew near to them it took all the doctor's strength to stop Bedelia from leaping out of the wagon as he reigned in the horse to a slow trot.

"Michael, Keenan," Bedelia called out. They turned to their names, and Michael caught his betrothed in his arms as she leapt towards him.

The doctor and Veronica carried on in the surrey while Bedelia, Keenan and Michael followed on foot. Bedelia never let up once to give either of the men a chance to speak. All the way home she told them what had happened in the time they had been away.

That night around the dinner table, Michael and Keenan recounted their search for work. There were plenty of labouring jobs requiring brawn, but Michael was not up to the task yet. They had tramped all the way to the east, to a beautiful valley that was being opened up for farming. The township had just been established and was well behind Nelson in its development.

Between them the two men had brought a small amount of money from the old country and decided to put it together to start a general store, much needed in a small farming community. They were considering taking out a loan with the bank and had started drawing plans to construct the building and had already sent back to England on a departing ship for supplies to stock the store.

Keenan, in his own quiet way, related the turmoil Michael had experienced when he had been turned away from job after job. "He was a sorry man, and I was quite at a loss for how to draw him out of it, so I was."

Veronica and the doctor smiled to each other and nodded, turning their heads to look at Bedelia.

Bedelia was excited at the prospect of life with her beloved in a new community, yet wary about what it would mean for her and her developing career. She felt she had a purpose in life here and was starting to make a name for herself and earn respect from the community she was serving. She had found her niche as a budding midwife. She felt more confident and competent, and she was learning new skills every day. What would happen to her, she thought, if she followed her heart to a life as a wife and probably a mother, in this world where only the man of the house earned a living?

She was so pleased to see Michael that she did not share her thoughts until she was in bed that night. "Vonnie, I have not a clue what to do. My heart strings have such a pull from the man I love and yet I have a real passion to help new mothers and babies survive. Giving birth and being born appear to be the most dangerous times in our lives. If I know how to help prevent the troubles that I can, then I must do it. I can't think of a more rewarding thing to do in my life. Is it at all possible to do both?" Bedelia added.

"I do believe that is something for you and Michael to decide together, Dee. No one can do it for yer. Rest and leave it for tomorrow. Sometimes decisions like these need to be slept on." With that, Veronica turned over and closed her eyes.

For Bedelia, sleep was more elusive and her night was not at all restful.

Michael and Keenan had turned down the offer of staying in the house. "Why, we will sleep in our bivvy the night," Michael had insisted. "We are quite used to a good night's sleep in this balmy weather under the canvas, as long as we can keep the night's dew off our blankets." In the morning they had boiled up their own billy, cooked their breakfast and eaten it on the log outside.

"They seem more comfortable with that arrangement than eating with us," Bedelia said, slamming her plate of cooked oats on the table so hard that the milk slopped over the side.

"Dee, they're just used to making do like that," Veronica said.

"They are just plain rude," Bedelia responded with a tear in her eye. "I was so happy to see them and now look how I feel. I'm sure they'd rather be elsewhere."

"Not at all, my dear," the doctor interjected. It was so unusual for him to share his opinion that the sisters stopped what they were doing and listened carefully. "Sometimes words cannot express the uneasiness a man feels when he has two minds about something. We're not as free in the tongue as you ladies are, for telling it how it is. It is a gift I have noticed women have."

Veronica and Bedelia glanced at each other with a bewildered look. Bedelia had a faint memory of their mam chiding their da for not speaking plainly and expecting others to understand what was going through his mind. "Men!"

their mam would say with that exasperated tone the girls weren't quite able to understand at the time.

Later in the morning Keenan and Michael could be heard chopping wood. They were stacking it neatly in the small lean-to the doctor had erected. The sisters decided to leave them to their task and set to preparing lunch.

They chose to bake a cake and cook a hearty soup made with leeks, potatoes and milk from the cow one of the local farmers had loaned them out of gratitude. Bedelia had tended his wife giving birth and the doctor ministered to their sick children.

The smells emanating from the kitchen drew the men in, and Veronica poured each of them a strong brew from the big teapot on the stove. After eating they sat around the table with not much being said until Bedelia blurted out the question that had been sticking to her tongue, so ready to be said.

"Well, what of it, Michael? What's it to be? Are we ready for the banns to be read or just be done with our plans?"

The others discreetly exited the room with excuses of tasks they needed to attend to.

"I cannot yet fulfil my promise to take care of you in the way I mean to. My damaged hand changes everything, and I must be sure that I can provide for you and the family we may have. I love you, of that I am sure and that is why it must be so."

"But I want to and can help. I am needed to help these women in their troubles, and I have learnt so much. I know I can help." Bedelia looked at Michael with such sincerity.

Michael took Bedelia's hands in his and said, "No, my dear. I must be the one who earns the money, for I am hoping that there will be a large family to provide for. You will be needed at home for them. Have patience and it will work out for the good. Now let's finish up our cake, for there are things to do."

They sat at the table in silence. Bedelia nibbled at her slice of cake, then she cleared the dishes from the table, clattering the cups and plates and slamming them down on the bench.

"Damn him," she said to Veronica in bed that night. "I am not going to be one of those poor women that I tend, who keep churning out babies until their bodies get too tired to go on. I have a gift, and whether he likes it or no, I'm going to use it."

This prompted no reply from Veronica. The sisters bid each other goodnight.

An uncomfortable silence reigned over the household, and the two men made plans to leave. There were no promises of when they would return. They had plans and needed time to organise these and take action.

That night at dinner, after they had all complimented Veronica on her cooking, the doctor spoke. He had stayed quiet with all the tension in the air in the last few days.

"I want to make a proposal. Would you be prepared to hear it and then ponder your decision?"

The other four turned to each other, surprised looks on their faces, and nodded.

"I am the only son of a wealthy family. Once both my parents died, I inherited a large estate. I have very few happy memories of my life in England. Therefore, when my great friend Stephen wrote telling me of his life in New Zealand, being curious as to its possibilities I decided to take the unprecedented move to emigrate.

"With what I have experienced here and the people I have met so far, I am sure I will lay down my roots in this country, as the land of my birth has no longer any hold on me. I have been fortunate to have found an ideal place to live and work and have formed lasting connections like the ones I am making with you and the community that is burgeoning before our eyes."

The others sat there stunned. This dialogue was the most they had ever heard at one time from the doctor. They listened intently as he continued to speak.

"So, to get to the point, this community is lacking a general store for supplies. We have to wait for them to come from Nelson or further afield. Michael and Keenan, you are looking at setting up such a facility and service further away. Would you consider an offer from me to finance the building here in this community, with you as long-term tenants? I would benefit from it in more ways than one. The first would be as an investment, and the second, of course Michael, is if you would agree to have your future wife continue as my assistant and midwife. I have seen that Frau Schwass has produced a large healthy, happy family and worked to serve her community as their midwife. I have every faith that we can assist Bedelia to do the same.

"So, there it is. I will leave you all to go away and discuss my suggestion. I can assure you this is something that will be of mutual benefit to us all."

Bedelia burst into tears, overwhelmed that a solution to their dilemma was right under their nose. Michael stood and went to her, embracing and reassuring his weeping betrothed. The doctor, Veronica and Keenan slipped quietly out of the room. As Bedelia sobbed Michael patted her back. "There, there, everything will be all right. We'll make it work Delia, I'm sure we will." After some time Bedelia looked up, and the love of her life kissed her.

When they finally separated, they sat at the table and started making plans.

After they had absorbed the doctor's offer and given a unanimous "Yes", there was much to do to build their store and stock it with all the requirements of a fast-growing settlement. Keenan and Michael listened to suggestions from the young ladies as to what women would wish to purchase when visiting the store. The sisters were excited to have some input in the plans. It did create a little hope for Bedelia as to what her future would hold, but there was still that nagging doubt as to her role in the new life Michael had envisioned for them both.

Michael and Keenan needed to spend some time away sourcing all the materials and skilled people they would need to build the store. After they and the doctor had found a suitable site close to the surgery that was available for purchase, all three men went to town to set up the necessary legal and financial matters involved in a business agreement.

Bedelia felt sure that the community would continue to grow as more settlers arriving in Nelson harbour made their way throughout the land. Each arriving family needed to travel further afield to find a place for themselves and a job, or if they had enough money, to purchase some available land. A general store would be an asset and a necessity.

As the population increased, so the doctor's surgery become busier. When she was not needed for births Bedelia was employed by the doctor in many different nursing and assistant roles.

Women would come in to organise for her to attend their births as the families continued to grow. Bedelia was constantly amused by the clandestine language of pregnancy. "Taken poorly". "In the family way". "The arrival of a little stranger". It was not plainly talked about other than behind the closed doors of the surgery. The design of pregnant women's clothes would hide any bulges. The physiology of conception, pregnancy and childbirth were taboo subjects, even between the expectant couples.

Bedelia's name and reputation as a competent midwife spread throughout every kitchen, sitting room and bedroom in the district. Her forthright advice on all matters to do with reproduction was kept solely between the women. She continued to work alongside the *Hebammen* when required, but she was also consistently working alone. There was plenty of work for everyone.

Sometimes she would take Veronica with her as an extra pair of hands, but her sister would always find something that needed doing with the rest of the family they were attending, or would help in their kitchen, away from the birthing sounds coming from the bedroom. It was only on rare occasions that Bedelia would summon Veronica to help.

On one of these occasions Bedelia had managed the birth, but she needed Veronica to watch the mother, whose bleeding was continuing to be of some concern. Bedelia called out for her sister. "This is Hope, Vonnie," she said as she showed her how to rub the top of the uterus, explaining to both women why it was required. Bedelia needed to tend to the baby boy, who had been through a prolonged and difficult birth and was having trouble breathing.

Bedelia had learnt from the doctor how to find the baby's heartbeat with her fingers, what this would feel like and how fast it would normally run. This baby's pulse was much slower than she knew it should be and the baby was gasping for breath. Bedelia knew she needed to act fast.

The baby was still quite blue. The reassuring progression to pink of a healthy newborn baby was not happening. Bedelia tried sucking, in the way she knew how, to dislodge any mucous that may be obstructing his windpipe, to no avail. She tried gently puffing air into the baby's lungs, but neither the colour nor the breathing improved.

Bedelia felt for the heartbeat again. It was still only about as fast as an adult's rate, and it had an unusual beat that Bedelia did not understand. There wasn't an even rhythm to it. She wrapped the baby in more warm cloths after changing the wet ones and continued to puff air to fill the baby's lungs. The heart rate became faster, but the baby remained blue.

The mother's bleeding had settled and her growing concern for this baby's well-being motivated her to send Veronica for the doctor. "Just ride the horse. Please get him back quickly, for I fear for this little one." The surgery was only a twenty-minute ride away. The horse was in the family's barn with the surrey unhitched.

The urgency in Bedelia's voice alerted the mother to the dire situation. "What's happening to my baby? Is he all right?" she said. "Please ask Geoffrey to come in." Bedelia nodded to Veronica as she left the room, and in only a few seconds the woman's husband entered.

Bedelia explained the situation to the new parents as best she could between the ministrations to their baby. "I'm not sure what's happening with your baby. He has had a difficult journey into this world, he has, and he's not acting as I know he should. I have sent for the doctor who is skilled in the care of babies."

The baby started gasping again, so Bedelia resumed helping him to breathe. She wondered how effective this was, but she couldn't just sit back and watch the little boy struggle.

Within the hour the doctor arrived. He rushed in with his medical bag and found Bedelia close to tears as she continued to grapple to keep the baby alive.

She had wrapped the little boy in a woollen blanket with only his chest visible. With a cursory glance at the baby's blue lips and hands, the doctor nodded to Bedelia and tapped her reassuringly on her arm. He took over from Bedelia, who slumped down on the chair.

The mother, by now, was sitting up in bed. The concerned look on her face remained, her husband's face mirroring hers as he sat beside her holding her petite hand.

The doctor completed a full examination of the baby. He then listened to his heart with his stethoscope, a hollow wooden and brass tube about twelve inches long, which splayed out like a bell at one end. He placed this on the chest of the newborn infant while he put his ear to the opposite end. He explained to Bedelia his findings and he directed his words to the new parents also. "Listen to the heart sounds, Delia. They are not the usual lub, dub as the little organ pumps the blood through; there is an audible whoosh. That means the valve in the wall between the two chambers of the heart has not closed. This needs to happen at birth when the baby takes its first breath. Rarely, it does not."

"What are you telling us, Doctor?" said the baby's father. "Please tell us our son will live."

"I'm very much afraid that I cannot tell you this. The baby cannot survive. He needs the oxygen from the lungs to be pumped through the body and this isn't happening. There's nothing I can do to save your son. I suggest you hold your baby and spend his last hours with him. I'm sorry that I can't do more for you. If that is too painful for you, Bedelia and I can take him into another room until his time on this Earth is done."

"Are you wishing to have him baptised? There is no priest handy, but I do know the words and that will help his soul to pass beyond the gates," Bedelia said.

The parents chose to spend their son's last minutes with him cradled in their arms. They asked Bedelia to bless their son in the way she knew how. Bedelia and the doctor then left the room to give the parents time with their dying son.

Tears were streaming down Bedelia's soft cheeks. The emotion and the futility of this situation was not lost on the doctor. They sat in silence for some time before the wailing from the bedroom told them the inevitable had happened.

They took their time before they re-entered the bedroom, where both parents were sobbing over the lifeless bundle in their arms. Bedelia very gently took the little boy from his mother and father. She washed and dressed him in the gown that had been prepared before the birth. She put a bonnet on his head and wrapped him in the shawl that hands had knitted in anticipation of his arrival. She laid him in the wooden crib his father had lovingly made for him and placed it beside the bed.

After seeing the doctor off with reassurance that she would rest soon, Bedelia tended to the mother. She fed Hope and Geoffrey and they all fell into exhausted sleep, Bedelia in the bed in the room next door.

Bedelia stayed on for the wake, which was a grim affair. It is so much harder when death happened to one so young, so loved and anticipated. Bedelia took some days to come out of her exhausted silence on returning home. Despite knowing there was nothing she could have done, her mind was still full of the "what ifs".

"Why was the baby blue, and what made the heart sound so unusual?" Bedelia didn't wait for the doctor to answer as she carried on. "Why did he struggle to breathe and how long can a baby like that stay with us?" Still Bedelia left no time for reply. "Was there anything more we could have done?"

The doctor spent some time combing through the literature in order to show Bedelia what had happened. They found the sections on the circulatory system of a baby before and after birth, and that critical reversal of the flow of blood through the heart, lungs and body when the baby took its first breath.

"We cannot know why the miracle of life happens or doesn't, Delia. God moves in mysterious ways and we, as his servants, only have a small role to play in that," the doctor said.

Chapter 22

Veronica and Mrs Pentwick had conversed by mail. Veronica shared the letters with Bedelia and the doctor. The Nation family were pleased that the older woman had decided to make her home in Nelson and accept their offer to be their housekeeper. She felt another long ship journey back to a life without her husband was not the best choice at her age.

The doctor was more than pleased to share his home with Veronica and Bedelia. They were now well-known in this small settlement and the arrangement appeared to quell unwanted gossip.

Days turned into weeks. The doctor and his two companions made the most of their free time exploring the surrounding beaches. The area had a temperate climate. They had their favourite picnic spots, and even if they came across some of their patients, their time off was well-respected and they were mostly left alone.

The doctor had become completely relaxed in Bedelia and Veronica's company. He told them, "It is like a breath of fresh air having you around. I have never been so content." At first their open discussions had been quite foreign to him, but now he joined in. "Your laughter is free and contagious. You make me feel as if I have been welcomed into your family," the doctor said.

The sisters smiled at each other. Bedelia said, "Well, George, you were a tough egg to crack, but you have been such an asset to my life and learning."

"My skill for human interaction is the reverse of yours," the doctor said. "I may have a full and comprehensive intellectual knowledge, yet I lack the understanding of a person's emotional needs."

Bedelia saw him differently. "When you talked to Hope and Geoffrey about what was happening with their baby, you showed true compassion. I heard how caring you are," she said. They were having their usual post-dinner discussion, re-living the profound experience for them all.

The doctor looked rather pleased with the compliment, although he said to the sisters, "I have a lot to learn. I am hoping to pick up some of your natural ability to interact with others from all walks of life. My life has been peppered with disdain. My brother and I were often disciplined for the most minor of misdemeanours and we were strongly discouraged from spending time with our parents and their peers. After my brother died it was easier to just spend time alone. That way, I didn't open myself to ridicule."

"Well, I am surely pleased I didn't grow up with money and status," Bedelia said. "Even the girls in the workhouse and then Therese and the others on the ship: we all had nothing, yet we had so much fun and laughter. Jesus, Mary and Joseph would have been shocked at what came out of our mouths sometimes, now wouldn't they, Vonnie?"

Veronica nodded, then raised her head and her eyeballs at the same time. "I quite gave up trying to set Dee straight. It just seemed to spur her on to blaspheme even more."

Veronica started giggling, as if remembering the futility of trying to tame her unruly sister.

"Initially I was shocked at the openness of your language, Delia, but it wasn't long before I was intrigued and a little envious of your ability to call a spade a spade. Sometimes you seemed so light and innocent, yet in the next breath so worldly and forthright," the doctor said.

Bedelia shrugged her shoulders, "No use beating around the bush, George. If you've something to say, it's best to say it right then and there."

One night the discussion changed abruptly as Bedelia recounted the story of the old Irish midwife telling her mam about a very young girl she was tending. The young colleen said "I'm so afeared. I'm not sure what to do as I don't know where the baby will come out." The midwife replied, "The same feckin' way it went in." Bedelia and Veronica roared with laughter.

The doctor quickly excused himself and when he reached his room he let out a whoop of suppressed laughter even the sisters could hear from the kitchen, above their din.

They had received only the occasional visit, but towards the end of summer Michael and Keenan spent the day at the doctor's home. Michael was more serious during this visit.

"I am ready to settle down now, Delia," he said. "We have the store almost ready for trade, with an area upstairs to live. Stock is arriving from the old country and we have agreements from local farmers to sell some of their produce. I will meet with Father McGillivray, who I hear is in Nelson, and will post the banns over the next few weeks. I have decided that you can help in the store, and when our family starts, well, you'll be right there."

Bedelia couldn't hide her feelings as she blurted out, "Well, Michael Mahoney, is that it? You have decided for us. What about myself, do I not have a say in the matter?"

"Well, I thought ..." Michael stammered, stunned by Bedelia's reaction.

"You know what thought did. He followed a muck cart and thought it was a wedding." Bedelia spat the words out.

Yet again the others in the room made a hasty exit with even more inventive excuses as to the tasks they needed to perform.

Michael sat there unable to answer Bedelia's questions. She sat opposite him, her lips pursed and her arms on her hips.

"So, what about me? I have made a name for myself here and I'm liking it. I don't just want to be the wife popping out babies for the Pope, I want to mean something to folks who need me. I love you Michael, but I love my midwifing and I am getting good at it. I can't just throw that away now."

Michael slowly looked up from his hands and said, "A man must be the provider for his family. Otherwise, what will people say?"

"We can do things differently. This is a whole new world. We have left the old one behind. We can make a new start, and if we have that real love for each other, we can do anything, so we can.

"Why," she continued, "I have seen how strong and brave women are, and I know I can be a good wife, have a few babies and care for others in the family way as well. But I can tell you now, and that's for sure, I am not going to be popping babies out every year until I die from it.

"Please Michael, let us just try to work this out. We love each other enough to weather the storms and other people's opinions. There are sure to be plenty of mountains on our way, but we can climb each one as we come across it."

Veronica returned to the kitchen to prepare lunch. She found Michael and Bedelia crying in each other's arms, big smiles on their faces.

"Come now, we can't have that unseemly behaviour in here. Be off with the both of you and walk the matters off. It will give you some time together, something that has been sorely missing by the both of you," Veronica said as she shooed them out the door.

When they arrived back at the house, the smell of fresh buns was coming from the kitchen. They both sat on the free bench and tucked in.

"We've decided to have a talk to Father and go ahead with the banns, then we will have the wedding when he's here next," Michael said. "That way it will give us more time to prepare our new home."

Veronica clapped her hands and she embraced her sister. "Oh, thank Jesus for that, but I was so afeared that you would call the wedding off."

Keenan and the doctor joined the congratulatory exchange and then resumed their meal. The conversation immediately went to the organisation of the event, and where they would hold the ceremony and the wedding feast. The doctor insisted on paying for the food and was rather overcome when Bedelia asked him to lead her up the aisle.

Veronica wanted to discuss the stitching of her own dress and which shoes she would wear. She had all of two pairs to choose from. The sisters giggled and huddled together making plans for the guest list.

"Of course, we'll ask the German families and the Nations. Do you think we should send a message to Mrs Pentwick? What about asking if we can use the Lutheran church and hall?" Bedelia carried on with her staccato chatter as she thought of more and more things to consider.

Veronica smiled while she listened to her younger sister prattle on. She was so pleased for her, and only hoped that she, too, would meet a suitable husband before long.

Life continued as usual, other than the added excitement of the preparations for the wedding and the shift to the new accommodation where Michael, Bedelia and Keenan would establish their new home and store.

Michael and Keenan took their leave to complete setting up the business. Keenan was a dab hand at carpentry, and had talked about his intention to set to making items required to furnish a home. He would also add partitions to the area on the floor above the store so the living, kitchen and dining area was separate from the bedrooms.

Bedelia wished to see where she was going to be living and to make plans as to what she would need to set up her home. She said she wanted to leave the men to organise the store and the merchandise they would be selling. Michael returned for her, and they set off together for a day.

The general store was only three miles away from the surgery, within easy walking distance. It was positioned on a rise in the road opposite a hotel under construction, which was also nearing completion. Keenan and Bedelia discussed the layout of the rooms and where he would need to put up the partitions. The vista from the store and the hotel was quite spectacular, Bedelia thought. From the upstairs room where she chose their sitting room and bedroom to be, there was an uninterrupted view of the bay. It was north facing, and would capture most of the day's sun.

Michael and Bedelia had seriously discussed how they could incorporate Bedelia's working with running the store, and the possibility of working around an ever-growing family. Veronica had offered her help, and they all agreed there would be enough suitable people looking for work to assist in the running of the business.

Bedelia burst into the kitchen to tell Veronica all about the store, the home she was to share with Michael and who knew how many children, and how Keenan would be a part of their lives and help with the children or the store when she was called to births. She hardly drew breath with all the news.

It was minutes before she realised there was a fundamental change in her big sister. There was a lightness in the way she performed her tasks in the kitchen. There was almost a little skip in the way she moved around the room.

The doctor walked in after hearing Bedelia's breezy entrance. So much had happened in one day, but it had been devoid of Bedelia's exuberant presence.

Bedelia turned towards the doctor, who had joined Veronica at the side of the table, gently taking her hand.

"What's going on here?" Bedelia said. "I leave you both for a jiffy and … Hold yer horses. There is something going on here, and that's for sure."

Veronica was the first to answer. "We are to be married, Dee."

Bedelia threw her arms around the doctor, for he was standing closest to her. When she was done shocking him, she took her sister by the waist and they danced around the kitchen table, squealing, laughing and crying in jubilant celebration.

The doctor stood there with a smile so broad Bedelia thought he looked like a cat who had just swallowed the cream. When the din finally settled and normal conversation was able to resume, the doctor joined the sisters at the kitchen table and told Bedelia of their day.

While Bedelia had been away, a young lad had been brought in from his farm. He had been harvesting hay with his father and brothers when the scythe his brother had been using sliced his tendon at the base of his calf. The doctor had been impressed with how the family had done all the correct things at the time of the accident. They had washed the wound out, tying a very tight strip of cloth at the knee to stem the bleeding and brought him directly to the doctor.

The brothers carried him in and the doctor ushered them straight to the table where he could tend to the wound. He praised the family for their quick thinking and set to work, preparing a clean area to perform his repair. He called out for Veronica to come and assist, giving her clear instructions as to what he required.

Veronica continued the explanation. "I told George not to ask me to look at the wound, at all. I said if I so much as sensed the blood and the guts, he would have to pick me up off that floor, so he would. I handed the doctor each requested item from an arm's reach away."

The doctor picked up the thread of the story. "Without showing my mirth, as it was rather comical to watch, I needed Veronica to help. So I bit my lip to avoid laughing, as I sensed her discomfort.

"The ligament had been partially severed, so the repair was only going to serve to stem the bleeding and give the patient a little use of the damaged leg again. Ligaments are difficult to mend as they are needed for strength in the use of the leg, especially those of the Achille's heel. I told the lad that he would need to rest for months and only expect a little return to normal function once that wound had mended."

The doctor took Veronica's hand and stroked it tenderly.

"With the operation completed, I no longer required Veronica's help so I dismissed her and noticed that she was gagging as she left the room. I could hear her rushing out through the back kitchen door and supposed she would be heading for the outside privy. I still had to dress and bandage the leg, so I carried on completing the task you would normally do, Bedelia. When the surgery was all tidied and the rescue party and the patient sent on their way, I went in search of Veronica. I found her lying on the path that led back from the privy, just coming round from what appeared to have been a faint. Her face was ashen and her lips pale. Her hair was in disarray and her skirt was muddied from the puddle she had landed in."

He told Bedelia that his concern was allayed when she attempted to rise by herself, but his natural reaction was to pick her up and find a resting place inside the house. She looked so fragile. "I carried her through the door leading to the kitchen," he said.

Bedelia could read his eyes as to what had happened next. Veronica's heart was laid bare on the table alongside his.

The doctor told Bedelia that he had placed Veronica carefully in the chair beside the cooking range and busied himself setting her dishevelled dress in order, washing the mud from her slender hands and skirt.

"I told him to stop his fussing. That I was quite all right now. It was just a moment," Veronica said.

"George was in a bit of a dither, so he set to and prepared some food from the pantry, laying it out on the table and slicing the mutton and bread in thick, uneven slabs. He made a pot of tea, but forgot to put the leaves in," Veronica chuckled. "We talked a bit of nonsense and then George burst out that he loved me and some more that I will keep to myself, if you don't mind, Dee. And I had a bit to say that is also just ours to know. Then he asked me to marry him and guess what I replied?"

"I can't wait until I tell Michael your news. Why don't we have a double wedding? We would be inviting the same guests. Oh, and doctor, would you be up to having a priest?"

"George, please, Delia. And yes, Veronica and I have already discussed that. The Church of England means nothing to me but bad memories, so I will take instruction from a priest and be married as a Catholic for Veronica's sake."

It wasn't a lavish affair, but it was a truly joyful occasion. In their short time in New Zealand the two couples had gathered many friends.

The Lutheran church was bursting at the seams. Despite the doctor's initial offer, the German community had come together in true fashion to provide a wedding feast befitting their friends. The celebrations and gifts included blends of the many cultures of the settlers and the indigenous people the couples had so far spent time with. They had all been included in the widespread invitation to the wedding.

The sisters were a picture of simple beauty in their hand-crafted gowns. The material included a shared part of their mother's wedding gown, which had been among the treasures transported in their sea chest. Each bride wore a pounamu the colour of grass carpeting the valleys of their home in the Emerald Isles. They were carved in the shape of a heart and gifted to them by Keenan.

Stephen Nation had been honoured to walk both brides down the aisle, with Lilian and Rosemary following behind. Mrs Pentwick was excited to have helped with preparations for the ceremony and took the front pew of the church with the Nation boys.

The grooms looked so proud of their beautiful brides. The sisters had fulfilled the company's scheme setting out to sponsor immigrant women of good character to become suitable brides. What lay ahead of them in this untamed landscape was for all to guess. The toasts from the guests were for a long life of good health, good fortune and abundance.

Keenan finished his speech. "May the road rise under you. And here's that you may always have a clane shirt, a clane conscience and a guinea in your pocket."

Glossary

Plattdeutsch, or Low German, appears to be a language in its own right. Some say it is a dialect of German, but it shares its roots in Anglo-Saxon with English.

Because it is a spoken rather than a written language, a word in Plattdeutsch may vary slightly in spelling and pronunciation from East to west, across North Germany.

Plattdeutsch	English	German
Bitte	Please or Pardon?	Bitte
Dat is Fru ...	This is Mrs ...	Das ist Frau ...
Dat is good	That is good	Das ist gut
Dat is bannig good	That is very good	Das ist sehr gut
Doller	Harder (Massage)	Stärker / mehr
	Congratulations	Glückwunsch
Hebamm (s)	Midwife	Hebamme (s)
Hebammen (pl)	Midwives	Hebammen (pl)
Ik bün ...	I am ...	Ich bin
Ja / jo	Yes	Ja
Mien lütte Broder	My little brother	Mein kleiner Bruder
Mien Baby	My baby	Mein Kind
Mien Mudder geiht dat nich good.	My mother is unwell/ doesn't feel well.	Meiner Mutter geht es nicht gut.
Mein Fründin	My friend	Mein Freund
Moin /Moin, moin	Hello	Hallo
Nee	No	Nein
Schoop	Sheep	Schafe
Tschüüs	Goodbye	Tschüß / Guten tag
Slaap	Tired	Müde
Twee Hannen	Two hands	Zwei Hände
Utpressen	Push (baby out)	Rauspressen
Ni pressen	Don't push	Nicht pressen
Veelen Dank	Thank you very much	Dankeschön
Willkomen /	Welcome	Willkommen (More commonly used is-Schöön, dat du dor büst)
Twölf Kinner	Twelve children	Zwölf Kinder
	We are doctors	Wir sind Ärzte
	Good night	Guten Nacht

Irish

Ceann milis	Sweet one
Ceilidh	Social event of music and dance
Cac	Poo / faeces
Wean	Baby
Macushla	My darling
Garda	Policeman / constable

Scottish

Nae	No
Wee bairn	Little baby

Maori

Mānuka	Bush with small white or pink flowers
Pounamu	Greenstone / Jade found in South Westland NZ
Whare	House / houses
Raupō	Reeds in a swamp

French

In flagrante delicto	Caught red-handed breaking rules or committing a crime.